THE UNDOING OF THISTLE TATE

THE
UNDOING
OF
THISTLE TATE

BY KATELYN
DETWEILER

MARGARET FERGUSON BOOKS
HOLIDAY HOUSE · NEW YORK

Margaret Ferguson Books

Copyright © 2019 by Katelyn Detweiler

All Rights Reserved

HOLIDAY HOUSE is registered in the U.S. Patent and Trademark Office.

Printed and Bound in May 2019 at Maple Press, York, PA, USA.

www.holidayhouse.com

First Edition

10 9 8 7 6 5 4 3 2 1

Library of Congress Cataloging-in-Publication Data

Names: Detweiler, Katelyn, author.

Title: The undoing of Thistle Tate / Katelyn Detweiler.

Description: First edition. | New York : Holiday House, [2019] | "Margaret Ferguson Books."

Summary: Seventeen-year-old Thistle Tate, a bestselling author with glowing reviews, diehard fans across the globe, and more, struggles with secrets that threaten to unravel her seemingly perfect world.

Identifiers: LCCN 2018036658 | ISBN 9780823442393 (hardcover)

Subjects: | CYAC: Authorship—Fiction. | Fathers and daughters—Fiction. Single-parent families—Fiction. | Secrets—Fiction. | Fame—Fiction. Dating (Social customs)—Fiction.

Classification: LCC PZ7.1.D48 Und 2019 | DDC [Fic]—dc23

LC record available at https://lccn.loc.gov/2018036658

To Carebear and Denny, the reason I can and do write.

To Danny, the inspiration behind this love story and all love stories to come.

THE

UNDOING

OF

THISTLE TATE

one

Fifteen-year-old Marigold Maybee remembered everything and nothing about the moment she almost died.

It could have been five seconds; it could have been five hours.

Metal crashing and glass smashing, screams and sobs and sirens, so many sirens. Violet, her mom, was next to her on the road, under the blue January sky. Marigold could feel her own hand wrapped around her mom's cold, stiff fingers.

"Be brave, Marigold," her mom said then. Marigold wasn't sure how she knew exactly, but she was certain she hadn't heard the words with her ears—she'd heard them inside herself.

"I'll try, Mom," she whispered. "I want to be brave."

Marigold took a deep breath, squeezing her mom's fingers tighter.

And then she opened her eyes.

—EXCERPT FROM *LEMONADE SKIES, **BOOK 1: GIRL IN THE AFTERWORLD***

I have lots of dreams, but I've only ever had one nightmare and it's always exactly the same.

I haven't had the nightmare in a while—a good thing, I'd thought, a *wonderful* thing. But I was wrong. Because it came back with a vengeance tonight, making up for lost time.

If it were up to me, I'd choose a common, run-of-the-mill nightmare every single night instead—spiders crawling all over my skin or a zombie attack or stumbling off a cliff. Anything else would be a treat in comparison.

But it's not up to me.

And so here I am again: heart pumping ten beats too fast, tears running down my cheeks—the nightmare still gripping me like it never wants to let go.

I sit up, turn on the lamp next to my bed, and take deep breaths.

I'm not surprised I had this dream, not tonight. Liam was here earlier, lying next to me on the bed watching *National Lampoon's Vacation*, our legs and arms so close but still never touching. His pick, because he loved the *Christmas Vacation* one and figured this would be just as funny. But there's a scene, less than sixty seconds long, where the Griswold family is in the car, fighting about getting lost in the middle of nowhere—when *boom*, just like that, they're off the road, crashing through signs, nearly flipping over. It's a comedy, so everyone is fine, of course, besides the car. But just seeing it, hearing it . . .

The nightmare is fading now, but there are still tears in my eyes.

That's how it goes: I'm sobbing and then—a *crash*. Shattering glass. I'm in a car, I suddenly realize, a car that is colliding hard and fast with something else. After a few seconds of dizzying explosions of noise, everything stops. It's quiet and too bright and I am alone.

And then I wake up, crying, as if I've just somehow managed to crawl out of the car alive, as if it all really happened, exactly like this.

Dad says I wasn't even there when my mom died in the accident fourteen years ago. But that's all he'll say. I asked about it a lot, back when I was younger.

I look at the clock now—a little after two in the morning.

I won't be falling asleep again.

I pick up a book from my nightstand. The words blur and I put it back down.

I stand up, moving over to the window, my hand reaching for the bucket of yellow Ping-Pong balls I've had on the sill for as long as I can remember.

Liam. My best and only friend. I want him to come back. He

sleeps here some nights, but only when we accidentally fall asleep in the middle of a particularly long Netflix binge.

I pull the curtain aside and push up the window. I toss one, two Ping-Pong balls at Liam's closed window and wait. We live in Philadelphia where the houses are crowded close together, so there's only a few yards of space between us, a narrow area of ground that leaves just enough room for a thin brick wall that separates our properties.

I could call, of course, or text. But this has been our preferred system of communication since Liam moved here the summer we were both four. A few more seconds and there he is—his black hair sticking up in bird wings all over his head, eyes squinting at me in sleepy confusion. I give a shrug.

He knocks his fingers twice against his window, code for *coming now.*

I get back into bed and pull the covers up to my chin.

Liam has a key so he can walk our old hound dog, Lucy, when my dad and I are away, and I soon hear the soft *click* of the front door opening and closing.

He comes upstairs and opens my bedroom door. I reach my arms out and, without any words, we're hugging. It's maybe the best hug of my life.

Then again, every hug with Liam feels like the best.

He eventually pulls away, settling himself next to me on the bed.

"Missed me already?" he asks, his deep brown eyes peering at me.

"I had the nightmare again," I say. "It felt so real, Li. I mean, it always feels real. But this time it's like . . . every part of my body remembers my mom's accident. And it wants to make sure my brain remembers, too, even if I wasn't actually there. Maybe there's more to it, there's something I'm supposed to understand from the dream . . ."

"It's just a dream, Thistle." Liam leans into me, wrapping an arm tight around my shoulder. I scoot over the last few inches between us and let my head fall onto his chest. It's warm and familiar and it's mine—but it's not. Not *mine*. Not really. "I think you're reading too much into it. Every time you dream it, it feels like the worst time, but that's just in the moment. It'll fade. By tomorrow morning you'll barely remember it."

I nod, even though I know that's not true. I always remember.

He's wearing a Phillies pajama set, which is adorably dorky, but it looks good on him, his dark olive skin seeming even more radiant against the clean white of the red-striped shirt and shorts.

Stop, Thistle.

Now is not the time to reflect on his attractiveness. Not when he's this close to you on your *bed*. Not when you woke him because your terrible nightmare was maybe the worst of your life.

"I grabbed something for you on my way out," he says, shifting to reach into his pocket. "My mom bought more of those chocolate-covered caramel pretzels from Reading Terminal Market that you love. I swiped one for you." He hands me a balled-up napkin and I slowly unwrap it, let the pretzel fall into my hands, sniff it, and poke at it with my tongue.

"Just eat the damn thing, weirdo."

"This is a sacred moment. It can't be rushed."

"Mhmm." He pulls away and stands up, walking to my bookshelf. I pop the pretzel in my mouth as I watch him, and my night is suddenly feeling impossibly better.

"Let's not watch anything else that might have crash scenes in it, okay?" he says. "And besides, I'm more in the mood right now for good old *Sorcerer's Stone*. 'Harry—yer a wizard.' God, I love that moment. Hagrid is the freaking best."

I smile. The dream is still there, but it's fading. *This*, Liam and me, is what's real.

"I was inspired by your pajamas," he says, grinning at me as he pulls the book from the shelf. "They are seriously enchanting."

It's only now that I realize I'm wearing ratty red pajamas with various Quidditch-related items scattered across my body: Snitches and Bludgers and Beater's bats, Hedwig, and Harry's spectacles, too, for good measure. It's too late to do anything but laugh, and besides—it's *Liam*. He comes back to the bed then, and props the book up against his knees.

"Chapter one, 'The Boy Who Lived,'" he says, clearing his throat loudly—too loudly, maybe, given my dad is just a wall away from us. Though Dad never seems worried about how late Liam and I stay up together—he knows we're just friends.

I know we're just friends, too. That we'll always be just friends.

I snuggle in closer.

He starts reading about the Dursleys and life on Privet Drive, and I don't know how far along he gets before my eyes close, but they do.

I fall asleep again after all, because Liam is here.

⚽⚽⚽

He's gone when I wake up.

Hopefully I wasn't a creep while I slept—accidentally kissing him, accidentally whispering *I love you*. We do love each other. But not like that. Or at least he doesn't.

I'd learned that the hard way when we were twelve: we'd decided to practice kiss, just once. I don't remember whose idea it was now, but I do remember how scared I felt, how worried I was that he'd notice my sweaty, clammy, disgusting hands. It lasted for five seconds, tops. Just a peck.

"Too weird," he'd said, jumping back as if I'd held a match to his skin. "Way too weird. I mean, you're like my *sister*. I can't kiss you. It's wrong."

The words had stung, but I'd made myself laugh and agree. And now I've spent the last five years trying—and failing—to convince myself that it will never happen again. That it's silly to keep thinking about it.

I put on some old overalls and a green T-shirt and head downstairs for breakfast. Lucy is waiting for me at the bottom of the stairs, tail thumping against the wooden floorboards. She's getting old—she was my Christmas gift the year my mom passed away—and her back legs are too stiff to climb the steps. She sleeps downstairs in the office now, instead of on my bed. I rub her ears for a moment before we both head into the kitchen.

"Hey, sweetie," Dad says, not bothering to look up from the stack of printed pages spread across our kitchen table. He has a highlighter in one hand, coffee in the other, and a red pen tucked behind his ear. "I had oatmeal and almond milk delivered yesterday, if you want that. Some fruit, too." He's back to work then, likely already forgetting I'm right here.

I nod, not that he can see me, and pour some Chocolate O's—a weekend-only treat—into a bowl and carry it over to the table. I swirl my spoon around and watch the milk turn grayish brown.

"Dad," I say quickly, before I can stop myself, "I had that nightmare again last night. About the accident."

He puts his mug down, but he doesn't look up. I'm staring at the shiny pink peak of his bald spot.

"I'm sorry to hear that—I was hoping you might have outgrown it." He sighs. "But it's just a dream. You know that, Thistle."

"Maybe if I knew more about Mom, I wouldn't keep having it."

It's an old, familiar, worn-in conversation. We both have our part to play. Me: *Tell me more about the human who is half of my DNA.* Dad: *Not right now. Maybe later.*

I want to know more about my mom so maybe I can actually miss her. Miss *her*, Rose Lockwood Tate, specifically—not just the idea of having a mom. Dad hates to talk about her—not just the accident and her death, but her life, too. I know he's still sad, fourteen years later, even if he's smiling. Even if he pretends our life as a duo is good. But still. I'm her daughter. If we don't talk about her, then she'll be completely gone. So I keep asking, keep trying. I need to.

"You know the important stuff," he says.

"Which amounts to almost nothing."

He finally looks up, staring at me with his light brown eyes. My eyes are blue. Like Mom's. I know from photographs that I look exactly like her. "That's not true," he says. "We just really need to focus on the big tour starting Tuesday, and the deadline, and . . ."

I tune him out then, as he probably anticipated I would. That was his goal. Eventually he stops talking, and I finish my soggy cereal, and it's like our chat never happened.

"I'll be out in the garden," I say, dropping my bowl in the sink.

"I'm sorry, Thistle. I'm distracted."

"That's okay." He's not a bad dad. He's really not.

I head outside to our tiny backyard with my even tinier garden. My mom grew up in this house, spent her whole life here except for college and then a few years in an apartment when she first moved in with Dad. This was her garden. It died along with Mom, until I was old enough to take over. Now it's my favorite thinking spot, out here with the beautiful flowers in an array of colors—all except for yellow or orange or gold, not anymore. It's my own miniature world that I've created. A perfect balance of order and chaos.

It's a gorgeous day in mid-October, the kind of balmy weather that almost makes you believe summer isn't actually over and winter may never come. I zone out weeding, the sun warm on my back.

"There you are," someone says from Liam's yard, startling me from my trance.

It's his mom, Mrs. Caruso. I can't see her, but I know she must be on their back patio for her morning coffee. She insists on going out there even in the winter, bundling up to savor her brew under the sun and the sky. She grew up outside the city, in a small rural town somewhere, and she takes any snippet of nature she can find here.

"Your father told me he ran into you early this morning—that you were slipping in the front door just as he was coming down to start the coffee. You slept at the Tates', I take it?"

"Yeah," Liam mumbles. I crawl over closer to the brick wall, holding my breath to be as quiet as possible. "Thistle . . . she was upset about something, so I went over to cheer her up. I was reading to her and we accidentally fell asleep."

"It seems to me this has been happening a lot lately. You go over to hang out, and suddenly it's six in the morning and you're tiptoeing back up the stairs here. Sleepovers were one thing when you were kids, but now?" I can hear the accusation in her voice, picture her raised eyebrow without needing to see it for myself.

"It's not like that. It's no big deal."

"Hm. It's not like *that*?"

"She's my best friend."

Even though I know this, it still makes me feel warm and fuzzy to hear the label out loud. Unlike me, Liam has other friends, people from his prep school. And I'm the *best*.

"Good lord, Liam. Please. You live and breathe for that girl. Don't act like I'm stupid."

I gasp. *You live and breathe for that girl.*

"No more sleepovers, and no more sneaking out after eleven."

I wait for Liam to deny it. *She's like a sister, Mom! Don't be gross. Nothing will* ever *happen between us. Ever.*

But he doesn't say that. He doesn't say anything.

He just stomps across the patio. The kitchen door opens and then slams shut.

He didn't deny it.

For the first time since that kiss five years ago, I feel it, and it's magical—better than flowers, better than Harry Potter and chocolate-caramel pretzels:

Hope.

❁❀❁

I float inside to wash up.

He didn't deny it. Liam. Didn't. Deny. It.

But then my dad calls out to me from the office—"Sweetie, could you come in here for a minute?"—and I deflate. Instantly.

We have a rule in the Tate house: I never have to work on weekends. Not even when there are deadlines. And no work means not setting foot into the office, unless it's to check on Lucy.

It's like, for forty-eight precious hours a week, my nemesis Marigold Maybee doesn't exist.

"Thistle? It'll just take a sec. Good news! Very good news."

"Yeah?" I'm leaning on the door frame, my feet still squarely on the hallway side.

"Five starred reviews! *Between Two Worlds* just got its fifth star! It's a new record for us! This is a great way to kick off pub week and the tour on Tuesday. Five!"

He's beaming up at me and waving his hands in the air. I guess he expects me to start tap dancing around the room next, twisting and twirling in glee, but I don't. I can't even bother to smile.

"Thistle?"

I ignore him. My eyes go to the bookshelves instead: rows of *Girl in the Afterworld* in English and every other language I could ever think of. Plus some that I would never have thought of.

And now, the second book in the series: *Between Two Worlds*.

Titles change on foreign editions, but the author is always the same: *Thistle Tate*.

Me.

There's only one book up there that's different from the rest, and I walk across the room to pick it up: *The Princess and the Pizza Delivery Man*, made out of construction paper and ribbon. Apparently when I was little—according to Dad, at least—I'd get bored with whatever picture books he'd try to read to me and make up my own stories instead. I hadn't quite mastered the alphabet yet, so he wrote down this particular story for me, and I drew the pictures. I guess I really loved pizza. And princesses.

I had written three words of it on my own, though: *By Thistle Tate*, in bright red crayon on the front cover. My *s* and *e*'s were backward.

By Thistle Tate.

Those three words may have been true then.

But they're a lie now.

two

Marigold had always hated the abandoned house that faced the street where the accident happened. It was less than a mile from where she lived, entirely unavoidable, and she hated how sad and empty it made her feel to see it. Abby and Sam used to call it the Death House. Now they didn't say anything when they passed by it on the rare times Marigold hung out with them.

Marigold dreamed about the accident—and that house—every night. But instead of lying on the road next to her mom, she was sitting in the old rocking chair on the rotting porch of the house, watching the accident come to life. There was crashing and wailing and flashing, a body tumbling through glass, and then—her mom stood up from the road and turned toward the house.

She looked at Marigold and smiled.

—EXCERPT FROM *LEMONADE SKIES,* **BOOK 1:** *GIRL IN THE AFTERWORLD*

I can still remember everything about the day my dad and I made the decision, two and a half years ago, a few weeks after my fifteenth birthday.

The day we chose to lie.

I was painting a map of the Holy Roman Empire for my Latin "class," to include in the end-of-year portfolio for my homeschooling evaluator—Mrs. Everly, an English teacher we hired from a local high school—and trying not to worry about my dad. He'd been distracted the night before and all that morning, too, and after he'd given me my assignment, he'd disappeared into his office with the door closed.

When my mom died, my dad quit his job as a high school English teacher. He wanted to be home with me, and that didn't change when it came time for kindergarten. He was a teacher, so he could teach me himself. Homeschooling, home everything else, too. We rarely left the house, except to go to the grocery store five blocks down and the Chinese take-out restaurant across the street. Sometimes we went to the library or the park or one of my favorite local museums—the Please Touch Museum and the Franklin Institute. Dad didn't even replace the car Mom had totaled in the accident. He began to stop seeing old friends, eventually cut off any former social life altogether. I was too young to understand that Dad was too sad for friends, and that he was scared. Scared that more bad things would happen if we stepped outside—another accident, another freak tragedy he couldn't control. It was safer to stay home.

My universe was tiny but lovely, at least in the early years. Dad channeled his energy and grief into doting on me—reading me books for hours every night until I fell asleep, working tirelessly on homeschooling lesson plans, cooking me chocolate chip pancakes anytime I asked, watching online tutorials so he could learn to braid my hair and paint my nails. He was so good at being a dad that sometimes I almost forgot to miss my mom. Almost.

I'd work on assignments while he tried and quit a whole slew of stay-at-home jobs—online tutor, virtual assistant, customer service agent, audio transcriber. There was no mortgage to worry about because my mom had inherited the house from her parents, one stroke of luck in our favor—if it can be considered *luck* that both of her parents died too young. And my parents had me later in life, well into their thirties, so they'd had some savings by then. Life insurance also helped. My dad tried to explain it to me once, when I'd asked why he didn't have to go to work like Liam's parents. But still, even when I was a kid I wasn't dumb. I knew there were bills to pay.

Writing was my dad's only constant. It had always been his dream, though he'd gone into teaching because it was the practical thing to do. But it was a side bonus of quitting, he said: fewer papers to grade and more time to write. At first he tried a memoir—single dad coping, raising a daughter alone. He submitted it to literary agents nonstop for a year. No takers, though. So he tried picture books next, then chapter books, then middle grade novels, evolving as I did. Adventure, fantasy, science fiction, historical, mystery. He tried everything.

Over ten years of writing, and not a single sale. Every rejection made him sink just a little bit lower and took him just a little bit farther away from me. As I got older I realized it wasn't only the rejection letters. It was as though the more time passed, the more real life got, the harder it was for him to pretend that everything was okay. He missed my mom—sometimes I heard him crying in the middle of the night—and he was worried about money. I'd eavesdropped on him talking to a Realtor about selling the house, but neither of us wanted to leave. This was *her* house. If she was anywhere still, it was here, not at some ugly pink gravestone that we never visited. I offered to start going to school so he could teach again, but he said he'd rather be at home with me.

And then, finally, there was hope. A new manuscript, the best I'd read yet—*Girl in the Afterworld*. The idea had come from one of my dad's English assignments for me: *Create a scene in your own afterworld*. His prompts tended to be a little on the dark side.

But I'd loved the concept, and I'd spent more time on the story than I ever had on any other project. I wrote about a never-ending skyscraper up in the clouds, every floor filled with people who had died. I was alive and could transport there through a portal—the porch of an abandoned house in our neighborhood—and return home anytime I wanted. I searched for my mom while I was there, of course, making new friends from across the world. And at the very end, for one glorious moment, I'd found her. Mom.

I hadn't known it until a few months later, but that was the start of Marigold Maybee. My dad slaved over the manuscript, and when I finally read it, I was stunned.

The story opened with fifteen-year-old Marigold just barely surviving a car accident that killed her mom, Violet. But then Marigold found a portal, a second chance—just like the one I'd described—to a place called the *Afterworld*, where it was beautiful and dark and perfect and so similar to the world I'd created for my assignment.

My dad had been reluctant to send *Girl in the Afterworld* out, no matter how much I told him I loved it. He was terrified of more rejection, kept saying it needed more work. I believed in him, though. And in Marigold. So I'd pushed. But he kept saying no.

That had been just a few weeks before. Had he sent it out after all? Was he drowning in more rejections?

I was too worried and curious to keep working. I put down my paintbrush and walked to the office. Lucy followed at my heels, bumping up against my ankles as I stopped in front of the door.

"Dad, everything okay?" Silence. I was about to turn the knob when the door swung open.

"Everything's fine. I just need to talk to you about something."

"Something good?" I was afraid to hope.

"I think so, but . . . it's complicated." He looked away, his brow furrowing.

"Tell me."

He stepped back into his office and gestured for me to take the love seat. He sat in the desk chair, rolling it over until he'd stopped right in front of me. Lucy had already settled at my feet, perched on her haunches, watching my dad as closely as I was.

"So I listened to you," he started. His eyes were fixed on his hands, clenching and unclenching on top of his knees. "I sent the Marigold story out to literary agents."

"What? Dad! That's great!" I leaned forward to hug him. He wrapped one arm loosely around my back, giving me a few light, quick pats.

I sat back, frowning. "Okay. Well, that was a lame hug. What's the catch?"

"Right. Perceptive as always, aren't you?" He forced a laugh. "So I decided to send the manuscript to only ten agents this time—my dream agents, really. But when I sent it, I . . . er . . ."

There was a pause. I squinted, confused.

"You . . . ?"

"Well, I was so afraid this one would be rejected, too, that I decided to do an experiment. I was curious to see how much biography and background play in to their consideration of manuscripts by unknown authors. So I—um . . . I decided to switch it up a bit, I guess you could say? I told them someone else wrote it."

"You're losing me," I said. "If you didn't say you wrote it, who—?"

"You."

I laughed. "That makes no sense. *Me*?"

"Yes. I wrote the cover letter as *you*. I said that I had just turned fifteen, and that I'd had the idea for Marigold because my own mom had died in a car accident when I was little . . . and I sent a photo, too. Of you."

I stared at him.

"It was the one of you in your garden," he continued. "You're watering the marigolds. You know the one? From last summer?"

He took my silence to mean that no, I didn't know exactly what photo he was talking about. He rolled back to the desk, picking up a frame from next to the computer monitor.

"This is one of my favorites of you—you are so much like your mom."

He shoved the frame into my hands, and all I could do was stare. I looked so young, my thick black curls falling out of a messy braid, clear blue eyes without a trace of mascara on the lashes, pale skin with a smudge of dirt along my forehead. I was fourteen then, but I could have passed for eleven or twelve, easily.

"But no one would ever believe that," I said, words finally coming back to me. I pointed to my face behind the glass. "I look like a kid in that picture!"

"Well, Thistle, that's the thing. They must have loved the photo, the idea of you. And most importantly, they loved your story."

"But it's *not* my story. It's *yours*."

"Well, I mean, technically, yes, I wrote the words . . ." He ran his fingers over the top of his thinning gray-black hair. "But it was your idea, remember? You thought of the Afterworld, and the portal . . ."

"I wrote a ten-page story, Dad. You wrote a whole book."

"You were the *muse*, though. This story wouldn't have happened without you."

"That's beside the point," I said. "And what are you even saying? They loved the story? And me? What does that mean?"

"Well, I sent it out two weeks ago, and now there are five agents fighting for your story."

"*Your* story."

"No, *our* story." He looked me in the eyes for the first time. I fought back another defiant *your story*. Because as nervous as he was, he also looked hopeful. Excited even.

I barely recognized those emotions on his face.

"Thistle, I've been thinking about it, and . . . I know which agent I want to pick. Who *we* should pick, but only if you agree."

"If I agree to what? To lie? To pretend to be the author? They'd meet me and they'd know."

"I'm not sure that's true, sweetie. There are a few teen authors out there these days. Successful ones even. Publishers love it, readers love it. It feels more genuine that way. Much more relatable than if the story were coming from someone like me—a fat, schlubby fifty-something-year-old guy, trying to write a fantasy love story for teen girls."

"You're not fat," I said, on instinct. But we *did* need to eat less takeout. His clothes were looking uncomfortably tight lately.

"Chubby."

"Okay, but not the point. If they like it so much, why does it matter if it's you or me on the book jacket?"

"They get hundreds of manuscripts a week, Thistle. They're only going to notice a few of them, tops. And this . . . it caught their eye. The story, yes. But the author, too. It's a package deal. The publicity people will love having this hook."

Agents, publishers, publicity people now, too—it was too much, too bizarre to take in. It was all happening just a few hours away from us, in New York City, but I'd never been there before. I'd barely been outside of Pennsylvania, except for a few vacations with Liam's family. Publishing might as well have been taking place on the moon, it felt so far away from our quiet little world in Philly.

Still, I understood enough to know that we couldn't do this.

"No way, Dad. I'm not agreeing. Obviously. It's . . . *wrong*."

He moved his chair closer, resting his hands on my shoulders.

"It would only be for this one book. That's it. Anything else I write in the future will be under my name."

But what if they find out? I almost asked, but didn't. That question was way beyond my ability to process.

"I can't even lie to you when Liam and I raid your change jar. I could never ever lie about something this huge."

My dad shook his head. "I need something, Thistle. For *me*. It's—it's knowing that something *I* wrote is actually good enough. That someone thinks it's worth making into a real book. And this is only the first step. We don't know what will happen next. Maybe publishers won't like it."

I didn't say anything to that, which he must have taken as a green light to keep going.

"The agent I want to work with, Susan Van Buren, is very picky. She's a big deal. It's a dream opportunity, Thistle. A *dream*. So what do you say? Do we give it a shot?"

"I'm sorry, Dad, but no. Maybe it's not too late to tell this Susan that it's actually you? If she really loved the story?"

He shook his head slowly. "It's this or nothing. There's no backtracking now. I just . . ." He trailed off.

"You what?"

"I haven't wanted to worry you, but we need money—I know we both want to stay in this house, but selling it and downsizing might be the only option we have soon, and we'd get an advance if the book sells to a publisher."

The words burned deep down in my stomach.

Bills were piled up on the kitchen table. We needed money. It was just one book. But he deserved to have it published under his name: *Theo Tate*. If he couldn't have that, maybe this was the next best way.

"I only want this if you want it, too. We'd do it together, you and me. Teamwork. I'm sure we'll have loads of revisions to do. I think that could count toward your English requirements for the year. Mrs. Everly would no doubt approve." He gave me a weak smile. "So what do you say?"

We sat there staring at each other. Silent. Both of us waiting to hear what I would say.

I didn't want to live a lie.

But I loved him. I wanted him to be happy. I wanted *us* to be happy. And I also wanted to stay in Mom's house.

"Yes," I said.

Yes.

❁❁❁

One month later, *Girl in the Afterworld* sold at auction to one of the six big publishing houses competing for it. All of them trying to impress us with the most money, the most promises for huge publicity and marketing campaigns.

But the winning publisher didn't want just one book. They convinced my dad—and my dad convinced me—that it had to be a series. He had a detailed synopsis for two more books ready the next day.

Three books in total: The *Lemonade Skies* trilogy.

But that would be the end. Just this series.

Only Marigold.

Elliot Archer, our young but brilliant editor at Zenith Publishers, had us come to New York City to meet him. That was the first time I had to wear my lie like a second skin.

From the minute I stepped off the train into Penn Station—filled with the smell of deli coffee and greasy pizza and pastries, rotting garbage and urine—I wanted to be back in Philly. I wanted to skip our meeting with Elliot and go home to my own quiet corner of life. The need to disappear only swelled as we climbed into the waiting limousine and traveled through massive throngs of cars and people, passing through Times Square, buildings growing taller and shinier and grander as we went.

This wasn't my city. This wasn't me. Why was I doing this?

Dad. Money. Our home. Mom's home.

"You're a wonder, Thistle," Elliot had said, toasting me with sparkling apple juice in his office. "This is one of the most perfect first drafts I've ever read. Just think, if you're writing like this at fifteen, imagine what you'll be writing as an adult!"

My dad looked like he might combust with joy. They were both too preoccupied with their own delight to realize how undelighted I was, thankfully.

I'd chugged my juice as Elliot grinned at me, my throat burning from the fizz.

We're lying! I wanted to scream, before it would always be too late. But I didn't.

I didn't say a word.

three

Marigold knew it had only been a dream, but she had to go to the old house. She snuck out at night, when her dad was asleep.

Once she was there she sat in the rocking chair on the porch. Closed her eyes. Breathed in the early spring air. When she opened her eyes, she wasn't anywhere near that awful road. There was only one thing she could see, in the middle of a strange field.

It was a skyscraper—so tall it appeared to go up endlessly through the sky. And the sky wasn't blue—the blue was left for the grass, rolling fields of deep azure. The sky was yellow, dotted with stars in every color of the rainbow.

There was a sign above tall golden doors: THE AFTERWORLD.

Could her mom be here? Marigold walked up to the building and eased the doors open, stepping into a silent atrium lined with expansive windows. Then she heard footsteps and turned quickly to see who was approaching.

The boy was about her age, with dark brown skin and bright golden eyes.

"I'm Colton," he said, staring at her. "Are you lost?"

—EXCERPT FROM *LEMONADE SKIES, BOOK 1: GIRL IN THE AFTERWORLD*

I didn't have much time with Liam before kicking off my *Between Two Worlds* tour that Tuesday, the day the book was out for the world to read. I'd be gone fifteen days—first Illinois, then Minnesota, Colorado, California, Washington State, North Carolina, Massachusetts, and DC, wrapping up with a big hometown show in Philly. It would be a nonstop blur of planes and trains and classrooms and bookstores and fans, with school assignments from Dad filling any small windows of downtime Zenith's schedule permitted me.

Liam came over at five in the morning just before our car to the airport arrived, and I could barely string two words together I was so surprised. Especially when he left me with a plastic bag of tightly folded paper footballs—notes for the tour, he'd said, one to open up each day I was gone. "Seriously, only one a day. No cheating. I know how much you really hate this part of it, so I wanted to make it better," he'd said, and then hugged me good-bye.

Dad had asked me not to tell Liam about our secret, said it was safer that way. I promised him I wouldn't and then immediately broke that promise, telling Liam the truth as soon as we signed on with Susan Van Buren. I'd told him before the book deal, before the *New York Times* bestseller list, before people all across the world cared about Marigold Maybee's fate. Before it became my whole universe. I don't regret it. Liam and I don't keep secrets. We never have. Liam doesn't love that I have to pretend—doesn't love that I have to *lie*—but he supports me. Liam's nice enough to my dad's face, but he blames him for starting this whole mess. Of course, we've never told my dad that he knows. Dad keeps up the charade when Liam's at the house, covering his writing tracks.

Liam's notes got me through the tour, the smiling and signing and talking about books I didn't actually write to rooms filled with adoring fans. I'd read one note just before each event, and it was as if I had Liam with me, even if he was hundreds of miles away.

Remember that summer we were maybe eight or nine and out of our minds bored, and you pinned me down and smeared peanut butter on my face for Lucy to lick off? She was so fierce about that PB I remember thinking she'd probably end up chewing my lips off. But we were both laughing so hard, and finally you ended up peeing a little in your pants, screaming about it just as your dad walked in. I mean literally *peed your pants. We could both see the stain soaking through. SO AWESOME. I laughed even harder and then I started peeing MY pants. Man. Your dad thought we were crazy. But I'm not sure I've ever laughed harder than I did then.*

Remember that Halloween we were fighting because we both wanted to be aliens? And I said it'd be nerdy to be matching and you got hurt and said, "Fine, aliens are so last year, anyway." I knew you didn't mean it. And I also knew you weren't a big fan of Halloween, but went trick-or-treating for me. So when you told me you were dressing as a slice of pizza instead, I begged my mom to help me look like a can of root beer because you ALWAYS insisted on drinking root beer with your pizza. I looked pathetic—we painted aluminum foil brown and wrote "Root Beer" on it and wrapped it on a big paper tube that I wore. I had about a thousand dents in me. You didn't care, though. You were so happy. That was my favorite Halloween ever.

Remember that time my parents surprised us with a trip to Disney World for my eleventh birthday, and the second day there you got a fever and were throwing up everywhere? (Ugh, that chili dog from the night before did NOT look pretty coming up.) My mom said she'd stay and watch you so I could still do the park, but I refused to leave. We spent more time at the hotel than on rides, but it didn't matter.

We were allowed to watch movies ALL. DAY. LONG. And
that felt like a freaking awesome vacation to me. You and
Back to the Future (parts I, II, AND III), what more could
I have wanted?

Liam didn't make any grand, sweeping declarations. No *I love you!*
I'm IN love with you! Be mine forever please, Thistle!!! (I only *slightly*
expected this reveal on the last day.) But still, that didn't mean it
wasn't true. Because, of course, I hadn't been able to stop thinking
about that conversation I'd overheard. What Liam's mom had said
and what he *hadn't* said.

Maybe he was waiting for tonight. My big Philly bookstore
finale. Dad and I got home too late last night for me to see Liam,
and I'd slept in this morning past the time he leaves for school. But
tonight. Liam and his parents always come with us to lend moral
support at local events.

I had saved my favorite new dress for this appearance. Bright
yellow top—all my tour outfits are in marigold colors—with intri-
cate, shimmery beading swirling along the neckline, and a short
gold-tinted tulle skirt that flares out when I walk. I bought heels,
too, and I never wear heels—gold, open toed, with thin straps that
wind around my ankles.

Maybe Liam will take my hand after the event, tell me that he—

My dad knocks on my bedroom door, ripping me from a lovely
image of Liam and me, moonlight on my gold tulle, looking at each
other in a very unsibling-like way.

"Thistle, I need you in the office. We took way too much time
off with the tour. I don't have to remind you that we have just over
two weeks to nail down this conclusion. I'm still thinking Marigold

should bring Colton back with her mom, too, that they test out the portal and . . ."

I follow him, but I've stopped listening. It doesn't really matter—he'll write the ending he wants to write.

One more year.

One more year and the last book will be out in the world. I'll tell my fans that I've decided to stop writing so I can go to college. I don't care what I study, as long as it isn't English. Environmental studies. Biology. Botany. Maybe I'll become a professional gardener, spend my day with plants and soil. No paper, no ink. No words.

One more year. And then I'll have my life back.

Dad promised.

❀❀❀

I blow-dry my hair and get dressed. I even put on new gold eyeliner that may or may not be way too much. I wish I had a mom to help me with my makeup, my clothes. But then again, if Mom were still alive, I wouldn't be parading around at a book event—I wouldn't be doing any of this at all.

The doorbell chimes. I race down the stairs, only narrowly avoiding a wipeout in my heels, and smooth down my curls before grabbing the doorknob.

Liam. My stomach flips like it's been two years, not two weeks, since I've seen him.

He has on an orange-and-blue-plaid button-up shirt, brown corduroys, and the tan suede shoes he only wears instead of his beat-up Adidas Sambas for very special occasions. His usually messy hair is combed back, still wet from a shower, and his face is freshly shaven, his skin smooth and silky looking. I want to touch it, but I can't.

"You look nice," I say softly. I feel too shy now after the days apart. The notes. The hope. "That shirt looks new. Is the orange for me or Marigold?"

He smiles, flashing his bright white, almost too-perfect teeth. "Of course it's for you. And I, uh—I wanted to bring flowers, too, but nothing I could find looked as nice as anything that'd come out of your garden. So I—I bought you some bulbs instead." He pulls a small paper bag out of his pocket. "Tulips. The lady at the flower shop said they're still okay to plant this time of year. The idea seemed so cool at the time, but now, handing you a brown paper bag instead of a bouquet, I . . . it feels lame." He's blushing, his eyes focused on the faded red welcome mat that we've probably had since before I was born.

Liam has never given me flowers—or bulbs—before. Not for last year's tour. Not for a birthday. Not ever.

I reach out for the bag. "Li, this is perfect."

He glances up at me, still not convinced.

"Seriously. Perfect. I can wait until spring for your flowers to bloom."

We stare at each other, and I suddenly forget how to use words.

"You look nice, too," he says finally. "You look beautiful, actually."

Beautiful. He's also never called me beautiful before. He's never called me anything.

Liam's parents, Frankie and Aileen, step out onto their front porch, and Dad yells from the office that our car should be down the block. I turn to put the bulbs on the table in the hallway and then grab my jacket. Now I'm the one blushing.

This. Us. I can't think about it—I need to put my mask on. For the next few hours at least, I need to be Thistle Tate, wildly successful prodigy author. Not Thistle Tate, moony and desperately crushing seventeen-year-old girl.

It's a silent car ride to the bookstore, except for my dad rattling off the latest sales updates for Liam's parents. I'm published in thirty-five countries now, apparently.

The driver drops us off just as I'm supposed to be starting. Which is fine, because I don't like to get there early—I much prefer to head straight up front, put on my grand rehearsed show, sign some books, and call it a night. Avoid any excessive mingling. The pretending: it's way too exhausting. I don't know how professional actors do it every day.

We walk into the bookstore and maybe two seconds later I hear her, that sharp, needly voice—"Thistle! Darling! *Surprise!*"

Susan Van Buren. Her glossy silver hair is pulled back in a severe chignon, and her deep orange—no doubt Prada—dress is in stark contrast to her usual wardrobe of black and dark gray. "Only for you do I wear such a garish bright color," she says, and laughs. But I know it's not a joke.

Her direct opposite, my editor, is just behind her, wearing a yellow suit that I have no doubt is part of his regular rotation. Elliot is an eternally sunny, happy man. At least he has been, ever since Marigold made it to the top of national bestsellers lists.

I look around for Liam and his parents, but they've disappeared into the crowd. Dad is still here, of course, greeting Susan and Elliot like they're all lifelong best friends.

"We wouldn't miss your last night for anything in the world," Elliot says to me, leaning down to kiss my cheek. "Standing room only, zero tickets left."

"And it's your second week hitting number two on the *New York Times* series bestseller list! We had to celebrate our rock star!" Susan says, wrapping an arm around my dad as they both gaze at me with a look of pride. "I can't wait to see you shining up there tonight. It's all so fabulous. Fabulous!"

They talk around me as we move toward the audience. Planning, strategizing, raving about the third book as if it's already complete—as if it's already the best book yet. My dad is chiming in a little too much and a little too loudly.

"Thistle is so excited for you to read it soon," Dad says. "She'll be glad to finish, I think. Glad to start on something new."

I freeze. *Something new.* The words tear at me like tiny icy fingers. It's not happening again. I can't let it. I won't. Last time was different. I didn't understand the consequences. I know better now.

"Ooooh, Theo," Susan practically squeals—and Susan is not the squealing type—"that's wonderful news!" I don't have to look up to see the glint in her eyes. The hunger.

"A new book!" Elliot squeals back. "Best news of the night! Is there anything more you can tell us, Thistle, hmm . . . ?"

I have no idea how to respond, so I say instead, "We should probably start the event, right?"

My dad pats me on the back. "Of course. You got this, sweetie. I love you."

I keep moving toward the front, trying to take deep breaths. I should be used to it at this point, two books in: the crowds and the fanfare, my larger-than-life face beaming on the banner strung from the ceiling. Giggling, whispering thirteen-year-old girls—dressed in all shades of gold, orange, and yellow T-shirts, dresses, scarves, hats—their wide eyes mesmerized as I step up to the podium.

It's her! It's Thistle Tate! It's really her!

But no. Still just as scary. Just as surreal. My heart feels like it's a pump or two away from beating itself right out of my chest, sky-rocketing into the audience.

While the owner of the bookstore introduces me, I think about my first reading, at the New York City launch for *Girl in the Afterworld* last year. It was the worst day of my life. Apart from the day my mom died. I had been sweating rivers through my too-frilly new orange dress—which was appropriate for a seven-year-old girl going to church on Easter Sunday, not for a supposedly sophisticated sixteen-year-old-prodigy author, but Dad had insisted. It set *the perfect tone*, he'd said, *sweet and young*, in case anyone managed to somehow forget just how old I really was. Susan and Elliot and their entire team had been huddled together in the front row, watching, waiting, expecting. Expecting so much. Too much. The lying had felt excruciatingly painful that night—physically so, not just emotionally, as if my stomach was being sawed in half while I stood up there at the podium, tripping over the words I was reading from my "own" book. I had to excuse myself halfway through the Q&A to dry heave in the bathroom for ten minutes. *Stage fright*, I'd said afterward, nervously laughing for the crowd. They seemed to warm to me even more after that, because now I was just a normal girl—shy and stuttering and insecure. I was real to them. Marigold Maybee was a happy dream, smoke and light and glitter. But Thistle Tate was flesh and blood.

That had also been a two-week tour, but it felt like two years. Two eternities. My dad never left my side—we slept in the same room, ate every meal at the same table, rode side by side on planes and trains and in smooth black cars. My lips and cheeks felt broken by the end, bruised from the inside out from too many fake smiles.

I take a long sip of water and stare at the audience. My hands are shaking and a drop of water splashes on my dress. If only Marigold were real. If only she could be up here instead of me, addressing her adoring fans. It's Marigold these girls love. Their moms, too, and the scores of twenty-somethings and above who read these books. *My* books. The bookstore owner is shushing them all as they eagerly await my first word.

"It's so good to see you," I say, plastering on the dazzling but still humble smile I've practiced for hours in my bedroom mirror. "And so great to be back home in Philly."

There are some cheers here—pure Philly pride.

"For those of you who are new to the books," I start, dreading the intro my dad has insisted I use for each event. The *heartstring hammer*, he calls it, to *make fans feel closer* to me. I keep my gaze just above the front row of the audience and force myself to keep going. "Marigold's story was created very much from my own life. Just as Marigold loses her mom in a car accident in the first book, I lost my mom the same way when I was a little girl."

I look around for Liam. I need his eyes to reassure me. I say the same exact words in every city, but they feel more real here, more horrible. This was her city. Our city.

When I find Liam, he's sitting with his parents, but he's not watching me. His eyes are squeezed shut and his face is tilted upward, toward the ceiling. If you didn't know him, you might think he looks thoughtful, like he's carefully considering my words. I know better, though. He's anxious for me. Worried. He knows how much I hate being up here.

A loud cough comes from the audience, throaty and purposeful. My dad. It's not the first time he's used that particular cough to nudge me along.

I start again, smile switched back on. "I wrote about Marigold because she . . . she can do what I only dream of doing. Because she can go to the Afterworld. Where her mom is. Marigold can search for her—she can have the hope that she'll find Violet, see her again."

My eyes lock with the eyes of a boy who looks to be about my age, in the front row. Shaggy bright red hair down to his shoulders, hundreds—thousands, maybe—of freckles scattered across his pale face, his neck, his arms. He's wearing a black T-shirt with the name of what's probably an obscure band I'm not nearly cool enough to have ever heard of, tight black jeans, black boots. Black messenger bag at his feet. Susan would approve of his choice in wardrobe, at least. I can't look away because his type is so unexpected here—far too young to be a father escorting an enthralled daughter, but too old to openly admit to reading my books for himself. He's at the end of the row with an empty seat next to him, so he's seemingly on his own. No girlfriend dragging him along.

"Marigold," I start again. *Shoot.* What had I even been saying?

The boy is smiling now, and there's a smugness to it that I don't like. He's amused, apparently, by my lack of cool. I keep my eyes on him, determined to show that I'm capable of being poised and professional.

"Marigold will hopefully have a second chance with her mom. If only the real world were like that, right? If only we had just thirty more minutes to sit down and talk to a person we loved and lost. I was three when my mother passed away. There were so many words, ideas, and feelings I wasn't capable of expressing yet. So many important conversations that my mom and I will never have. I wrote these books so that I could live vicariously through Marigold—feel her excitement, her hope. But still . . . it's not enough. Not really. I'd give everything to trade places with Marigold. Swap out my real life for fiction." I take a deep breath as I finish, feeling strangely triumphant. I even managed to end my speech with truth.

The boy looks away now, the smile gone.

I do a short reading and the Q&A without any more slipups. The signing is uneventful, too—until I look up to see the boy standing in front of me, copies of *Girl in the Afterworld* and *Between Two Worlds* on the table.

I feel myself flush, though I'm not sure why. I open my mouth. Nothing comes out. He has piercing light green eyes and I can't quite read his expression. I squirm in my seat, smoothing my dress across my legs, waiting for him to speak first.

"It's for my sister," he says finally, smiling. Of course that's all this is. He wouldn't want me to think *he's* actually interested in Marigold.

"Don't worry." I reach for the books. "I had a feeling you weren't a rabid superfan." He laughs, and I feel myself start to relax. "What's her name?"

"Emma."

"Where is Emma tonight then?" I ask, my pen starting to glide across the title page of the first book.

"She's, uh . . . been pretty sick. She was hoping she'd be well enough to make it tonight, but it didn't work out." I pause midsignature and look up at him. He's watching me, frowning, but he shakes it off when he sees me notice. "You wouldn't believe the crazy tears that happened when my parents told her she wasn't allowed to come. She's had a calendar going for the last hundred days, crossing off every date to count down to this. Just so you know, Emma Flynn may very well be your most enthusiastic fan in the universe."

I glance down, unable to look him in the eyes now.

"Well, then, that makes up for Brother Flynn being less than ardent," I joke, hoping to change the subject. He'd seemed too cool, too hard at first glance, dressed in all black, that wry smile that had made me itch to prove him wrong—I wasn't prepared for the conversation to turn so personal. But I should know better than anyone that appearances can be deceiving.

"Oliver. Though Brother Flynn has a nice ring to it. Sounds kind of medieval."

I finish autographing the second book and put down my pen. This one got a personal message: *Feel better soon, Emma. I look forward to meeting you next time.*

There has to be one *next time* in Philly for the final book.

"Well, Oliver, I hope this wasn't too painful for you. Tell Emma she's lucky to have such a selfless brother."

"Not painful at all," he says, shoving the books into his messenger bag. "Not my usual Wednesday-night entertainment, but that's okay. I mean, it's pretty wild that you're—what, seventeen? My age? And you've already written two books? Wow. I feel like such a pathetic underachiever standing next to you."

Of all the things fans say to me, this is the worst. Especially coming from someone my own age. They compare themselves, and of course they fall short. *Don't feel bad! I'm not really better than you!* I want to scream. *I'm worse, actually. I'm a total impostor.*

I glance behind him at the long line of people still waiting for signatures, hoping he gets my hint.

Oliver takes a step back, but he's studying me again with those green eyes. I don't know what he's trying to see.

"Well, thanks again, Thistle. Hopefully you'll meet Emma

someday." He's turning toward the door when he abruptly stops, grabs my pen. He pulls a promotional flyer with my face printed on it from the stack at the end of the table and flips it over, scrawling for a few seconds.

"What's this?" I ask as he slides the paper and pen over to me.

"I know you're superbusy, but—if you ever have a free minute—it would make Em's day to hear from you. She's not doing so great, but every good thing helps, you know? No problem if you can't," he says, backing away. "The signed books are already awesome."

I nod and look down at the paper. Emma's name and e-mail address, in neat capital letters, so there's no possibility of me misspelling. If I were to actually e-mail, that is. I fold it up and slip it into my canvas bag with the extra pens and water bottles at my feet. I wonder what's wrong with her, and I start to open my mouth to ask, but Oliver is gone when I look up.

Then I see Liam watching me from the back of the room, and I smile. He smiles back.

And I forget about everything else.

four

Marigold kept returning to the old house, and, from there, the After-world. The more time she spent exploring that impossible skyscraper with Colton—desperately hoping her mom was there—the more she was certain of one thing. She couldn't let herself fall for him.

As alive as Colton seemed in the Afterworld, Marigold knew he wasn't really alive. He had been, though, only a few months ago. He'd been riding his bike down Broad Street in Philly, following his twin brother, Jonah, when a ninety-year-old man had a heart attack behind the steering wheel and plowed through a red light, hitting one of the quickly moving bicycles.

Of all the dead boys there might be, she found one who'd lived a short train ride away from her house in the suburbs. But Colton still looked real, sounded real, felt real—she'd brushed against him, and he definitely was not vapor. He would probably taste real, too. But that . . . No, she wouldn't let herself kiss him. There was only one person who mattered, only one person she needed to find.

Her mom.

—EXCERPT FROM *LEMONADE SKIES*, **BOOK 1: *GIRL IN THE AFTERWORLD***

I strip off my beautiful dress as soon as I'm back in my bedroom, hanging it on my closet door and smoothing out the soft tulle skirt.

Susan and Elliot had surprised Dad and me with dinner plans after I finished signing. Liam and I didn't have a moment alone before they'd swept us away to a fancy restaurant with tiny portions and huge prices, where they regaled Dad and me with *Lemonade Skies* updates until just after midnight.

It's too late now. Liam's lights are already off.

I put on pajamas—Harry Potter again, because everything else is still packed in my tour suitcase—and settle into bed with my laptop and a handful of iced gingersnaps. They're not my favorite cookies. I mean, no chocolate? But they're Marigold's obsession, which is why Elliot and his boss, Martin Davis—head of Zenith Children's Group—had them delivered to our door this morning to welcome us home from the tour. But my dinner was nearly microscopic, so even gingersnaps sound excellent now.

I skim over my e-mails, flip through social media. There are easily hundreds of alerts—tags, private messages, fan photos. I stand up and snap my laptop shut, set it on the dresser. Lately, when Liam's not over, I spend my nights searching through college websites. I've already made a list of the colleges I want to apply to, a handful of Ivies and some more mid-list schools, too, all over the country, even a few abroad. I had considered adding University of Pennsylvania, my mom's alma mater, but that was quickly ruled out. I need a break from Philly. Liam and I joke about going to the same college—though I'm only partly kidding, because it's hard to imagine a life that doesn't involve Liam by my side. Otherwise I have no clue where I really want to go, what I want to do, but that's not what matters. It's just the idea of it. The freedom. I could go to California, or Massachusetts, or Texas. I could go to London if I wanted, Sydney, Florence—Dad tells me I can go *anywhere*. I've earned it, he says.

And that is the one *Lemonade Skies* perk I can't deny: the money. I'm not strong enough or principled enough to refuse that, not when it comes to college. My getaway. What started as a way to save our house and pay off some bills went way beyond all expectations. We could buy five houses now, each nicer and newer than this one. But only this one was Mom's.

I'm too exhausted tonight, though, to think about the future. I lie down on top of my blankets, ignoring the stack of books on my nightstand—advance copies from other YA authors who want me to give them a blurb, bless them with the Thistle Tate golden seal of approval. My dad politely declines most requests on my behalf, only letting through a few judiciously selected stars on the rise—we don't want to *dilute our brand*, he says—but I still end up reading most of the books anyway. Books, my best friends and my worst enemies.

I lean back against my pillows and close my eyes, crunching on a cookie. Gingersnaps are way too hard. More like biscotti than cookies. Why did Dad choose them as Marigold's favorite? He certainly didn't consult me on that particular detail. Unless . . . were gingersnaps my mom's favorite cookie? Is that why my dad picked them?

I'm her daughter, and I don't even know what her favorite kind of cookie was. Or maybe she didn't even *like* cookies—maybe she loved salty more than sweet, potato chips more than chocolate bars. There are so many little things I don't know about her. Little things that add up to big things.

I push the question away and reach for another cookie, my brain replaying the night, and it comes back to me now, a fresh sting, what Dad said to Susan and Elliot: *something new.* There won't be anything new. Not ever. Dad promised.

I bite angrily into my gingersnap just as I hear a *thump* against the window.

A Ping-Pong ball. Liam.

He *is* awake.

I crawl out of bed and run to the window. I tap twice and Liam points to my backyard.

I'm wearing Snoopy slippers and covered in Quidditch accessories again and my makeup is washed off, but it doesn't matter. I step out into the hallway and see that my dad's bedroom door is shut and there's no light on. I tiptoe down the stairs, stopping for just a minute outside the office, listening to Lucy's guttural snore. It's a completely awful sound: *wheeze, gurgle, wheeze, gurgle.* She yelps sometimes, too, sharp squeals as her legs kick, running through the air, a happy puppy again in her dreams. The snoring I got used to, but those yelps would wake me up when she slept in my room.

I keep moving down the hallway, through the kitchen. I grab my coat from the hook and wrap it around me.

"Hey," I say, stepping outside, closing the door softly behind me. Liam is sitting on the brick wall that separates our yards, his legs dangling on our side, just above my patch of garden. The moon is only a fragile crescent tonight, so it's dark back here.

"What's up?" I take a deep breath, trying to force my face into an expression that looks suitably calm. I can't be sure without a mirror, but I'm most likely failing horribly.

"I couldn't sleep," he says quietly, kicking off the wall to stand, barely missing my lavender plants. "And I saw your light was on. Wild night out with your publishing crew?"

"So wild," I say, walking across the patio. "My dad offered me champagne! I said no, though, tempting as it was to erase my mind a bit. I don't want to end up hating champagne like I hate sparkling apple juice."

It's an ugly memory, and I wish I hadn't reminded us both of it now.

"Yeah. Well . . . I'll smuggle over a bottle of bubbles sometime. We can swig it together out here. That way, whenever you drink it for the rest of your life, you'll think of me."

That sounds potentially very romantic.

"And," Liam continues, "even if you puke it up all over the garden, it can't be worse than when you got sick at Disney World. Nothing could scare me away after that."

Less romantic, maybe.

"Gross," I say, shaking my head. But then I look at Liam straight on. "That reminds me of your notes. I didn't say thank-you before. So . . . thank you. Seriously. It was the only good part about being away."

He's stepping toward me, stepping until he's right in front of me. His arms are wrapped around his chest, shivering. It's cold out tonight, and I notice suddenly that he's in his pajamas, too—ratty sweatpants and an unzipped Phillies hoodie over his decade-old *Reading Rainbow* T-shirt, which only still fits because it was more of a dress when his mom first bought it for him. I had made fun of him endlessly, but he'd insisted on wearing it anyway. He even wore it to 7-Eleven once when we went to get Slurpees, just to prove that he wasn't embarrassed. It was his favorite show, after all, and his favorite color, neon green. It's tight against him now, finally. It looks just right.

"What are you grinning about?" he asks. He's smiling, too.

"That god-awful shirt."

"Huh. Well, do you want to go next door and ask Mrs. Rizzo which of us is more likely to win a beauty pageant right now? Because I feel pretty confident that my sweet vintage *Reading Rainbow* shirt will beat out your mangy Harry Potter flannel any day."

Mrs. Rizzo lives in the other house next to mine and she's not my biggest fan. She's no one's fan, really. Well, except for my dad's. She comes by at least once a month, wearing her pink housecoat embroidered with blue-and-white parakeets, to bring him a tin full of bird-shaped shortbread cookies. Each one is covered in a different color of sugar crystal. I call them her *fowl* cookies, although I've never actually eaten one. Otherwise, Mrs. Rizzo is mostly known for keeping tabs on the neighborhood from a bright yellow lawn chair on her front porch.

"We probably don't even have to go over to ask," I say. "She might be spying on us from her bedroom window."

"Solid point. So in that case," Liam says, "we should make her evening more interesting. Don't you think?"

Liam steps in front of me, studying my face. He's only a few inches taller than me to begin with, and he's leaning down now, so close there's barely more than a finger's width of space between us.

"Oh?" I whisper. I'm numb suddenly, stunned, watching Liam as if this exact moment hadn't occurred to me a thousand times before. A million, maybe. As much as I wanted it to happen, I don't think I actually believed that it would. Liam's lips, my lips. Together. Kissing.

Liam hovers just in front of me. I realize he's waiting for me, to make sure I want this as much as he does.

I've fallen into him, my lips on his, before I've even made the conscious decision to move, my body knowing before my brain that THIS IS IT, THISTLE. *This is your moment.*

Thirteen-, fourteen-, fifteen-, sixteen-year-old Thistles would all be dying right now.

Seventeen-year-old Thistle is dying, too.

He gently touches my back, pulling me even closer, and my arms find their way around his neck—so naturally, smoothly, as if it's not weird at all that this is happening. We might as well have been in this exact place a hundred times before.

And the best part, I think, as I smell cinnamon gum and Old

Spice and the winter pine soap that his mom has in every bathroom, always, a scent I'd recognize anywhere—is that he knows the truth.

He knows the truth, and he wants me anyway.

❄❄❄

I wake up grinning, and it takes me a few seconds before I can remember why. As soon as I do—*Liam!*—I shoot out of bed, blankets exploding into a heap on my floor. I run to the window, pulling my curtain aside to look at his window. Of course he's not home. It's Thursday morning, and he has water polo practice before school.

I realize now that we didn't actually make any plans after he finally pulled away, giving me one last peck on the nose before saying good night. But it's Liam. I see him pretty much every day. We have our Ping-Pong balls. We don't have to do anything as formal as arranging a time to go out on a date. *Date.*

I take more time than usual getting ready, showering and braiding part of my hair into a headband, pinning the rest of my wet curls into a loose bun. I scour my closet for a long time, realizing that far too many of my clothes fall into one of two categories: fancy dresses and skirts and blouses for tours and appearances, yoga pants and hoodies for every other kind of day. I go for black yoga pants that technically could be leggings if you don't study them too closely, and a light gray wool sweater that is the only thing my dad saved for me from my mom's closet. I've never worn it outside my room. I was waiting until I grew into it, and then when I finally did, it still didn't feel right to actually *wear* it. I hate the idea of overwashing it, ruining it somehow. Losing some last trace of her that could still possibly linger.

But today is a special day. If my mom were here, I'd want us to be close enough that I could tell her everything about last night. Liam, the kiss, *finally.*

(41)

Wearing her sweater is the best I can do.

I head downstairs and find my dad in the kitchen, flipping a pancake. I pause, surprised. We don't make breakfast. I mean, we pour cereal and milk into a bowl or microwave some oatmeal. A toaster strudel is about as elaborate as it gets. But there's already a pan of bacon set off to the side, and a bottle of maple syrup on the counter.

He turns to greet me, spatula in hand, smiling big. But his face instantly falls.

"That sweater."

"I'm sorry—" I start, already turning back toward the stairs to change.

"No." He shakes his head. "Don't be sorry. Keep it on. Please. I love that sweater. I gave it to your mom for her fortieth birthday."

Her last birthday.

"I'm glad you're wearing it." Dad looks like he wants to ask me more, but he doesn't. He turns back to the pancakes.

I ask an obvious question instead. "What's the special occasion? It smells delicious in here." I move closer to the stove, leaning in to pick a piece of hot bacon from the pan. There are even chocolate chips in the pancakes. I can't remember the last time we had them. But now, standing in this same kitchen, watching Dad at the stove, breathing in the smell of chocolate and batter, I am six years old again.

My dad is my superhero. My best friend.

I move to hug him from behind, burrowing into his back. We don't hug enough these days, I think.

"Well, it is Halloween today," he says. I'd forgotten. Dates tend to be a blur around here—the only ones that matter are deadlines and tours. And even as someone whose world revolves around the afterlife, the idea of creepy ghosts and ghouls has never appealed to me. "But I'm sad there has to be a special occasion for a dad to make his daughter some pancakes."

I pull back, forcing a smile even though now this sentimental moment is leaving me feeling more wary than grateful. "I mean . . . no offense, but we ate a box of doughnuts from Wawa on my last birthday."

He laughs, but it's a sigh, too. It doesn't sound quite right. He flips the last pancake onto a plate and puts the spatula down.

"I don't know, Thistle. You seemed so quiet at dinner last night with Elliot and Susan. This tour has been hard on you, I can tell. These last two *years* have been hard on you. But last night, you just . . . you looked so exhausted. I'm worried that something I thought was *our* dream is only my dream now."

It's true, completely, but I won't say that. I can't. He's trying so hard this morning. He realized that I was upset, and he's doing something, no matter how small, to make me feel better.

"It's not just your dream . . ." Had I ever wanted this? Not really, not even in the beginning. But I had wanted to give him a reason to smile, to feel good about his life. Our life. I'd wanted to save our home.

"I love our time together," I say, as diplomatic as I can be. "I love Marigold. I just . . ."

He waits, his brow furrowing deeper.

"I want to be able to have a more normal life. After it ends. College, friends other than my dad and my dog—no offense to either of you—and the boy next door." I toss a piece of bacon down to Lucy as an apology. Just in case she understood. There's a very human wisdom in her eyes—so much so that as a kid, I was convinced that she was a girl like me trapped in a dog's body. My dad even tried to write a picture book about it years ago, but that manuscript never found a home. Just like so many others.

Lucy inhales the bacon in one bite, gives the floor a few swipes with her tongue to make sure there isn't any residue left, and then sits down on my foot.

"I need you to understand how I feel," I continue, my eyes still on Lucy. "I worry sometimes, that . . . that this won't be enough for you."

"Thistle, you know I want those things for you, too. I want you to go to your dream school, make your dream friends. And you will. You will have all of that."

"Then why did you bring up another book? Last night with Susan and Elliot?"

"Okay, you're right. That was out of line. It was a big night, and I got myself too hyped up. Let's focus on this last book for now. Making it the best it can be."

For now.

I dislike those two words.

"Enjoy the food while it's hot," Dad says, before I can respond.

I fill my plate up with a stack of pancakes and bacon, and we sit and eat in silence.

There's a lot I want to say, though: *No way, Dad. There's no for now. This is over. No more lying. We have all the money we need. And you proved it to yourself—you are a writer. Even if no one knows but me and Liam.* Of course I would never say the last part out loud to him.

I take another huge bite instead, warm butter and maple syrup oozing down my fork.

But even chocolate chips can't make this Halloween breakfast taste special.

five

Marigold opened her eyes, safely back on the porch, curled up in the rocking chair. The shift between worlds surprised her every time. There with Colton one minute, alone at this sad house the next. Minutes passed the same way in both places, but she liked her minutes with him much better.

She still had no idea how the porch and rocking chair created a portal. It didn't matter if she went at night or during the day. She also didn't understand why she, a living girl, was allowed to go to the Afterworld. Was it because she'd almost died the day of the accident? Or could others use the portal and go with her, too? She didn't know. All that mattered was that she could and would keep doing it.

But tomorrow, she wouldn't go to the Afterworld. Marigold would do what she'd just promised Colton—she'd find his twin, Jonah, so she could tell him that Colton wasn't resentful, that he was glad Jonah had been on the lucky bike. That he loved him. Marigold would tell her dad she was hanging out with Abby and Sam—he didn't know that she'd barely talked to them outside of school in weeks. She had to do this, for Colton.

—EXCERPT FROM *LEMONADE SKIES*, **BOOK 1: *GIRL IN THE AFTERWORLD***

Dad and I are sitting down for take-out Thai that night, *Sherlock* playing on the TV—the one show we can both agree on watching—when the doorbell rings. We don't usually get trick-or-treaters, but there's no pumpkin on the stoop and our front lights are off and the curtains pulled closed just in case anyone is tempted to try.

I jump up, nearly knocking over my full plate of pad see ew in my frantic need to get to the door. "It's probably Liam," I say mid-leap toward the hallway, trying and failing to sound casual. I've been staring at the clock since four, his usual return time on Thursdays when there's no water polo game. It's six thirty now. I was starting to lose hope.

"Liam as in the same Liam you see every day?" Dad asks, one eyebrow cocked. "You seem oddly excited."

"Oh, he—he had this project at school today that I wanted to hear about. It was on . . ." My eyes flash to the TV screen, where Sherlock is investigating a conspiracy in an episode based on *The Hound of the Baskervilles*. My dad and I love this one. "It was on the use of dogs in literature. From the *Odyssey* to *Oliver Twist*, *Old Yeller*, *Where the Red Fern Grows*, *Sorcerer's Stone* . . . Cool, right?"

I'm proud, almost, of how quickly the lie came together. Maybe my dad isn't the only creative one in the family. Or maybe these last few years have made me a better liar than I ever wanted to be.

"Dogs, eh?" Dad is looking from me to the screen, where a large demon dog is lunging.

"Ha! Weird timing. I'll have to ask if this made the cut!"

I'm out of the room before Dad can ask more questions. I walk down the front hallway, open the door, and see *him*. He's bundled up in his plaid jacket, cheeks pink, eyes bright under the streetlight. I have to remind myself that this is just Liam, only Liam, that I've seen him literally thousands of times before tonight. Kiss or no kiss, it's still the same Liam.

"Trick or treat," he says, smiling. "I figured I'd actually use the front door today instead of a Ping-Pong ball." He looks nervous, or at least I hope he is—maybe it's just wishful thinking. But I'd rather not be the only one standing here sweating.

"Hey," I manage to respond. I debate hugging him, but I wouldn't typically greet him that way, so I decide against it.

We stand for a minute, staring.

"So . . ." he starts, his grin growing wider.

I should be asking him in. He could sit with Dad and me until we finish dinner, and then we could push onward with one of our Netflix marathons like we were doing before the tour. But the idea of it—of lying side by side on my bed like we do—feels like way too much today. The same, but still so different.

"Want to go for a walk?" he asks.

"Yes," I say, nearly floating off the stoop in relief. A walk feels safer. "Let me grab my coat."

I yell to my dad that I'm going out and shut the front door before he can say anything.

Liam and I are quiet for the first few minutes. I'm not sure if he's leading me somewhere in particular, or if we're both just aimlessly walking for the sake of being together. Two mini-ghosts and a Wonder Woman pass us on the sidewalk. A small cluster of glowing jack-o'-lanterns grin and grimace from a nearby stoop.

"Are you hungry?" he asks.

"Sure," I say, thinking about the delicious mound of pad see ew that's sitting on the TV tray. I hope my dad remembers to put it in the fridge so it's still good for tomorrow's breakfast.

"I was going to say we could grab some sandwiches from Wawa and sit on the art museum steps, but it's probably too cold for that. How about Juan José's?"

I nod, smiling. It's one of our favorite local spots, a Mexican dive that everyone but us seems to think is viable for take-out orders only. I'm pretty sure it's the painfully bright plastic floral tablecloths and fluorescent lights, but that's fine by me. Whenever we eat there, we're the only customers, like it's our own private restaurant. They always bring us complimentary cups of some delicious mango concoction.

We've been going for years and I still don't know the name of the drink, but it tastes like sunshine and laughter and world peace.

We don't talk again during our walk, but luckily it's only a few more minutes until I see the Juan José's sign, a flashing neon-yellow sombrero. Liam picks up his pace just as we're closing in, beating me by a few steps. He opens the door then, a cluster of bells at the top chiming loudly, and holds it, waiting for me to go through first. Liam has never gone out of his way to open any doors for me. Ever. Not to say that he's lazy or selfish or anything like that, but there was no need for chivalry before now because we were just two best friends. It's another first. Flowers. *Beautiful.* And now this . . .

I realize that Liam is watching me stand frozen in front of the door. He looks mildly confused, maybe mildly amused, too.

"Oh," I say. "Thank you."

We sit at our usual table and place our usual order—six tacos, a quesadilla, and a burrito, all to be split down the middle. And chips, with two different salsas. Pineapple for me, spicy chipotle for Liam.

"So," I say, after I've nearly finished my first cup of the mango-flavored nectar of the gods. "How was school today?"

I never ask that question. Just like he never asks about my day at home with Dad. There's not enough common ground—too many kids, teachers, classes I will never really know about or understand. And for me, every day is more or less the same, and talking about the writing only makes me cranky. So we talk about other things, movies and celebrities and politics. College. Dreams. And hypothetical questions—we love hypothetical questions. For example: *Who would you rather see as president, Miley Cyrus or Taylor Swift? Would you rather watch only Nicholas Sparks movies for the rest of your life, or eat nothing but chocolate for a hundred straight days? Never fall in love, or never find a job that makes you happy?*

We can play this game for hours.

"Okay," he says, making himself a paper ring out of the straw wrapper. "Had a Calc quiz, started *Gatsby* in English Lit, watched a ridiculous video about the reproductive habits of spiders in Bio. Best part of the day was when Brian Bender stood up on his chair and asked Kyle Reynolds out on a date in front of the whole cafeteria. But you don't know Brian . . . or Kyle . . . so it loses some of the effect, I guess. Kyle's been very out since elementary school, but Brian, not so much. The whole cafeteria broke out in applause."

"That's cool," I say. "This guy, Kyle, he said yes, then?"

"Yep." Liam grins. "It was awesome."

"Great." I bite down on my straw, grinding it between my front teeth.

"Would you rather . . ." Liam starts, his dark eyes twinkling, "win a two-week trip to South America, all expenses paid, with a personalized tour of Machu Picchu, or . . ."

I laugh. My dream trip, as he knows, though my dad's been too busy to agree to go. Yet. "How in the world will you top that? Lame question, I can already feel it."

"Or go on a date with me?" he finishes.

"Oh."

"Not as easy as you thought?" He's still smiling, but it's more anxious now. I can tell because his left eye is crinkled just a little too much, making his gaze a smidge lopsided.

"Well, that depends," I say, hoping my cheeks aren't as red as they feel. "That's a two-week trip but a one-night date. That doesn't seem fair. Is there a chance for more dates?"

His neon grin flashes. That's what I've always called it: *neon*. His brightest, fullest, highest-wattage smile that only comes out when it's incredibly deserved. Like when he won free Diamond Club Phillies tickets last year, right on the field behind home plate, or the time his parents surprised him—and me—with that infamous trip to Disney World.

"I'd say there's a very high chance of multiple dates then," he says. "If that helps in your decision-making."

I nod, pretending to look serious and thoughtful. But on the inside I am nothing but high-pitched squeals and fist pumps and high kicks that could probably get me a place with the Radio City Rockettes.

"How about we go on a date to Machu Picchu?" I ask.

"Nope. It's South America or me. One or the other. I should have emphasized the small print on that. My bad. If you go on the date with me, you can never go to Machu Picchu. And vice versa." There is *always* fine print to our hypotheticals.

"Well, then, after careful deliberation . . ."

He pretends to hold his breath, waiting.

"You. I pick the date."

The neon smile is back, lingering this time, like it might become his permanent expression.

"I like that decision."

"Me too."

"And the bonus to that decision? It's effective immediately! Thistle Tate, we are now officially on our first date—with more to come."

If we were any other two human beings on this planet right now, I'd be making myself gag under the table. We're every cheesy dialogue that Liam and I have ever made fun of, watching bad rom-coms or old episodes of *The OC* or *Gilmore Girls*. And it feels good.

"I think that this is our first hypothetical situation that actually became real life," I say, my smile no doubt just as neon as his. "And thank goodness. Because last month when I picked eating nothing but mushrooms for every meal for the rest of my life so that I wouldn't die the next day, that would have sucked in actual practice. I definitely might have regretted that decision."

"Not this one, though," Liam says. He reaches across the table and grabs my hand. His palm is hot and sweaty, just like mine. "I hope."

"I'll have to go on a few more dates before I can say for sure. I don't want to give you a rash answer."

"Fair. I'll give you that. But I still can't believe you'd pick me over Machu Picchu. You've been obsessing about going there ever since we were ten and saw that documentary on the History channel. You couldn't stop worrying about whether or not it was aliens who built it all. It was pretty hilarious."

"No worries, plenty of other mysterious old ruins I can see."

"So is there something else you would have chosen over me?" He gives me a big, terrible, adorable wink. We've both always been notoriously bad winkers.

Before I can answer him, the waitress comes over with our food, lining up the overflowing plates between us.

Of course not, I think first. But then I realize, that's not quite true, is it?

Because what if I could go, like Marigold, to the afterworld? See my mom again. A date with Liam or a chance to see my mom . . .

My mom, of course. The afterworld.

But I don't tell him that.

Instead I say, "I think I've already given you enough compliments for one night. Let's eat before that cute round head of yours gets any bigger."

❀❀❀

When I get home Dad's bedroom door is shut and his lights turned off. I take a flying leap onto my bed, my hands stretched above my head as I bounce off the mattress. My fingers knock against something—the full glass of water on my nightstand.

Usually I'd be cursing and ranting, but I'm too giddy about my *date* to feel concerned about anything right now. I roll over to assess the damage. The glass didn't break and most of the water seems to have spilled on top of the canvas bag that I used at my signing last night. I stand up and start to pull everything out—a few spare books, pens, water bottles—still mostly dry, so that I can hang the wet bag on my desk chair. Then my fingers wrap around a last scrap of paper at the bottom. A crumpled old receipt or flyer probably. I start to reach for the wastebasket when I see the handwriting. *Emma Flynn.*

My stomach twists with guilt. But I hadn't actually agreed to e-mail her, had I? I shouldn't. Somehow lying to a sick girl feels infinitely worse than lying to a healthy girl.

On the other hand, it would take me thirty seconds to shoot off some generic message. And her brother had said it would make her day.

I sit down at my desk and open up my laptop. Just one quick note. My good deed for the day.

Dear Emma Flynn . . .

I write a few short lines and hit Send. It was the right thing to do. Now I can forget about it, clear conscience.

But then I picture her telling Oliver, how happy he'll be. And strangely, as I lie in bed, drifting off to sleep, I don't think about Liam.

I think about Emma and Oliver Flynn.

❀❀❀

I wake up a few hours later, 3:37 according to the bright blue numbers on the clock on my nightstand. I sigh and roll over, hoping I can get back to sleep. I'd been having such a nice dream, a grand adventure with Sherlock—starring Benedict Cumberbatch, of course—involving mermaids and sirens and a crumbling castle by the sea.

But then I hear him, and I realize why I woke up.

My dad, crying in his bedroom, across the thin wall that separates us. It's a sound I haven't heard in years, not since before Marigold came around.

I slip out of bed and into the hallway. I knock once, twice. The crying stops, and the house is suddenly too quiet. I can just barely hear Lucy wheezing steadily from downstairs.

"Dad?" I say.

"I'm fine, Thistle," he responds quickly, and then coughs, clearing his throat. "Nothing to worry about, sorry I woke you. You can go back to bed."

I take a deep breath and ignore him, turn the knob, and push the door open, blinking my eyes a few times as the room comes into focus. The light is on, and my dad is in bed, the blankets covered in photos and papers and women's jewelry. It must be my mom's.

"What—?" I start, but then move closer to the bed.

"I'm sorry, I'm fine, I really am," my dad mutters, gathering up a thick pile of what look like handwritten letters. "It was just seeing you in her sweater this morning . . . it made me think about her even more than usual."

I pick up a photo I've never seen before—my mom and dad on a beach, laughing into the wind, hair blowing wildly. "What is this stuff? You've never shown me any of it."

He's silent for a moment before saying, "I know, sweetie. I haven't even let *myself* look at these things in a long time, but you're right, I should share these pictures with you. Not tonight, but soon, okay?"

I put the photo back down on the bed. "What are those letters? Can I read them?"

"They're—they're a bit private, actually."

"Did Mom write them?"

"Yeah. She loved writing letters, especially ones she would never send."

"I want to read them. Please let me?"

"Maybe someday." He sighs, dropping the letters into a red metal box.

The anger is seeping in, slow and heavy, and I'm gritting my teeth, deciding how much of a fight I'm ready to start right now. But then I see a photo that's fallen to the floor just below me, and I pause, bending down to pick it up so that I can study it more closely.

My mom, waving from the driver's seat of a bright blue car. It takes me another few seconds, but then I realize I'm there, too—tiny two- or three-year-old me—smiling out the window in the backseat.

"Was this the car . . . ?"

"Yes." He's clearing the rest of the bed, the last traces of my mom quickly disappearing back into that red box. "It's very late. You should go back to bed."

I want to say more, push harder. But I go to my room instead, slamming my door behind me.

After restless tossing and turning, I eventually fall back to sleep. There's no more Sherlock, though, no more Benedict. I'm Marigold now, or Marigold is me, I can't tell—it's so blurry, bright, like a photo overexposed in the sun. But I'm climbing up a flight of stairs inside that grand skyscraper toward my mom, I can tell that much—I can feel it deep in my bones.

Closer, closer.

Close, but never quite there.

six

Marigold felt like a stalker.

She'd taken the train into Philly and had been waiting on a bench outside Jonah's school for over an hour now—a Thursday afternoon, because Colton had told her that was when Jonah's debate team met, and she wouldn't have to find him in the usual afterschool crowd. That this would be easier.

At 4:25 he finally emerged. He was alone, preoccupied with something on his phone. Marigold knew Jonah would look exactly like Colton, of course. They were identical twins. But still, she hadn't been prepared for the utter exactness of it all: their tight black curls, their dimpled cheeks, and their dark-lashed golden eyes like perfect mirror images.

"Jonah," she said, standing up.

He looked at her, startled.

"My name is Marigold. And I know your brother."

—EXCERPT FROM *LEMONADE SKIES,* **BOOK 1: GIRL IN THE AFTERWORLD**

The next morning, my dad and I pretend the night before never happened. And I can almost believe it, too. We're so good at acting around here.

He works on the book while I sit next to him and occasionally nod when he asks for an opinion. Usually our mornings revolve around Marigold, and afternoons are reserved for homeschooling curriculum—but it switches some days, depending on when Dad is struck by inspiration. He tinkers without me, too, but only when he's obsessively rereading or editing or polishing, not when he's working on new material. It makes him feel less guilty, I think. I'm always *included* in the creating, not that my opinions count for much.

Dad tells me to take a break after lunch, so I curl up on my bed and start reading. I have just a few pages left of an advance reader's copy for a debut author, a sort of Wild West space-opera mash-up. I finish, too quickly, and decide that this one is worthy of a blurb, no matter what Dad says. I sit at my desk and write the quote, then open my e-mail and send it off to the author. I scroll through a string of publicity requests next, about to close out when I see it: a message from Emma Flynn.

I'd forgotten about the e-mail already. And for some reason, I hadn't actually pictured a scenario in which she would respond.

> Hey, Thistle. It's Oliver. Emma's in the hospital right now, so she had me checking her e-mail. She's okay, nothing too serious, just had to be stabilized. Should be a few days. I didn't tell her you e-mailed yet because I wanted to ask if maybe you could stop by? Just a quick hello. Tomorrow or Sunday maybe? I know this is a huge favor to ask. So no pressure, seriously. But just in case you can, she's at the Children's Hospital. Give her name at the front desk. If not, totally cool. E-mail was great. Thanks again.—O

I close the e-mail. Maybe I can pretend it slipped into spam. Let my e-mail be enough, like Oliver said. Because I shouldn't go. I really shouldn't.

I run through the possibilities: I do go, and she's so super-appreciative that I feel even more terrible than usual for days. I don't go, and Emma is fine, she reads the e-mail later and thinks I'm great. I don't go, and Emma *dies*, and I regret forever that I didn't brighten her final days. Ugh. I want to erase that last possibility from my brain. Because it's the only one I can see now.

I'll think about it. Sleep on it tonight.

But I'm distracted during my homeschooling lessons all afternoon. My first *date* with Liam. The late-night conversation with Dad. Mom. Emma and Oliver. Dad's too busy to notice, tinkering with our latest chapter while I work on calc. Two weeks until the deadline, he reminded me earlier, as if I could somehow forget.

Two weeks, and four chapters to go.

Dad was way ahead of schedule for the first two books, but not this time. The stakes are higher, crafting the perfect ending for the series. He deletes more than he writes each day.

Somehow the afternoon actually passes, and Liam comes over after dinner. Again, no Ping-Pong balls. As much as I love tradition, I like that he's using the front door now. I like that it marks a new era for us. My dad's holed up in the office tonight with the door shut, so we claim the sofa. We're deep into a fierce game of Scrabble—I'm just an *i* away from crushing him with *quixotic*—when I tell him about Emma.

"So, wait," he says, after I've started briefing him about Oliver, his eyes still squinting at his row of tiles. "This was the ginger guy you were talking to at the signing, right? I wondered why he was there. I assumed it was for a sister or a girlfriend or something like that. No offense. Not your usual demographic."

"Right," I say, nodding, "and he said his sister was sick, and she'd love if I wrote her an e-mail. So I did. Last night. Just a short note saying I hoped she felt better. But then I heard from Oliver today, and she's in the hospital, so . . ."

"He wants you to visit?"

"Yeah. He said no pressure, though."

"Yeah, easy to say *no pressure*, but he's putting pressure on you just by asking. What's wrong with her?"

"I don't know. I assume cancer, but who knows? She's sick enough to be in the hospital. That's what I can't stop thinking about."

"Wait," he says, turning to me. He's frowning, his eyebrows pinching together in one heavy dark line. "You're not actually considering going, right?"

"Well, I don't—" I stop, reach down to pet Lucy, using her as an excuse to look away. I do this a lot, I realize. She's my crutch. "Maybe? I don't know. I haven't decided anything yet."

"I mean, I know it's not up to me, it's your call. But . . . you don't want to lie to this sick girl, do you? It just seems—I don't know, even more wildly unethical than usual."

"*Wildly unethical?*" I turn to face him.

"Well, I mean . . . come on?" He's looking at me like he doesn't have to say the full sentence. Like of course we both know exactly what he means.

And I do. Oh, I do. I know it's *all* unethical—wildly unethical, as Liam put it. I knew from the day I said yes, we could go with Susan Van Buren—and I know it a thousand times more now. The truth is sharp and heavy and suffocating. I wear it all day, every day. It's why I hide from most people. Why my world is so small. Too small.

I don't need Liam to remind me. And his judging me out loud for the first time ever makes me say, "I'm going to do it," the words spilling out before I can stop myself. "I'm going to go see Emma in the hospital. I know I'm a lie—it's a lie—but maybe it'll make her happy. Is that so wrong? To use the lie for one good cause?" I'm still not sure I want to go, but now I have to. The line has been drawn—by me, like a thick black Sharpie marker on a bright white sheet of paper. I can't back down.

"I'm sorry, but . . . I just don't get it," Liam says quietly. "I try so hard to be supportive of you, I really do. But I guess you have to do what you need to do. It's your life."

My anger is fading, and I'm not sure what I'm feeling now. Fear, maybe. Fear that I've permanently damaged this tenuous new bond with Liam. Because what he said is true. And he's upset because he cares. Because he has morals. That's part of what I love about him. But if everything I do is unethical, why not use it for some good once in a while? Why not make one sick girl just a little bit happier?

He smiles at me, small and hesitant, and then says, "I'm gonna head out, Coach is making us come in tomorrow morning for extra practice. I hate early Saturdays, but we have some big meets coming up. We're okay, right?" His already dark eyes look even darker than usual, wide and unblinking.

"Of course we're okay," I say, grabbing his hand. "Though I am mildly upset I didn't get to properly win this round . . . I'm saving the tiles."

We kiss by the door, but it's a quick peck tonight.

"I'll see you later tomorrow," he says, giving me one last hug before stepping onto the porch.

"Tomorrow," I say back. *After I go to the hospital*, I think.

I watch him through the glass pane until he disappears behind his side of the brick wall. And I decide: I'm not going to let Dad in on what would usually be an official Thistle Tate Team Decision. I'll say I'm in the mood for a long walk, or that I'm going out to see a movie. The thought sends a tiny thrill through me, which is pathetic. It's a pretty unrebellious way to go against your parent, visiting a sick girl in the hospital.

I check the Post-it with Emma's room number. I've only been to the Children's Hospital once before, a charity read-a-thon that I signed at, along with two other local authors. I was in a cheerily decorated common area then, though, not a hospital room.

Yes, definitely the door in front of me. I'm here, even if I'm still not sure I want to be. I step closer, easing in along the wall so that no one inside the room can see me. I pause, listening. A low beeping, TV news, a woman laughing. I can't tell what's coming from Emma's room and what's coming from the other rooms around me. I take another step, now just inches away from the partly opened door.

I hear another laugh, but it's a guy this time. Oliver maybe? I'm not sure how well I remember the sound of his voice. But I do remember that smile on his face when I stumbled at my event, talking about my mom. How much I had resented him for it. And now I'm here, about to visit his sister—and him, it would seem.

I lift my hand, my fingers squeezing into a clammy fist. But I freeze there, my knuckles nearly grazing the door frame. *Ten minutes. You only have to stay for ten minutes.* I'll say I need to get back home to write—Marigold deadlines and all that. Emma will appreciate that reasoning.

I knock on the doorframe. A second passes, two tops, and then I catch a glimpse of Oliver's bright red hair, his freckly face as he pokes his head out of the room.

"Whoa," he says, looking completely stunned. "You actually came. That's so awesome."

He steps into the hallway—in black again, head to toe. There's not even any type or logo on his shirt this time to break it up. Black, black, more black.

I want to ask him now—to mentally prep myself—*Why is Emma here?* But she can probably hear everything from the room.

"Is this a good time?" I ask instead. "I don't have long . . ." I let the sentence drop off, not wanting to blatantly lie.

"Sure, totally great." He gently grabs my arm, nudging me a few feet away from the door. "Emma is doing okay," he says, his voice much lower this time. "Crohn's. Nasty rough patch right now."

"Crohn's . . . ?" Not cancer then. Crohn's. It has something to do with the intestines, I know that much. It's a word I've heard but never actually thought about.

"Crohn's disease. Inflamed GI—gastrointestinal—tract, essentially. Emma's had it for a few years now. Sometimes she seems perfectly fine, barely has any symptoms. But then other times, like now . . ." He shakes his head. "It can get pretty bad. She has something called a stricture, which means she has so much swelling in her intestines that they became blocked and don't work right anymore. She was in a lot of pain, but they've been reducing the inflammation since she got here. The good news is that she probably won't need surgery. Not now, at least."

"I'm sorry," I say, though I wish I had something more insightful or more meaningful to offer him. "That sounds pretty terrible."

"It is, but she's a trouper. She'll get through it. And she'll definitely feel better now that you're here. You'll be a temporary miracle cure."

I give a weak smile, and we stand there for a moment, staring at each other in the cold fluorescent light of the hallway.

"Should we go in?" I ask finally. "I'm sure she's wondering who in the world you're out here talking to." *Ten minutes*, I remind myself. *Ten.*

"Yeah, of course," he says, smiling again. "Our mom had to run some errands and my dad—he's a lawyer—is busy working on some big case, so it's just me and Em." He's already walking back through the door.

I peer into the room slowly, cautiously, hoping to see Emma before she sees me so that I have a second to mentally compose myself. But Oliver's female clone is already staring at me from the bed. She's a few years younger and a bit skinnier, I can tell, but other than that and an extra ten inches of that flaming-red hair, they could be identical twins.

"Hey there, Emma," I say, my voice embarrassingly high-pitched and squeaky. "I'm—"

"Thistle Tate!" she finishes for me, jerking upright from her pillows. "Oh my god, Ollie, how the fuck did you get Thistle to come here?"

"So crude, Em, cursing in front of our esteemed visitor," Oliver says, but he's chuckling.

Emma turns to me. "Hospital rules. Mom and Dad let me curse here, as long as it's not directly to a doctor or nurse. They know it sucks, so they tell me that the least I can do is say fuck and shit and hell as much as I damn well please."

"I keep telling them that it's a terrible rule," Oliver mutters.

"I totally fucking support it," I say, feeling bold enough to step right up to her bedside.

Emma squeals with laughter. "Oh man, I didn't think you could get any cooler. You just nailed it!" She lifts her hand to high-five, and I slap it, but lightly. I can't stop looking at the tube sticking straight into her arm, her skin so white it's nearly translucent.

"Trust me, these things are much more secure than they look."

"Sorry." My cheeks feel hot. I force myself to meet her light green eyes, the exact same shade as Oliver's. "I've just . . . I've never visited anyone in the hospital before."

"I hate that I had to ruin your lucky streak. But I was so bummed to miss your event the other night. I thought Ollie was a god just for getting me the signed books, but *this* . . . ! This is pretty ridiculously outstanding, even for him. Your book is what's making this particular episode even remotely bearable. I can almost forget about the shitty things going on with my body when I'm hanging out with Marigold."

She's pointing to the table next to her bed, where there's a copy of *Between Two Worlds* propped open. She's more than halfway through.

"What do you think so far?" I regret asking this the second I hear my words out loud. I wanted to avoid book talk as much as possible. Stick to general niceties—the weather, hospital food, whatever it is you talk about when you're visiting someone in the hospital. But not Marigold.

"This is my second time reading it. I started again yesterday. It's perfection. Thank god she's found her mom—I was hoping you wouldn't make us wait until the last book! I seriously bawled. Also I have to say, and I know you probably get this all the time and you're sick of hearing people geek out on you, but . . . totally on Team Jonah."

I can't help but grin at that. "So am I. But don't tell anyone, okay?"

"Is that a teaser for the next book?" There's a machine beeping quietly behind her, and I swear the beeps are getting faster. "It is, isn't it? I hope she picks Jonah instead of Colton. You can just tell when they're together, what they have is so much more real. Colton tries to act all perfect, but he's so clingy and sulky and he's totally got an ego. Even if he wasn't dead and some weird ghostly thing in the Afterworld, he's like the guy that every girl thinks she wants, sexy and brooding and whatnot, but not the guy they actually need. You know?"

"Spoken with the vast wisdom of a thirteen-year-old," Oliver says. I glance at him and see that he's smirking at us. Now this is the attitude I expected from Oliver.

"Hey," I say, putting my hands on my hips and attempting my best glare. "I happen to be seventeen and have had barely any romantic experience either, but that doesn't mean I don't understand feelings and relationships. Women are intuitive about these things. Your sister is right. Colton is the dream, Jonah is the reality. And reality doesn't have to be a bad thing."

Oliver puts his hands up in mock surrender.

"Again, just when I think you couldn't possibly get any more awesome," Emma says, shaking her head. She sticks her tongue out at Oliver. "It's not like you're one to talk about experience, Ollie. How many times do I have to tell you, secretly watching a few episodes of *The Bachelor* doesn't count as actual real-life dating experience."

I grin, resisting the urge to demand another high five. Her praise makes me proud—too proud, probably. But she likes the me that she's meeting right now, not just the me that she thinks wrote the book she's currently obsessing over.

"So what else do you like to do, besides writing?" Emma asks. "I've read loads of blog interviews and other posts that you've done, and you talk a lot about your writing life and whatnot. And I know you're homeschooled. But what about the rest of your time?"

"I, uh . . ." *I have no friends, really, so I spend most of my time talking to my dog, talking to my garden, or talking to the boy next door. Occasionally* kissing *the boy next door, but that's a new development.* I'm fairly certain this isn't quite the answer she's looking for, though. So instead: "I read a lot of YA . . . besides *Lemonade Skies*, that is. I get a ton of advance reader's copies, so my shelf is always well stocked."

"You're so fucking lucky! I would never want to leave my room."

"Okay," Oliver says. "I think you're taking advantage of this rule right now. It's supposed to be when you're in pain and life at the hospital sucks. It doesn't suck right now."

"I don't remember that clause, Ollie," Emma says, shaking her head. "Take it up with the judges." She turns back to me, one very inquisitive-looking eyebrow raised. "Besides reading, though, I mean. Something that doesn't involve words or ink or paper."

"I have a garden in our yard," I say lamely. "Well, *yard* is a stretch. So is *garden*, really. I grow a few plants out there. Let's say that."

Emma nods, smiling encouragingly.

"And I . . . watch a lot of TV? I'm on a *Sherlock* kick right now. But yeah, I'm afraid my life isn't that glamorous, really."

"Huh. And here I was, picturing you traipsing around the globe with other famous YA authors, taking selfies in front of some pyramids or hiking around Loch Ness, looking for Nessie. But this is okay, too. I kind of like that you're really just as boring as me."

I want to laugh. Of course I don't have any author friends. For obvious reasons. They're friendly enough at events, sure, and some have reached out about grabbing a coffee when they're in town. But I always have an excuse, some deadline or other obligation.

"Em," Oliver says, leaning in closer to the bed. I glance over to see him frowning at her, wagging his finger. He looks adorably parental.

I laugh. "It's fine. Really. That's the first time anyone's ever called me boring as a compliment. But I'll take it. There are worse things."

Much worse things, I think. Like dishonest. Fraudulent.

My good mood disappears. The conversation isn't fun anymore. Emma isn't just a nice girl who laughed at a few of my jokes. She's a nice girl who would be horribly disappointed if she knew the truth about me.

"I should go," I say, probably too abruptly. Emma's face falls at the words, but she recovers quickly, forcing a small smile.

"Of course. You must be ridiculously busy."

I nod. "I'm glad I could come, though. I'm really happy we could meet. I—I hope you feel better and get out of here soon."

"Me too. But at least I have Marigold with me to help the hours go faster."

"At the rate you're going, you'll need something new before this afternoon unless you want to read *Between Two Worlds* for a third time. Oliver may have to make a library run for you."

"Oh, sure," Oliver says, grinning at me. "But she's getting Jonathan Safran Foer this time. Or maybe some Neil Gaiman."

"YA isn't intellectually stimulating enough for you?" I try to play it cool, to reclaim some of my boldness from earlier, but I mostly end up sounding annoyed.

"I'm not saying that! I just like to diversify."

"I'll read this Jonathan guy when you read some Thistle," Emma chimes in.

Oliver nods solemnly. "I will. When I get home tonight, I'll find the first one. I have to start properly."

"That's really not necessary . . ." I don't want to picture it, but the image flashes across my mind anyway, Oliver curled up in his room—probably with black sheets and black pillows, black walls covered in posters for bands that all look cool and edgy, long hair and beards and tattoos—cracking open the cover of *Girl in the Afterworld*. The cover that says *By Thistle Tate*.

"I'm a wannabe writer," he says, "short stories mostly. It'll be good for me. Give me something to aspire to."

Not me, I want to say. *No one should aspire to be like me.* Ever.

"This was really great," I say instead, already stepping backward, closer to the door. I'm waving my hand in jerky circles as if I'm cleaning an invisible window. I can't seem to make myself stop, though, and for whatever reason my instinct is to add a farewell curtsy, too. Just to make it even weirder. Oliver and Emma are watching me with eerily identical expressions, orangey-red eyebrows crooked up in amusement, deep dimples in their left cheeks, hands raised in slow, normal waves.

"Bye, Thistle!" Emma calls as I back out of the room, my legs still in some strange curtsy-like crouch. "You're the fucking best!"

I leave the hospital, hail a cab. I fight tears the whole way home.

Liam was right.

I shouldn't have gone there.

seven

Marigold was sitting in the rocking chair, her eyes just about to close, when he called out. Her name sliced through the warm summer rain.

"Dad." She tripped out of the chair in her rush to stand, steadying herself before she stumbled into the wobbly porch railing.

"What are you doing here?" he said. "I called Abby. And Sam. They said they haven't hung out with you in ages. Is this where you've been spending your time?"

"Maybe," she said, sighing. "Yes."

"Why?" He looked so tired, so old. So empty.

"I—" Marigold started and then she stopped. This was her chance. This was her moment to tell him the truth. But before she could say anything, a bolt of lightning flashed in the near distance. Thunder rumbled.

"We need to go home," her dad said, reaching out for her hand. "It's time for you to stop dwelling on the accident. It's time to move on."

—EXCERPT FROM *LEMONADE SKIES*, **BOOK 1: GIRL IN THE AFTERWORLD**

L iam doesn't ask about the visit, and I don't bring it up. Which is great, because I'm not ready to talk about it. It hurts too much. It hurts knowing that even if Emma and I had genuinely hit it off, felt a real connection for a few minutes, none of that really mattered. It meant nothing when the whole basis for me being there was a lie.

I spend the rest of the weekend hanging out with Liam, and if anything even slightly negative tiptoes its way into my thoughts, I squeeze his hand tighter or lean in for a kiss, focus on his eyes, his lips, his fingers.

We're watching *Goblet of Fire* Sunday afternoon—in the living room, because Harry deserves the big screen, not my laptop—when I hit Pause and turn to him, saying, "Let's tell my dad. About us. That we're together." I feel as surprised as he looks, but I do tend to get emotional during the Yule Ball scene. Hermione looks so beautiful in that pink dress with her hair all fancy. Her grand entrance! Her fight with Ron! So many feelings.

"I guess we can," he says, his eyes looking somewhere an inch or two above mine. "If that's what you really want."

"He's not dense," I say, suddenly feeling defensive. "I'm sure he'll pick up on something being different soon enough on his own. Right?"

"Yeah. Maybe." He still isn't looking at me.

"But if you're not ready, then . . ." I let it fade out, hoping that he'll jump in and save me, assure me that yes, of course he wants to tell my dad—he wants to tell the *whole world*, by golly!

"I—what are we going to say, exactly?" He's put an emphasis on *exactly* that I don't like, a lilting twist that draws out for a beat too long. I like the silence that follows it even less.

"That we're . . . dating?" I finally say, unable to bear the awkwardness of the moment any longer. "Aren't we?"

"Yeah. Of course we are," he says. "I just mean, do you think we're ready to put a label on it? *Official* boyfriend-girlfriend status? It's been a few days. There's no rush. Especially since this is the first time you've ever dated anyone."

"The first time *I've* ever dated?"

"Well, I mean, you know I had a few dates last year, at least. Arianna. And Riley."

Yes, he had told me about them.

Yes, I had promptly deleted the information from my brain.

"Okay, so you went on a few dates. That hardly makes you more experienced than me."

"Fine," he says, reluctantly nodding at me. I'm relieved to see that he's uncomfortable, too. It shouldn't just be me. "So we're both new to this whole thing. Even more reason to take it slow and not get our parents worked up. Right?"

I think about the conversation I overheard between Liam and his mom and decide he's probably right. There'd be rules, boundaries.

"Okay," I say. "But I wasn't going to tell my dad to start putting aside my dowry or anything like that."

"Dowry?" he asks, but he's smiling again. "Sounds a bit outdated for a self-proclaimed modern woman such as yourself."

"I did let you pay for me at Juan José's. I guess I'm not totally progressive. Because I'd be a liar to pretend I didn't like it a little bit. Feeling like a delicate lady and all."

"You can be my lady any day," he says. "Or you can be my *person*, if you prefer that."

I edge a few inches closer on the sofa, and so does he. There's a moment—or just a second, maybe, it's all one lovely blur—of staring into each other's eyes, Liam's palm brushing my cheek. And then we're kissing, faster and harder than we have before.

Just as Liam's hand starts to graze under my shirt, the tips of his fingers spreading warmth across my entire back . . . my dad walks in.

"Cough, cough, cough," he says, not even bothering to fake an actual coughing sound.

Liam flies off me so fast that he loses balance as he stands, tripping over a previously sound-asleep Lucy and slamming down hard against the wooden floor. Lucy is wide awake now, howling up at the ceiling. Amidst the chaos, I cover myself with a pillow, as if I have anything to actually hide. My shirt is snagged maybe an inch above my waist, but otherwise I'm perfectly decent. On the outside, at least. On the inside, I feel wildly, wonderfully indecent.

"So I suppose this means you two aren't *just friends* anymore?" Dad leans against the door frame, arms crossed.

"It's . . . recent," I say.

"Is it?" he says, his right eyebrow very purposefully cocked for effect.

"It really is," Liam says, wobbling slightly as he pulls himself up to stand. "Less than a week, actually."

"I see."

Liam looks explosively red. He turns, his eyes pleading for me to take over.

"Don't worry, Dad." My voice is surprisingly steady. All those readings have prepared me to handle anything with composure, I suppose. "We'll go slow. Okay?"

Dad opens his mouth, closes it again. His gaze flits everywhere but at me. I feel bad for him, like I always do when these monumental life conversations come up—my first bra, my first period, my first razor.

"We'll be fine, Dad," I say, more gently now. "You can trust us."

I'm not sure exactly what I mean by that. Trust us to not have sex? I can't promise that. Trust me to not get pregnant? That sounds more reasonable, with a tiny margin for error.

"We'll figure it out together."

My dad looks relieved as I say it, even flashing a very brief smile.

"So I'll just head back to the office then. I want to . . . catch up on your latest draft. Maybe give you some notes." A lie for Liam's sake.

Completely unnecessary, of course. "But maybe we can have dinner together, then? Sushi? Thai?"

"That would be great," I say. "And I vote sushi."

"Sounds good," Liam chimes in. "Thanks, Theo."

My dad leaves, and after a moment passes, Liam sits back down next to me. Not as close this time, though.

"Busted," I say.

"Busted or not, it's still probably good to take things slowly." He reaches out for my hand. "We have too much to risk. I care about our friendship too much to mess anything up."

"Slow is fine," I say, resisting the urge to lean in and nuzzle against his shoulder. *Slow is faster than I ever thought we would move.*

Liam grins. Not neon, but close.

I squeeze his hand and then reach out to tap the remote, the Yule Ball coming back to life, the Great Hall a bedazzled winter wonderland. "But for the record, next date, I'm paying for *you*."

❀❀❀

My dad doesn't mention Liam or our conversation over the next few days. For now, only one thing matters in the Tate house: our deadline, a week from this Friday.

Three more chapters, and a final reread of the whole thing to revise at least the most glaring problems. After that, there will be a few months of fine-tuning with Elliot.

I'm allowed to skip my "classes" until after deadline—at this point, Dad doesn't have a second to spare for anything but writing, and because we're a "team," that means I don't have time for anything but writing either. Right now I'm expected to dutifully sit next to him at the desk for the entire day, talking through each new passage as "we" write it. I watch him type a string of words, delete them all. Type a few more, delete half. Type again. Pause. Period. Next line. It's usually about three attempts to hone each sentence. He reads aloud at the end of every paragraph, and then again at the end of every new page. This is where all the reading I've done comes into play—I might not be able to write good sentences on my own, but I have a decent knack for recognizing other people's good sentences, including my dad's.

By Wednesday morning, our time together is notably less pleasant. I saw the same decline in spirits as the deadlines approached for the first two books—but with this being the last, the stakes vastly upped, tensions are running at record highs.

My dad starts to read: "'Colton,' Marigold says, breathless as she twists away from the window, the spectacular view of the rolling sky-blue fields of the Afterworld—'Colton, come with me. We have to at least try, no matter—'"

"Nope, none of that," I say, cutting him off mid-sentence. I push back from the desk a bit too aggressively, my chair bumping into the wooden filing cabinet. Lucy yelps and manages to skitter out of my path just as I bang my knee hard on one of the heavy drawers. My knee burns, but I pretend it doesn't hurt. "I hate that sentence, I hate this paragraph, I hate the whole chapter. And mostly, I hate that Marigold is still even *considering* bringing her mom and Colton home. First off, she clearly needs to be telling Colton about her and Jonah at this point. But beyond that, why are you so set on this ending anyway? You know this is it, right? There's no fourth book about Marigold and her mom back in the world living their happily ever after."

"Jesus, Thistle, stop," my dad snaps. He lifts his fingers off the keyboard, as if he's worried he'll pound it into pieces if he types another word. "This isn't about another book. It's about this one. We have it mapped out this way, all the teasers pointing to it. The old house is about to be demolished, the portal will likely close forever, and Marigold is determined to take her mom and Colton with her when she leaves the Afterworld for the last time. But she won't know if it works until they try. That's the suspense. If we don't end this way, so much of the plotline was superfluous and unnecessary and—"

"Nothing was *unnecessary*," I say fast, before he can keep rambling on. "Yes, Marigold wonders if it's a viable option—if maybe she should *try* to take her mom and Colton back home. But she doesn't. She doesn't test out the theory because she realizes it's ethically wrong to mess around with destiny. It doesn't matter whether it's possible or impossible, because the dead aren't meant to come back to life in our world. It's against the basic rules of our existence. We need that balance to survive."

"Honey, with all due respect, I hardly think that one exception will throw the whole world of the living off balance."

"But it's not just one exception," I say, flailing my arms around because I'm way too agitated to stay still. I swipe at the desk and knock a few papers to the floor, accidentally. But it feels surprisingly satisfying, and so I knock a few more off just for effect. My dad furrows his brow and frowns, but I keep talking. "If other people in the Afterworld see this happen, they'll try to leave, too. And even beyond that, outside of the fiction here, I think it's more important for the readers to see that Marigold makes this decision. They've lost someone, too, I bet. We all have. And we can't keep wishing that we'll find a way to undo that, to bring anyone back. We have to come to peace with it. We have to let the past be the past."

His frown softens at this. He flicks his eyes—a subtle movement, but I'm expecting it—to the photo of me and my mom hanging on the wall. I'm two years old, wearing, of course, a bright yellow sundress. My mom is in a yellow dress, too. Marigold would no doubt thoroughly approve.

"I think this is what your mom would want." He says it so quietly, I almost think that I've misheard. I *hope* I've misheard.

"What did you say?" I ask. It's masochistic maybe, but I need to hear it again.

"Your mom. I bet she'd want to come back to you. To us. If she could."

"Don't you dare use her in this." I'm up, out of the chair, in two seconds flat. "I realize I barely knew her." I shouldn't, but I look back at the picture again, and this time, seeing my mom and me together, so happy and smiley and carefree, not knowing our countdown had already begun—I can barely keep myself together. I feel the tears rushing forward, but I can't fall apart, not yet. I have to say these things before they burn a hole inside me. "But don't tell me that Mom would have picked your ending. Mom would never have agreed to any of this in the first place. She would have known how wrong this was. So you know what I think Mom would say?"

"You don't understand," Dad whispers, shaking his head. I should stop. Maybe. But I don't. I ignore him and keep going.

"I think she'd say that—if I have to go through this, if I have to be dragged into this mess because of you—then at the very least, I should get to have the final say. And she'd also tell us that she's not coming back. Ever. So both of us had better just accept that and move on."

I'm so angry that I literally cannot see the room around me. I can't see the bookshelves, the computer, the desk. I certainly can't see my dad's face. Lucy is hovering at my feet, but I push her back as I blindly stumble into the hallway and up the stairs to my room.

This is what your mom would want.

He had almost twenty years with her. I had three. But still, she was my *mom*. She would have defended me. She would have thought about my best interests, not hers, not my dad's. I have to believe that. It's all I have.

The one—the only—good thing about having a parent die when you're young is that you can spend the rest of your life believing that they would have been amazing. The best, most loving, most supportive parent imaginable. Because they never had the chance to let you down.

I'm not sure how long I've been looping these ugly thoughts, two minutes or two hours, when I hear a long, loud metallic scraping against the roof. I race down the stairs and run out the kitchen door onto the back patio.

"Dad?"

He's up on a ladder, hitting the rain gutter on the edge of the roof with a big rusty hammer. I haven't seen him do handiwork in . . . my entire life, maybe. Unless you count the way he duct tapes the AC units into the windows every summer, just to make them *extra secure*.

"Dad, what in the world are you doing?" I momentarily suspend my rage, but only because this scene is so ridiculous and unexpected. And because he's a good twenty feet or so in the air. Arguing from that height doesn't seem like the wisest idea.

"It's supposed to rain tonight, and I noticed that this goddamn gutter is loose. I'm trying to bang this nail back in so it doesn't crash down later."

"Why don't you ask Liam's dad to do it? He's good at this kind of thing."

"I can do it, Thistle," he says loudly, shifting on the ladder so he can look at me. "I needed to take a break from writing, from even thinking about writing, so I came out here to get some fresh air and noticed this. The whole house is starting to fall apart. Did you see the banister on the steps, how it's tilting at the top? And there's the broken tiles on the bathroom floor."

In the past few months, Dad has subtly—and not so subtly—started talking about the idea of a bigger, newer house outside the city. A change of scenery. But I've shut it down every time. I won't leave Liam. And I won't leave Mom's house. Even after I go to college, this is supposed to be home base.

"The house is fine, and we have the money to pay professionals to fix things."

"I don't *need* professionals." He's back to hammering, banging even harder now. It looks like, if anything, his attempts will knock the gutter off entirely, rather than somehow miraculously refasten it to the roof. "And once we hand this manuscript in, I'll have plenty of time to get to the other issues. Do at least some temporary fixes."

The gutter starts to shake. I back up farther in the yard so that I won't be under it, just in case.

"Dad, seriously, I don't think you're helping."

"Thistle, please. *Please* just let me do this."

"I'm just saying, it looks like it's about to—"

And as if my words somehow willed it, the gutter tears from the roof with a terrible, ear-splitting *clash* of metal on metal that no doubt the whole street can hear. It swings for a second, two, three, as if magically suspended, dangling in midair, before it spirals to the ground.

Before I can call out, before I can move, I watch as the ladder teeters and starts to fall away from the house. Dad makes a grab for the roof, hands frantically scrambling for an anchor. But his fingers slide off and he's slipping through air, a tangle of arms and legs.

There are screams, too—mine or his or both.

I hear his body hit the ground, the hard *crunch* of skin and bones against the concrete patio, and I can only think one thing:

I'm an orphan now.

eight

Weeks passed with no trips to the Afterworld because Marigold's dad kept a close eye on her. She had decided she couldn't tell him the truth, that he'd never for a second entertain any of it. So she'd wait it out. But that didn't mean she couldn't see Jonah. For Colton's sake.

"I still don't believe you," Jonah said one summer afternoon as they sat in a park near her house. "But let's pretend for a minute. Is he happy in the Afterworld?"

"I wouldn't say happy. Or sad. But he worries about how you and your mom are doing."

"Wait. Colt isn't watching us from up there or wherever it is?" Jonah asked.

"No, I wish, but—"

Jonah was looking at Marigold now, staring at her with Colton's beautiful eyes. "What's in it for you? That's what I don't get."

"I care about your brother. I want to help put his mind at ease."

"That's it? Purely altruistic?"

"That and—I lost my mom a few days before you lost Colton. I'm searching for her, and your brother is helping me."

—EXCERPT FROM *LEMONADE SKIES*, **BOOK 1: *GIRL IN THE AFTERWORLD***

Dad is awake in the ambulance, though he's in too much pain to talk.

I still worry that this is it, that Dad will leave me, too. Liam's mom had been working at home, so she came over before we left, and she had looked just as terrified as I felt when she waved us off in the ambulance.

We get to the hospital and Dad's whisked away into the ER. I'm alone in the waiting room, breathing in air that smells too antiseptic and metallic. Liam texts me for the first hour or two after school lets out, asking me nearly every five minutes if there are any updates. Then my phone dies and it's almost a relief when the screen goes blank.

After what seems like an eternity, a doctor finally comes out to talk to me. Dr. Pulice. She seems friendly and confident enough, even though she looks too young, like she must be fresh out of med school. But I trust her when she says that Dad will be okay.

It's not pretty, though: a fractured skull, two broken arms and a broken ankle, swelling and bruising just about everywhere. Dad's ankle is so badly broken it requires the placement of an external fixator, which Dr. Pulice has to explain to me: a metal device that stretches from his ankle to his knee, drilled from the outside into the bone. Both arms are in slings and will need to be immobilized to heal on their own. Which means he'll have very limited movement for the next six weeks, and that's just the beginning of his recovery.

I listen in a daze, nodding. Dr. Pulice takes me to see him in the ICU, and even though he's attached to a thousand machines and has IVs sticking out at awkward angles from his bruised, bandaged, broken body, I have never been more relieved.

"Dad! You're alive!" I walk quickly to the side of his bed, but I'm scared to touch him.

"I'm alive," he says, his voice scratchy and whispery. He looks exhausted. And drugged. His eyes are on me but he's not looking *at* me. "What happened? It's so . . . foggy."

"You fell from the ladder. But it's fine, you're fine," I say, leaning in to give him a soft kiss on his cheek, so light my lips graze more air than skin. "You just get some rest. I'll be here."

I sit down on the chair by his bed, watching as his eyes droop. I don't necessarily believe in a god, but I pray anyway because I'm so grateful and still so scared. Dad should never have climbed that ladder. But he wouldn't have been up there at all if we hadn't fought. If it weren't for Marigold.

Marigold.

How will he be in any state to finish before the deadline? What will we tell Susan and Elliot?

"Thistle," he says, interrupting my thoughts, and I'm ashamed that I'm worrying about Marigold right now, because she, for once, isn't the center of our existence.

"Is someone taking care of Lucy?" he asks, his eyes still closed.

"Yes, of course," I lie. "But I'll call and check in." I pat his hand, very delicately, and then stand and turn toward the hallway.

A particularly cheery nurse greets me at the front desk and lets me use the hospital phone. I dial from memory. Liam picks up after half a ring.

"It's me," I practically yell into the phone.

"Thistle? What's going on? Why did you stop texting?"

"I'm so sorry, my phone died, and I don't have a charger here, and my dad's pretty beat up but he's going to be okay." I feel tears welling as I say those words out loud.

"Oh thank god," Liam says, sighing into the phone.

I start telling him everything I know so far, and it's only when I finish and take a breath that I remember why I called in the first place. "Lucy. Is Lucy okay?"

"My mom brought her over to our house," he says. "She's great. I'm here, by the way."

"What? Here where?"

"In the cafeteria getting coffee. I got here right before you called. I wanted to be close if you needed me."

I drop the handset on the desk and walk as fast as I can without running, following the overhead signs toward the elevator bank, and then down to the ground floor. The fluorescently lit cafeteria is straight in front of me when I step off the elevator. I push through two wide swinging doors, and there's Liam, cell still in his hand, pacing in circles.

I swing my arms around him from behind, throwing my body against his. He turns and hugs me back just as fiercely.

"I was so scared for you," he whispers.

"I was so scared for me, too." I kiss his cheek and then pull back a few inches, glancing up to meet his eyes. They look just as tired as I feel. "It must be so late. What time is it?"

"Not that late. Just after ten."

"But it's a weeknight. You have school tomorrow."

He shrugs. "Doesn't matter. That's what coffee is for. My parents said I could come. They wanted to be here, too, but I said I didn't want to overwhelm you."

I feel a new rush of appreciation for Liam. Because right now, I can't imagine anyone or anything else in the world I'd rather see. I lean in and kiss him again, this time on the lips.

"I'm so glad you're here," I say when I finally pull away. I reach down for his hand and squeeze.

He tugs at my arm, pulling me over to a bench to sit. "In case you're hungry . . ." He pulls out a Christmas tin from a paper bag on the floor and takes the lid off. There's a pile of parakeet-shaped shortbread cookies, covered in sugar sprinkles, every color of the rainbow.

"My mom told Mrs. Rizzo. She came over right after the ambulance pulled away. She'd been napping when it happened, she said, but woke up to the sirens, and she was pretty shook up, Thistle. I've never seen her looking so—so fragile, I guess. Like without her usual witch mask on she was just some tired old lady. It was weird. I didn't like it."

For the first time in my life, I feel bad for Mrs. Rizzo, even if she can be a crotchety old gossip. She's always alone. Her husband died before I was born. And if there are kids, I've never seen them. I've never thought to even wonder about it.

I grab a parakeet and take a bite. I'm surprised to discover how completely delicious it is. I've been missing out. I eat two more before I stand up, brush crumbs from my lap. "I should see how Dad's doing. It'll only take a minute. He needs his rest. Will you wait for me?"

Liam stands, too. "Sure," he says, pausing to brush a stray curl behind my ear.

"I just . . . I need you here for a little longer." I have to take care of Dad. But I need someone to take care of me, too.

"Okay. Then here is where I'll be."

❀❀❀

Home. Finally.

Dad stayed at the hospital for eight days—he needed additional monitoring of his brain for bleeding. He's been engaging more each day, though we haven't talked about anything except how he's feeling physically, or what the weather was like outside the hospital windows. I couldn't bring myself to mention Marigold, but the fact that he hasn't said anything about her yet is unsettling.

The deadline is tomorrow. Twenty-four hours.

Dad's either lost an entire chunk of his memory, or he's in too much pain to care about anything but more sleep. He was supposed to go straight to inpatient rehab for the next six weeks, but he refused—he wanted to be home with me. He demanded a plan B. And he won. We'll have a nurse to stay with us around the clock for as long as he needs her, and an occupational therapist coming over weekly to help ease him back into everyday activities. He'll be in a wheelchair for at least six weeks. But because his arms were both broken on the upper half, he still has the use of his elbows and wrists . . . so I think that maybe, just maybe, he'll be able to at least hunt and peck on the computer keyboard. Things could be worse. Much worse.

The nurse, Mia, stopped by the house ahead of time to get ready for Dad's big return, which mostly involved converting the office into a makeshift bedroom so that he doesn't need to be moved up any stairs. She seems pleasant enough—a bit younger than Dad, I'd guess, with thick curly black hair spilling out from a long braid that hangs down her back, rosy light brown skin, and a soft voice that reminds me of summer breezes.

Lucy—who stayed at Liam's house so I could mostly be at the hospital, sleeping in Dad's room every night—looks as disoriented as I feel when we all come in together, Mia pushing Dad in his wheelchair through the hall, showing him his new room. Lucy sniffs frantically around Mia's hands, legs, bags, before she hobbles into the kitchen to be alone.

I follow her, grabbing a handful of her favorite biscuits from a jar on the counter. I'm groveling because I didn't visit her once this past week and I am the worst pet mother in the world. I cabbed home a few times, mostly to shower and change clothes and meet with Mia, and it never occurred to me to stop in to see Lucy. I saw Liam, but only at the hospital, not here.

Now instead of tripping over my heels like she usually does, she is very pointedly hiding under the kitchen table, sulking. I kneel under the table, too, offering her the biscuits. I'm the lowly servant bowing down to my deity. She sniffs for a few seconds—as if she's actually considering not taking them—before snapping up the biscuits, leaving my empty hands covered in gooey strings of slobber.

"I love you, old lady." I sigh, nuzzling my head against her ears. "I'm so sorry I forgot about you."

There's a list of about ten incredibly urgent things that I should be doing right now. I need to call Susan—or no, definitely e-mail, an actual phone call would be way too terrifying—so that she can break the news to Elliot. I haven't told her yet that we won't make the deadline because it all feels like too much, and because deep down, underneath my fear about Dad, there's something else I'm afraid of that is just as petrifying in its own way. With the deadline looming and Dad in his current state, I can't help but wonder what would happen if he can't write and we get caught.

And now that we're home, the fear is even more palpable. Could we be sued? Lose our money? The fact that my dad is the author doesn't make these books any less good, does it? Any less deserving of the praise, the fans all around the world? It was the writing that made them fall in love—it was Marigold and her beautiful world. But I'm not sure that Susan and Elliot and the rest of Zenith Publishers would look at it that way.

I feel dizzy suddenly. The kitchen is too warm, Lucy's breathing is too loud.

I push up off the floor and go to my bedroom, closing the door behind me. I'd deleted the e-mail app off my phone while I was at the hospital, so I'm not surprised when I log into e-mail on my laptop to see a long string of unread messages: Elliot and Susan, mostly; my publicist, my online-marketing guru, a few foreign editors. My dad is cc'ed on everything, as per usual. I decide to keep the app off my phone. Thank goodness Susan and Elliot both refuse to text their clients.

I skim the subject lines. There was a flurry of activity yesterday— apparently *Between Two Worlds* jumped to number one on the *New York Times* bestseller list for children's series. Even Martin Davis has e-mailed me personally with his congratulations. I should feel happy about it. Ecstatic. I should feel *something* at least, but I don't. If this were any other week, our whole life would have revolved around this news, but now it just feels empty. I click through the thread, the long lines of exclamation points and celebratory emojis. They must think it's bizarre that neither of us has replied yet, almost twenty-four hours since the news broke.

I keep scrolling down my in-box, stopping when I see Oliver's name smashed between the various *#1!!!!!!!!!!!!* subject lines. I open his e-mail.

Hey, Thistle—Thanks again for coming by to meet Em. You rock. Also, I am a man of my word and have just finished *Between Two Worlds*. Read *Girl in the Afterworld* last week. Almost considered faking a couple of sick days to read them straight through. Don't tell anyone I said that though, okay? (No offense.) Seriously, best YA I've read. (Technically the only YA I've read, unless *Catcher in the Rye* for school counts, but still. The best.) Emma and I discussed, and we are willing to pay you fifty bucks for a sneak peek of the last book. I mean that's almost the value of two and a half books, so total steal for you, right? Anyway, let me know if we have a deal.—O

I think about Oliver and Emma, who I'm not planning to ever see again. But I'll definitely never see them again if the truth comes out. And I picture it then, because I can't stop myself: Emma discovering that her idol is a fraud, her faith in humanity crumbling. Oliver hating me for deceiving his sister, hating me for wasting the time it took him to read two books—YA books at that, nothing fitting his normal sophisticated literary tastes.

No. They can't find out. No one can.

A *ping* goes off. A new message from Susan.

Her subject line: **VERY CONCERNED, PLEASE CALL ASAP, THANKS**

My whole body tenses as I open the message. It's short and to the point—she's distressed that she's heard nothing in over a week, especially given yesterday's bestseller news. She's also worried that she won't have the final manuscript tomorrow as promised. *Elliot and I absolutely cannot wait to read it!*

Yes, Susan and Elliot, I understand. Trust me, I can't wait to read it either.

But I won't be reading it anytime soon. No one will.

I take a deep breath as I click Reply. If anyone can fix this, it's Susan. Everything can be solved as long as we have more time.

Dear Susan, I begin. *I'm afraid I have awful news . . .*

nine

Marigold's dad stopped monitoring her soon enough—it was easier for him to think she was fine, and it left more time for his own sadness.

It had been over a month since her last visit to the Afterworld. She waited to slip out until she heard snores from her dad's room, and when she reached the porch, she practically jumped into the rocking chair. And just like that she was there—in her yellow-skied world.

Marigold raced to the tall golden doors. Colton was always easy to find, on the lower floors in an area that seemed to be just for teenagers. But there had to be other people, other ages, on the higher floors. People like her mom.

She spotted Colton on his favorite window seat in the atrium. He stood when he saw her, his expression so serious that he reminded her of Jonah, and said, "I thought you'd never come back."

Marigold did it then without thinking—she wrapped her arms around him, holding on tight.

—EXCERPT FROM *LEMONADE SKIES*, **BOOK 1: GIRL IN THE AFTERWORLD**

I wait until after breakfast the next morning to talk to Dad about it.

I gave him a night to settle into his new room, a night to adapt to the strange new routines, Mia helping him eat and bathe and relieve himself—a long list of unsettling intimacies. He hadn't gone on a single date since my mom, and now a complete stranger was undressing him and sponging him down in his office.

So yeah. He needed a night. That's what I told myself at least. An excuse to put off the inevitable just a bit longer. I had barely slept the night before, tossing and turning and wondering *what if.* What if the secret comes out? What if our whole life implodes? When I finally fell asleep for an hour or two, I dreamed that I was in court, getting interrogated on the witness stand. There were thousands of people in the audience, all of them decked out in Marigold orange. Only I wore black. My dad was nowhere to be seen. But Susan and Elliot were in the front row, their faces cold and fierce. I woke up before the jury announced their verdict, but the feeling had been ominous, like the whole courthouse was about to collapse all around me, brick by brick.

It was a new nightmare, at least.

Susan had called me yesterday—within minutes of my e-mail landing in her in-box, of course. I ignored her the first two times, but by the third I realized she wasn't going to stop, so I picked up. I had to act more convincingly than I ever had in my life. It was the ultimate test of my talents.

"Don't get me wrong, Thistle," she cut in immediately after my shaky hello. "I am deeply concerned for your father. *Deeply.* I'm relieved to hear he's going to recover, of course, and am just *sick* that you had to go through this. Dreadful! But surely you have help there providing for him? A caretaker? If not, I can look into getting you one, so that you can be freed of those responsibilities. You're a minor. They shouldn't be left to you to begin with, and more than that, this draft, Thistle, it's imperative that—"

"It's too much," I said. "I don't have the brain space right now. I'm too exhausted and stressed to be creative. If I could just have a little more time . . ."

"But there's not more time, I'm afraid," Susan said. "It was a tight schedule to begin with. The dates are locked in so that it can be out next summer before you start college. The back-to-back turnaround is hard, I know, dear, but if it's only just a chapter or two still to write . . . ?"

"I can send you what I have so far. Would that help? You and Elliot can read that, and he can get a jump on those initial edits. Then I'll send the rest as soon as I can."

She sighed, a long, cutting, abrasive Susan Van Buren sigh. "I suppose for the time being that would take some pressure off, but I'll have to call Elliot. I'll try and get you a two-week extension. That's the best I can do. Even if the ending is a bit rough, Elliot will work through it with you—and I'm happy to weigh in, too. We're here to help however we can. That's our *job*. To make this easier for you, as smooth as possible given these unfortunate circumstances."

I mumbled a thank-you and rambled on with a string of half-assed assurances. I can't even remember what I said now, but it must have worked some kind of magic, because the call ended, I sent the unfinished manuscript, and got an e-mail back from Elliot saying he was sorry about my dad and looking forward to seeing the last chapters in two weeks. So all was settled. Temporarily. Very temporarily.

"Dad," I say tentatively now, tapping at the office door. "Can we talk?"

I hear a grunt—something that sounds a bit like *urrgumph*—that I take to be a yes.

"Coming in, I hope you're decent!"

I push the door open slowly, my eyes in half slits in case there's anything I shouldn't see. But no, just Dad propped up in the rental bed, fully dressed in a loose button-up shirt and stretchy shorts to accommodate his slings and external fixator.

"How are you feeling?" I ask.

"How do you think I feel, Thistle?"

I bristle at the coldness of his voice. At his lowest points, he could sometimes be a monster—his forays into customer service jobs were typically short, given that his personal motto tended to be, "The customer is always wrong, I am always right." But he was never a monster to me. Never.

"I'm sorry," I say, almost in a whisper.

"In case it's not glaringly obvious, I feel like I've been run over by a mile-long freight train. I should never have touched that gutter. What was I even thinking? This house is a disaster, I shouldn't have bothered."

"I'm sorry. Maybe it's better if we talk later?"

He sighs. "Sorry. The doctor's taken me off the more *efficient* pain meds now. Mia tells me I don't need them anymore, but that's not how it feels. And from the absurd amount of money she's costing out of pocket, you'd think she'd at least be more sympathetic. I'd probably be better off if it was just you and me."

"I can help take care of you, too, Dad. Whatever you need." I take a deep breath and step closer to his bed. "We're a team."

His face softens, at least marginally. "Thanks, sweetie. I don't mean to take it out on you. Really. None of this is your fault. I just . . . I need to get used to . . . this."

"You're going to get better. It's temporary."

"They can't guarantee a full recovery—there could always be aches and pains. I'm not a spring chicken."

"And you're not a Thanksgiving dinner either."

"Stunning use of metaphor," he says with an almost smile.

"Ha. Yeah. So speaking of metaphors . . ."

He pinches his eyes shut and sighs heavily. "I know where this is going."

"The deadline, Dad. The manuscript was supposed to be done *today*. I called Susan yesterday and got a two-week extension, but what am I supposed to do now?"

"Two weeks?" He laughs. Not a happy one. "That's impossible. Not only are my arms broken and in slings, but my head is pounding. I ache in places I never gave a thought to in my life before. And this ending—it needs to be *perfect*. Absolutely perfect. And I can't do perfect right now. I can't do anything *close* to perfect. I'm not even sure I could do moderately shitty at the moment."

"I'll help," I say, moving in close enough that I can rest my hand delicately on his shoulder, afraid to graze a bruise and set him off more. "We could find a comfortable way to prop your keyboard up on a tray for you to type. You really only need your fingers, right? Or you could try dictating to me, I know plenty of authors do that if—"

"Thistle, *no*. We'll wait. *We* will do it right, when I'm myself again. If they have to push the date back, so what? Our fans will wait. They'll just be even more excited."

"Well, it can't come out much later . . . Susan said they've already built everything around next summer because of my going to college, and she thinks that waiting will—"

"I'm so tired, Thistle. I need a nap. How about I call Susan when I'm feeling up to it? I'm sure I can finagle the time we need. We can send the chapters we already have, they're pretty polished, and—"

"I already did that. Elliot and Susan both have the manuscript. But that's not enough. Don't you get it, Dad? Your being incapacitated doesn't explain to them why the book can't be finished now. It doesn't explain why I can't work on it. Not you. *Me*."

"You're taking care of me. I'll tell them it's a full-time job and I need you."

"I already said we have a caretaker here—Susan was going to send someone herself. She's convinced there's no reason I can't bang out a rough ending that we'll polish up during edits. I'm scared, Dad, and Susan said—"

"Thistle." He takes a sharp breath. "*Stop.* Susan works for *us*, not the other way around, and it's her job to fight for what we need. And what we need is more time. I appreciate that you got this extension, I do, but we both know it's not enough. We'll get her to understand, and then it's her responsibility to make Zenith understand. Everything will be fine."

"You can't know that."

There's a pause. And then he says, "I will write an ending that will blow Susan's and Elliot's expectations out of the water." He's talking too slowly, enunciating overcarefully, each word louder, heavier. "But I'll write it when I feel ready and capable. There's no other way. I don't think you understand how monumental this responsibility is, Thistle. The absurd amount of pressure. This is my whole *career.*" He breaks for a second, but even a second is far too long. "*Our* career."

"Is it?" I say quietly, two paper-thin words, floating, suspended in the air between us.

Dad doesn't hear, or at least he pretends not to.

"Go enjoy the free time. Read books. Watch TV. Hang out with Liam. Whatever—go be a normal teenager. You don't have to worry about any assignments. Maybe get some exercise, try out a yoga class, work on your physical education. It's only November and you're already so far ahead in your logged hours, and your portfolio is stellar as always. Mrs. Everly will give a glowing certification to the superintendent come June, I'm sure. Just, please . . . I can't take the deadline stress right now. Let it rest."

I don't bother responding.

Instead I walk out of the room, close the door behind me. I

have nowhere to go, no one to see, nothing to do. I hear Mia in the kitchen, the sound of running water and clinking glass, and turn toward the stairs. I go to my room, collapse onto my bed.

And I cry. Because Dad might be the author, but it's my deadline—and I don't know what to do. I don't trust his *solution* . . . but I have none of my own.

Maybe because no solution exists.

❀❀❀

It's three o'clock that afternoon when I finally roll out from under the covers.

I pull up a scan of the contract for *Girl in the Afterworld* on my computer. I squint at the far too tiny words jammed onto too many pages, trying to make sense of the dense legal language. *The Guardian, on behalf of the Author, hereby warrants to the Publisher, and to the Publisher's successors, licensees, and assignees, that: the Author is the sole and exclusive Author of the Work(s)* . . . And so on. Warranties and indemnities, claims, settlements, judgments. The phrases blur into one big messy knot. I read and reread sentences, two, three, four times. I stare at Dad's signature on the last page. *Dad's* signature, not mine.

I'd forgotten the details. There had been so much paperwork at the time. I'd needed to apply for a work permit, and we had both signed agreements for Susan. But it was Dad who put his name in ink on the Zenith contracts, acting as my guardian because I was a minor—Dad who guaranteed that I was the sole author, that I would meet all deadlines.

Dad may be the one legally in breach, but that doesn't mean my future won't be ruined, too. I'm the face people will remember.

My phone rings, startling me. I close the contract with one urgent click of the mouse. I can't look at it anymore. I can't think about it.

A picture of Liam is lighting up my phone. He's standing on a stadium seat, cheering at the end of a particularly epic Phillies game we had gone to—hands waving in the air, a blurry smear on the screen, and his eyes, his smile beaming down at me.

I shut off the ring, pushing the phone away. But then I think back to that game, how Liam had yanked me up onto the seat next to him after I'd snapped the photo—how I'd wished with everything in me that he'd get carried away by his excitement over what was happening on the baseball diamond and kiss me right then and there. I look back at my phone and frantically tap Accept to take the call.

"Hey," I say quietly.

"Hey! Thistle! I was worried, you never texted me back this morning."

"Yeah, it's been . . . a long day."

"I'm sorry. I have a water polo game now, outside the city, but can we hang tonight when I'm back? It'll be late, but I have to head out in the morning—it's my pop's birthday, so we're staying with him and Gram this weekend. I really want to see you before I go."

"Yeah. Sure. Of course," I say, before I can change my mind. Seeing him—seeing anyone besides my dad—is probably the healthy thing to do. I am supposed to be a *normal teenager*, after all. Dad's orders. "Toss a Ping-Pong ball when you're back. For old times' sake."

"Really? The ball again? I only started using the front door because . . . because I don't know, I thought you'd want certain things to be different. Now that we're . . . you know. I was worried you'd think I wasn't taking this seriously."

"Li, please. I'm a sucker for cute traditions. You have no idea how happy those *ping*s on my window make me."

"I do because they make me that happy, too."

I feel momentarily better.

But then we hang up, and I can't resist the urge to do some digging online. What were the fates of other frauds like Dad and me? The first name that pops up is Brandon Ball. He'd published his book—*Flies Over Alabama*—as a memoir, only to be called out later for it being much more *semi-fictional* than fact. A media storm ensued. What he did is called *literary forgery*. That is: writing that is either attributed to a made-up author or, in the case of nonfiction, writing about something that isn't true. My heart skips a beat because the sunny and warm and entirely happy-looking Thistle Tate who's grinning at fans in a photo on every book jacket—that girl is very much a made-up author.

I keep reading about Brandon Ball. I have to.

His publisher stood by him briefly, until it became clear that the book was fraudulent—so many pieces not adding up, people who had never existed. Statements were issued, and customers could return their copies with proof of purchase. I try to find what came next—what Ball did with his life *after*—but there's nothing. He's disappeared from the Internet entirely. A total nonentity.

Next on the list: Madeline Bingley. Her story makes my skin crawl, hot and prickly under my thick orange Marigold sweatshirt—promotional swag from Zenith. Like me, she found her literary agent when she was a teenager. By the time she was a sophomore at Yale, she'd landed a book deal for a rumored half million with a major publisher. Everything was going so well—she was touted as a hardworking student, a hot young writer on the rise—until it was reported that she'd plagiarized from multiple sources. Accusations flew, a handful of big-name authors throwing their claims into the ring. All copies of her book were recalled and destroyed. Yale suspended her, then dropped her altogether.

Her trail ends there.

At least Marigold's story is original.

I shut off my laptop. That's as much as I can take for today. Neither of these cases is quite like ours. But we've lied, too, to our agent, our editor, the publisher, fans. At the very least, we'd probably have to make statements in new editions, clarifying that my father was the actual author. That I was nothing but a muse at best. As for a potential recall . . . would Zenith really take that hit? The money they'd lose—I can't wrap my head around it. But fans could demand refunds. It might be inevitable.

The heat is practically steaming from my pores now. I tear my sweatshirt over my head and toss it on the floor. I need to do something. Anything. But what?

What the hell can I do about any of this on my own except write the ending?

Me. By myself.

I could write it the way Dad wants it or I could have my dream ending. What if—what if this one piece of the story . . . what if it could be *mine*? One piece, but the most important one yet. The last say. The final word.

I'd need to revise parts of Dad's earlier chapters to set it up right, pave the way. But then I would make things so perfect for Marigold—or no, not *perfect*, never perfect, because that's not authentic. No, I'd make her life be exactly what it needs to be instead. Good-bye, Mom! Good-bye, Colton! Hello, normal life in the real world—a sadder world without her mom in it, yes, but a world that still has her dad and Jonah and her friends. A world of the living, not the dead.

For a few seconds—a few glittering, shimmery seconds—I almost feel hopeful. I almost believe that yes, I can do this. I've helped my dad the whole time, watched him construct these books word by word, sentence by sentence. And there *are* other teen YA authors out there—I doubt that all of them are fakes like me. So it's not entirely far-fetched to think that someone my age is capable of writing at least semi-decent sentences.

Just as quickly, that golden bubble pops. Even if I could convince my dad to let me do this, I'm not a writer. I've never written anything besides essays for Dad to read and put in my annual evaluator portfolio. And besides, I wouldn't be able to seamlessly attach my work to his. Susan and Elliot would see that the writing styles were different. Of course they would. Fans, too.

Maybe I could start the process, though. Cobble together a thorough outline, and then help Dad write actual sentences and paragraphs in time for the deadline. Of course I'd also need to get him on board with my ending.

I turn my laptop back on, open my e-mail and find Oliver's last message. *Fifty bucks for a sneak peek of the last book.*

I could let Oliver and Emma read what we already have, pick their brains about how to pull the final scenes together. Emma as a superfan who probably knows the characters and the world as well as I do; and Oliver would no doubt be a great critic. I could say that I'm paralyzed by the idea of wrapping it up perfectly, that I need them on board as—extremely confidential—advisors. Before I can decide if any of this—the outlining, involving Oliver and Emma—is a good idea, a new message pops up in the in-box.

Hey, Thistle—Okay. I guess I shouldn't have attempted bribery in the last e-mail. Maybe that's not your style. I promise that Em and I will both be exceedingly patient and never ask about the last book again unless you want to talk about it. So . . . I guess that's it then? Unless you do want to talk sometime. About Marigold. Or about whatever really. The existence of other universes, the plausibility of reincarnation, the necessity of the quadratic formula. It must get lonely being homeschooled. Or maybe not, since you're like an über-international-bestselling author who has loads of admirers. Just shout if you ever wanna. Okay?—O

I stare blankly at the e-mail for a few minutes, hoping that the words will magically click together in a way that makes more sense. Is Oliver . . . flirting? Asking me *out*? Or is he just being friendly, hoping to strike up a dialogue for Emma's sake?

My brain is too tired to excavate the meaning. I haven't eaten anything since oatmeal for breakfast, which probably isn't helping. I have no appetite, though. Except—I pull open my drawer, and yep, it's still there, waiting for a moment just like this. My stash of dark chocolate, left over from the tour. I don't have to be hungry to eat chocolate.

I unwrap one of the bars and take a big, messy bite as I throw myself onto the bed, rich chocolate warming my throat. I have hours before Liam will be home. Empty hours. I can't think about Marigold anymore so I reach for the stack of advance reader's copies of new books on my nightstand, running my hand along the spines. I pick a book with a mosaic rainbow on the cover by an author whose name I don't know. I flip to the first page and start reading, not bothering with the description on the back cover. It doesn't matter what it's about. It just matters that it's something, somewhere besides here, my sad little bedroom in Philly.

Because I need someone else's world right now.

Any world, any life, but my own.

ten

Sometimes it was easy for Marigold to forget.

Easy to forget that the other kids she met up here—they were all dead. So easy, especially after that first hug with Colton.

From hugs, to holding hands, to this moment now: Colton pulling her against him, his eyes closing, lips parting.

I cannot do this, she thought, her heart pounding in her chest. *I cannot kiss him. Colton is dead. Dead. Dead like Mom. Who I still haven't found. But I will. And she'll help me with this—she'll make everything easier, clearer, just like she always did before.*

Marigold said none of this out loud, though, and she didn't move either. She didn't step back after Colton's lips pressed against hers, his arms wrapping around her waist.

This—this was crossing a line. A decision she wouldn't be able to take back. A single moment that could change everything.

She closed her eyes, breathed in the sweet Afterworld air.

And then she kissed him back.

—EXCERPT FROM *LEMONADE SKIES, **BOOK 1: GIRL IN THE AFTERWORLD***

I wait until I hear Mia close the office door, her white-tennis-shoed feet shuffling back into the kitchen, before going downstairs to say good night to Dad. It feels like the right thing to do, even though seeing him is low on the list of things I want from my night.

"Dad?" I nudge the door open slowly.

"Hey, Thistle," he says quietly. His eyes are closed as I step into the room, and there's a small frown on his face.

"I'm sorry. I didn't mean to wake you up."

"No, it's fine. I'm okay. Just woke up from another nap and I'm groggy." He opens his eyes, but the frown stays. "Too much sleep isn't always a good thing, I guess. But it's all I really want to be doing right now."

"Well, I just wanted to say good night."

"Thanks, sweetie." He pauses, looking away from me, and I'm about to lean in for one quick peck on his cheek good night when he starts again. "So I tried to write this afternoon, just to see what I could come up with—first with me typing, but I couldn't get comfortable with these slings on, feeling so restricted, and then dictating on my laptop with Mia's help. It was abysmal, Thistle. I did it for you, though. I wanted to try it out because I know how stressed you are. But . . . nope. Nothing. Not one decent word. Total failure."

"Oh." He tried to write for me. He tried, and it didn't work.

"It's okay," he says, turning to me again. "We both need time off. I work too hard. You work too hard. But I'll be better eventually. We'll figure it out. Go get some sleep."

I nod numbly, even if I don't agree.

⬤⬤⬤

When I hear Liam get dropped off that night, I don't wait for his *ping* on my window.

I pull a sweatshirt on over my pajamas and grab two Ping-Pong balls before I step into the hallway. I see a light under the door of Dad's old room—Mia's room now—and make sure to avoid the creakiest floorboards. Not that it matters if she catches me slipping outside. She's here to take care of my dad, not me. We've barely spoken to each other—not because I have anything against her, but because I'd rather be locked away in my room than making small talk with a stranger who's currently eating in our kitchen, sharing my bathroom, sleeping a wall away from me. It's just one more thing that makes my usually orderly, predictable life way too shaky.

I feel bad suddenly, ignoring her like this. It must be hard for her, too, having a job that constantly puts her into new environments. I'll try to chat over breakfast tomorrow. Exchange a few pleasantries, not run up to my room hugging my oatmeal bowl like I did today.

But for now I glide smoothly down the steps, past my dad's office, into the kitchen. Lucy startles from under the table, snorting and kicking her legs out in her sleep. She's unsettled, too, sleeping in a different room. I crouch down and smooth my hand across her ears. She doesn't wake up, but she seems to sleep easier, her feet going still as her breath evens out.

It's cold when I step out into the garden, the brisk November air stinging as it hits my lungs. I move quickly, pushing our picnic table closer to the brick wall. Liam's family very conveniently has a wooden bench just on the other side, and it works as a step down. I hoist myself over the wall, and then use his bench to hop to the ground. Liam's light is on and I'm about to toss a Ping-Pong ball when he appears at the back door.

"You're pretty eager, huh?" he says, grinning as he walks into the yard. "It got late, I'm sorry. Even my parents didn't wait up for me to see how the game went."

I don't answer. Instead I drop the balls on the ground and step up next to him, grab his warm cheeks with my cool fingers, and pull him down for a kiss. I need this. Him. A real connection. He's the one part of my life that I can rely on right now. The only piece that makes sense.

He pulls away, and I lean in even closer, wrap my arms around him more tightly.

"Do you want to come inside?" he says, his lips grazing my

forehead as he speaks. I can feel him smiling without needing to look up. "It's way too cold out here."

I nod and let him tug me along, through his kitchen and downstairs to the basement. It's a second living room, mostly Liam's, with a massive flat-screen TV and entertainment center, a foosball table, and a bar—though his parents only ever stock it with soda and iced tea. I'm pretty sure his friends from school provide the beer when they use his basement as an occasional weekend meeting place. But Liam and I have never talked much about that. He's asked me over a few times when they're here, but I almost always find a reason to pass. He's different around his school friends. Drinking PBR and rattling off Phillies or Eagles stats, laughing over crude jokes, dissecting parties and people I've never met before. I like it best the way it is now—just Liam and me.

But now that we're dating, I should start making appearances sometimes. Make an effort to get to know his other friends.

We fall onto the sofa, still tangled up. He's looking at me curiously, his dark eyebrows knotted, but I don't want to talk. I just want to kiss, to feel his warmth under my hands, to know that this part of my life is okay. Feeling, not thinking. Just *being*, without all the rest. I kiss him harder and wrap my hands around his neck.

"Thistle," he says as he pulls back. "Are you . . . okay?"

"Of course I'm okay," I say, already trying to stick my lips back on his, make the words disappear, but he shakes me off.

"Don't get me wrong, I like this new fierce side. But it just seems unlike you."

"I'm upset," I say, turning away to avoid his too-serious eyes. "My life besides you totally sucks right now. My dad couldn't have dreamed up this kind of drama in a *Lemonade Skies* twist. We missed our deadline and I got us a new one, but I can't make him understand that we can't miss this one, too. We just can't when everything is at stake—*everything*, the book, our future, my dad's entire well-being—and I have no one to help me, so *please*. Please just let me forget about all of it, at least for a little while. Just kiss me."

His neck stiffens under my hands. "You don't have 'no one' to help you."

"I didn't mean it like that. I know I have you, for the important life stuff anyway. But the book stuff—it's on me to figure that out."

"I can help you with that, too." I shake my head, thinking I should maybe explain more about the contract, the actual legal consequences, my idea for outlining the ending myself, but then he continues: "I wish your dad had never started this."

"I know," I say instead. "Me too."

"And I wish you'd never gone along with it—this lying. It's going to catch up with you, and then what?"

"That's the whole point, Liam. It can't. And it's not like I had a choice."

"Really?"

"Stop it. You're not helping." I roll off his lap, edging away from him on the sofa. "This is why I didn't want to talk to you about it. You hate the books, and I only did it in the first place to help my dad. To make him happy."

"Well, it's not fair that both of you are *always* choosing his happiness over yours."

We're both silent then and I realize that Liam can't understand, not really. He has two parents who are happy, healthy, *alive*. Grandparents, aunts and uncles, cousins. My last grandparent, my dad's mom, died in a nursing home when I was six. Both of my parents were only children.

Dad is my family. Tiny and pathetic as it may be.

"I just want whatever will make you feel better," he says finally. "I care about you, Thistle. I really, really care about you."

Maybe *I love you* would have made a small dent in my armor. But he doesn't say it.

And maybe it doesn't matter, that word. Because it's suddenly clear to me, the truth blazing bright. I don't know how to say it, though. I don't know how to suggest we take a temporary hiatus until this problem is all sorted out because right now, Liam is making everything so much worse. Instead I grab the remote and turn on the TV.

I curl myself back up against him and give myself this at least—this night of pretending that it's okay. That we're okay.

❀❀❀

Mia and I talk over breakfast. I learn a little more about her—she's new to Philly, and had been living with her sister's family about twenty minutes outside the city. She seems glad to be here, gladder than I would have expected given how unpleasant both of us Tates are proving to be.

Afterward, when I'm back in my room, I decide to e-mail Oliver. At first I tell myself no—nothing good can come out of more bonding with him and Emma, but if I'm going to try to outline those chapters, I really need their help.

> Hello there, Oliver. No, I don't believe in bribery. But I am sick
> of holing up every day to finish this officially overdue book. My
> dad's fine(ish) now, but he got in a bad accident recently, so

things around the house are rough. So what I'm saying is: yes. It gets lonely. And it would help me with the ending if I could talk through some of it with not one but two Marigold superfans. (I'm including you on the list now, don't even try to refute it. You don't try for bribery unless you're a stone-cold superfan.) So maybe the three of us could hang out sometime and brainstorm? If Emma's feeling up to it. Anywhere that's not my house is fine by me. But no worries if you're busy. Just let me know. Okay?—Thistle

I have to pry myself away from my desk to stop refreshing the page, waiting for a response. I sit on the bed and rack my brain trying to think of my other hobbies, all the other fun, entertaining, enriching activities I could be doing. Surely I must do things besides read, pretend to write, watch TV, hang out with my dad and Liam. There's my garden, but it's too cold for that now. Sometimes I listen to music?

This is sad. Pathetically sad.

My phone chimes, a text from Liam. I feel a nudge of guilt thinking about my e-mail—though, really, I did nothing wrong. I asked to hang out with Oliver *and* Emma.

I open the text.

I've been thinking about you all morning. I really am sorry for pushing last night. No more Marigold talk. Swear. I know everything else sucks, and I want to at least be the one unsucky thing for you.

I stare at the text for a few minutes.

Another chime, and: *I wish I wasn't gone this weekend. I want to take you on a proper date.*

A brief pause, and then a third: *Next weekend, whatever you want. I promise.*

I should be elated by this turn of events. Liam acknowledging he was wrong, vowing to be the happy light in my life I so desperately need. He won't bring up Marigold again.

I felt so sure last night, though. Sure about taking a break until I've sorted everything out.

I deliberate for a few minutes before I text back: *No worries. Have fun in the country with Pop and Gram! xoxo*

Vague and noncommittal. Maybe a few days apart will do us good.

I get up and walk back to my desk, refresh my e-mail. A response from Oliver.

> Thistle! Sorry to hear about your dad. Hope he's okay. And sorry to hear you're lonely. Kind of glad (sorry) to hear even a badass famous author can get down sometimes, too, like the rest of us normal humans. Want to meet us at four at Grumpy Lou's on Pine?—O

I tell him, yes, four o'clock would be great, even though it's the weekend and I'm breaking my own rules to work on book stuff.

After three outfit changes, I decide on old black jeans and a chunky black sweater. It looks socially acceptable for a coffee non-date, I think, far more appropriate than the two tour dresses I tried on first. Except Oliver will no doubt be wearing black on black, too, and I don't want other people at the café to think we're some sort of twinning Goth couple. I throw on a blue scarf for a pop of color, which improves the situation.

I pass Dad's room that is technically Mia's, and I think about the red metal box for the first time since that night. Pictures and letters, scraps of my mom that still exist. Dad's not there to guard it now. I wouldn't want Mia to catch me invading her space, but next time she's out of the house . . .

I put on my jacket and yell that I'm going for coffee and a walk. I don't bother waiting for a response. When I get to the front stoop, I pivot in the direction opposite of Liam's house.

Mrs. Rizzo is outside in her usual housecoat checking the mailbox, and as I pass I prepare for a lecture. But instead she says, "How's your father?"

"Good," I lie. I look down at my boots. "Not that good, actually. He's in pretty bad shape. It's going to be a rough few months."

"But you have someone helping? I saw a woman smoking in the backyard. Disgusting, really. You should tell her that's not acceptable, especially with a recovering patient in her care!" She shakes her gnarled fist and squints at me with beady brown eyes, magnified to alarming proportions through her thick glasses. "You better not ever think about smoking, young lady. I'll see you if you do, and I'll be sure to go right up and knock on your door to tell your father."

"I won't," I say, almost smiling now. "Promise."

"Hmph. All right." She pauses, running a hand along her tightly cropped hair, bright moon white against her deep brown skin. I nod my good-bye, assuming she's done with me.

But then: "You come knock if you need anything. Okay? I'll make some cookies for your father tomorrow. Rainbow sugar, extra-special."

I smile for the rest of my walk. Smiling, because of Mrs. Rizzo! And not sarcastically! I never would have expected this day to come. I won't ever joke about her delicious *fowl* cookies again.

I look around when I step into the café, soft bells ringing from the door. The only other customer is a college-age-looking guy wearing bright purple Beats, fervently staring at his iPad.

No potential Marigold fans here. Wonderful. I order a mocha cappuccino and am taking my first frothy sip when Oliver steps inside. I put my mug down and wave, waiting for Emma to come in after him. The door bangs shut. No Emma.

A knot of panic pulls in my stomach, that delicious cappuccino foam instantly curdling. Emma was the vital element making this get-together feel perfectly okay. Necessary, really, because she is a vast treasure trove of *Lemonade Skies* insights. This was a work excursion. It was not a one-on-one hangout with Oliver.

"Where's Emma?" I ask quickly as Oliver gets to the table. And then I remember to say, "Hello! Good to see you."

"I wanted her to be here, too, but she started feeling sick this afternoon. I hope it's okay I came alone." He shakes his head and sits down, gazing intently into the swirls of my cappuccino. "It just sucks, seeing her fight through this. Makes me feel guilty for being so healthy sometimes."

"I'm sure she doesn't see it that way," I say quietly.

"I know. But it still sucks. She used to be the healthiest kid. She could eat anything and everything. Soda, pizza, burgers, birthday cake. I can hardly remember what's okay and what's not okay for her diet anymore. Feels like the list of not okay is growing every week."

We sit in silence for a moment. I want to say something comforting, but anything that comes to mind feels too blasé and artificial.

"Sorry," he says finally, attempting a smile. "That was a lot to hit you with. I don't think I even said hello, come to think of it. So—hey, Thistle! It's nice to see you again. Even if you won't accept a bribe."

"I was actually going to give you guys a teaser if you bought my cappuccino, but I beat you here, so no deal."

He cocks an eyebrow at me and grins before jumping up from his chair, heading toward the counter. I pretend to be watching something interesting out the window to keep myself from staring at him.

As anticipated, he's in all black today. Faded tight black jeans, scruffy hoodie, and a T-shirt with what looks like some sort of demonic silver octopus on the front. Instead of making him look serious or somber or death-obsessed, the black somehow makes the rest of him glow even brighter. That skin that looks like it would burn in five minutes of direct sunlight, the big green eyes and flashy white teeth—slightly crooked, I see now, as he catches me glancing toward the counter and grins. He walks back to the table then and hands me a chocolate-dipped chocolate chip cookie that's roughly the size of my head.

"How about this in exchange for that teaser? Not to be tacky or anything, but it cost twenty-five cents more than your cappuccino. Which means I'm giving you an extra quarter. Just saying. Quarters are like gold now that I can drive and have to worry about parking meters."

"Having a car in the city is so overrated. We haven't had one since I was really young." I pause, redirect. "This cookie looks completely awesome, by the way. And I say that as a great connoisseur of anything that involves chocolate and cookies."

"I'm glad you approve," Oliver says, settling into his chair. "So you wanted to brainstorm about the ending?"

"Yeah. But it doesn't feel right if Emma's not here."

"Okay, fair enough, but I do have a question for you. Is the After-world supposed to be heaven? Because I don't really see it that way. There's no sense of a god, for one. No greater being. There are some shady creeps, too, that probably would have ended up in flaming fire pits, if that was a thing. And it doesn't seem all that ideal or paradise-like." He pauses, his freckled brow furrowing. "Am I reading that right?"

I break off a chunk of cookie and dip it in my mug. "It's whatever you want it to be."

He folds his arms across his chest, squinting at me. "That feels like a half-assed response for some lame blog interview. I want the real info. The behind the scenes."

I swallow the cookie and take another sip of cappuccino. "To be honest . . ." I start. *To be honest.* Right. Because that's exactly what I am. *Honest.* I try again, my eyes glued to my cookie as I talk. "I don't have a neat answer for you. I was never raised to believe in a god, to believe in anything besides what we have right here and now. But not having my mom around . . . I guess I want to believe in something, you know? I want to believe there's a piece of her still existing, that she isn't totally gone. Though the idea of ghosts has always freaked me out."

"I hear you. Ghosts are terrifying. Not because they could hurt you or possess you or anything like that. But because of what it must be like, to haunt the same place forever. Never being able to move on. I'd take being gone for good if I had to choose between the two."

"Same." I look back up at him, meeting that sharp gaze of his. "So I tried to create a place that was removed enough from our world, but still not totally out of reach. And I liked the idea of my mom out there somewhere, making friends, building a whole new life." That's why I'd written my story for Dad—that's why this whole thing had started. Because I was desperate to pretend it wasn't really over for Mom.

"I bet your mom's totally out there right now, playing pinochle with my nan and talking about how she hopes she's got a good seventy years before you come knocking."

I smile at that. It's a nice image, even if I don't think it's possible. Wanting to believe and actually believing are two very different things.

"It's wild how many fan letters I get, asking me if everything in the books is true," I say, changing the subject. "If I somehow stumbled across a secret path to another dimension, called it fiction to keep the truth safe."

"I bet I'd have to buy you a lot more than a cookie to get that kind of truth out of you."

I laugh and say, "Listen, if I discovered that kind of secret, no bribery would get me to share it. The world would be too messed up if everyone could come and go from some kind of afterworld. No thank you."

"Point taken," he says, reaching forward and grabbing a big hunk of cookie. "How's your dad, by the way? You said there'd been an accident?"

I tell Oliver about the ladder, the hospital, the recovery. I explain about the deadline extension, and how it's impossible to write anything decent right now—and that's why I was hoping he and Emma could help.

At five o'clock the barista comes over to tell us the café is closing, kicking us out.

"You didn't give me a single teaser!" Oliver says, turning on me as we move to the sidewalk. "Spit that cookie out!"

"You need to be patient," I say, smiling in a playful way that doesn't feel familiar. "I'll send you what I've written so far. The *ultimate* teaser. And then maybe I can see you and Emma tomorrow for a brainstorming session?"

Oliver smiles back. "Sounds like a deal."

eleven

Fifteen-year-old Marigold Maybee had never celebrated anyone's birthday at a cemetery before.

It was Jonah's idea to visit Colton's grave that day. The twins should be together to ring in sixteen, after all. Even if it was far from sweet.

"I asked my mom to come," Jonah said, "but she burst into tears. So then I was going to ask you to try and take me with you to the Afterworld, to see Colt, but if something went wrong, my mom, she—"

"I'll go with you to visit Colton's grave," Marigold said.

It was a crisp, sunny fall day and Marigold followed close behind Jonah as they walked through the cemetery—the historic monuments, the views of the city skyline almost letting her forget where they were. But then Jonah stopped, and she saw the gravestone with the dates and: *Colton Jones. Beloved son and brother.*

I kissed you, Marigold thought. *I kissed you.*

She wanted to throw up, or scream, or claw through the six feet of dirt with her bare hands, discover an empty coffin and know that Colton was alive. But then she felt Jonah's hand on hers, his warm fingers against her wrist.

"I'm so glad you're here," he whispered.

—EXCERPT FROM *LEMONADE SKIES*, **BOOK 2: BETWEEN TWO WORLDS**

The next day I walk over to the Flynns' house, which is about thirty minutes away. Emma and Oliver haven't had a chance to read much of the manuscript yet, but none of us seem to mind that it's mostly a social call.

Their house is a messy but charming disaster zone because their mom, Siobhan, is a painter and has easels set up across the entire first floor with canvases in various stages of completion, and palettes, brushes, and stained drop cloths scattered around. When I meet her, she is busy mixing different shades of blues and greens, a line of white paint smeared across her cheek. Oliver leaves the room to take a call and Emma disappears into the bathroom, and I am suddenly left alone with Siobhan. She asks if I am really happy being a professional author—a professional anything—at seventeen. "Just blows my mind! I love my kids and think they're smarties, don't get me wrong, but I'm happy when they come home with a B on a big test. That's fine enough for me. You're kids still. You have the rest of your lives to overachieve." She smiles at me warmly, though, and I confess to her that I'm not as happy as one would expect, and then somehow end up talking about what it is like not having a mom for every bit of life I can remember.

Mr. Flynn—freckled and pale and red-haired, future Oliver in grown adult form—is there, too, and after my talk with Siobhan he makes us all some hot chocolate with homemade whipped cream.

Oliver is busy with a study group on Monday, but I go over again on Tuesday when he gets home from school. Emma's home, too—she hasn't been feeling well enough to go to school this week, though she's more than happy to hang out with us and talk Marigold. They'd both finished reading the manuscript Monday night, and most of our time is eaten up by their raving about all the things they love in it: Marigold's many happy, tearful conversations with her mom, her immersion in her mom's new life in the Afterworld; Marigold's growing feelings for Jonah, her failed attempts to tell Colton the truth about her and his brother, the simmering romantic tension beneath her time in both worlds; the discovery that the old house is to be torn down and the portal destroyed, the high stakes, the looming decisions.

They take my shame to be humility, luckily.

I've been actively avoiding the rest of my life—Liam got home too late for a visit on Sunday, and I told him I was sick the last two nights when he called asking to see me. Luckily he's had water polo games that have kept him too preoccupied to be more persistent. The lie slipped out before I could stop it. But I needed more time to wrap my head around how I'm feeling about us. I've barely spoken two words to my dad either. He's been eating his meals in his room and I even skipped good night yesterday, after he lit into me for stomping into his room too loudly on Monday. I'd been wearing my fuzziest slippers.

On Wednesday, Emma and Oliver and I retreat down to the basement, the only paint fume–free zone in the house. It's a space that is visibly claimed in equal parts by both of them, walls covered alternatingly in cluttered, toppling shelves of books and band posters, dark and vintage and completely alien to me. There's a desk covered with even more books, an entertainment center with a massive TV that looks to be about as old as I am—also covered in leaning piles of books—and a battered drum set in the opposite corner. And in the middle of the chaos, a beautiful deep green velvet couch and matching love seat that look like something from another century, overflowing with satiny pillows and crocheted throws.

I'm perched on the couch, bare feet kicked up on their coffee table, a mug of steaming tea in my hand. The basement is warm and toasty, with an old radiator hissing and clinking behind me. Emma and Oliver are debating an episode of *Game of Thrones* they watched last night—illicitly down here in their private lair, since Siobhan still deems Emma *way too young and pure of heart* for the show. I'm tuning them out, a happy humming in my ears, because I don't watch it and never intend to. Way too much gore.

Marigold. Now that they're up to speed, I should be asking them to help me outline the last few chapters. But it's easier not to, to give myself more time in this new world of make-believe—this alternate universe where I can almost pretend I'm the Thistle Tate I would have been if Marigold Maybee had never existed. If I had never lied. Not once, but over and over again. Though if there were no Marigold, I wouldn't be here right now. I wouldn't know Emma or Oliver.

I stare at my feet, at the chipped and ragged remnants of the orange polish I'd gotten for the tour. It should be weird to be sitting here, my naked toes wiggling around on the furniture of semi-strangers. Oliver is lounging just a few feet away from me, leaning against the opposite arm of the sofa, and Emma's across from us on the love seat. It doesn't feel weird, though. None of it. That's the weirdest bit of all. The Flynns' house has become my new happy place and if anyone else wonders why I've become an instant fixture—wonders why in the world I have nothing else to be doing, no one else to see—they're courteous enough not to say it.

"Emma, no way," Oliver says, looking up from his copy of *War and Peace* that he's flipping through for school—or maybe just for pleasure, knowing his tastes. "There's no way that Ned Stark is Jon Snow's father. No freaking way. It's too easy! That's what they want you to think! Don't be so gullible, baby sister."

"You're so wrong," Emma says, her voice suddenly much louder. She drags herself out of the nest she's built on the love seat. She looks paler today, even thinner if that's possible overnight. "I bet you six months' worth of washing the dishes that even if it's not Ned, it's not Rhaegar and Lyanna either. And you better not be cheating reading spoilers online since this is old news to the rest of the world. I've worked so hard to avoid them."

I feel my phone vibrating in my pocket. I don't look. I don't have to. It's either Susan—or Elliot, at this point—calling to ask about the book, or Liam asking to see me, and I don't want to pick up while I'm here.

"Need to get that?" Oliver asks.

"It's probably my agent—she's been calling a lot about the last chapters." I take a sip of tea, studying the rim of my mug very closely.

"Did she tell you what she thought of the rest of the manuscript?"

"Oh, yeah. Loved it. Best yet."

"But"—he looks up, all attention on me now—"you don't sound remotely excited? Because that's not amazing or anything?"

I shrug. "It'd be amazing if I had the end written. Seeing as it's due for real in nine days."

"Then let's get cracking," Emma says, grinning at me.

"Okay." I smile back.

"I've been thinking about it a lot," Emma says, "and I love most of what you've written, though I guess I'm kind of surprised with the direction you're going in, in the last chapters. I know Marigold wonders if she can take Mom and Colton back with her, right? Even if she can't know for sure until she tries. But I don't feel like Marigold's mom or Colton should decide to stay put out of fear—because they don't know what will happen to them if they try. I think it should be that Marigold decides she won't take them. It's never a question. It doesn't matter if they can or can't."

"Right." I nod. "I take your point—it would ruin the whole message. But the big thing I've been struggling with—does her mom want to try? With the portal closing, this is her last chance to go home, be with her husband again, see her house, her dog, her friends. So does she try to convince Marigold to take her back? Or does she understand? Does she get that this has to be it—the end?"

"What do you think?" Oliver tucks his messy hair behind his ears so that he can look at me straight on. "They're your babies. You know them inside and out."

It's true that I know Marigold. But her mom . . . she's always been as much of a mystery as my own mom. It was fun to help my dad fill in some of the smaller details: what she looked like, how she talked, what she chose to do with her free time up in the Afterworld. But the big things? That had been my dad. And I'd known from the look in his eyes whenever he was typing up words about her that this wasn't just a character, an idea in black-and-white on a page.

It was flesh and blood and truth. It was every dream of his coming true.

But what do I want to believe?

"I would hope she'd understand," I say, my eyes locked on Oliver's. "That's what I'd like to believe about my own mom, I guess."

"That's the right answer then," Oliver says, smiling now.

"Okay, so I maybe have to rewrite some of the chapters leading up to the end, because I was originally going for Marigold bringing her mom back. It's what the publisher wanted," I say, lying through my teeth.

"What about Colton?" Oliver asks.

"I think he'll want to try. He'd rather be destroyed than trapped in the Afterworld forever."

"Of course Colton is going to be a little bitch about it," Emma grumbles. She's scowling at me now, her lips in an angry pout, and for a minute I doubt myself, my idea.

"Save the language for the hospital," Oliver says, but he's smiling, amused by her fiery outrage.

"It's perfect, though," she says, ignoring him, "and exactly how it should be. I'm not angry at *you*, because you're just doing what you have to do to end that love triangle once and for all. I just hate Colton for being such a selfish, stupid prick all the time. I can't wait for Marigold to run straight into Jonah's arms."

"I gotta be honest, I'm not seeing what you guys hate so much about Colton," Oliver says. "I mean, they're twins. They're not *that* different."

"If the roles were reversed, Jonah would say he loves her, but she needs to go live her life without him. Fall in love with an actual *living* person."

They both turn to me, squinting eyes demanding confirmation.

"I don't think Colton is evil or anything," I say, letting myself feel more authoritative than I probably should. "He's bitter and sad and lonely. I'd be all of those things if I got crushed by a car and had to spend the rest of my existence wondering what would have happened if I'd gotten on my bike thirty seconds earlier. He just wants his one shot. I get that. It's just not the right thing to do, and he's too deep in his own pain to see it."

"So what you're saying is . . . is that I'm right?" Oliver asks, beaming up at me.

"I still hate him," Emma mutters. "Egotistical bastard." I'm not sure if the last bit is about Oliver or Colton, but I laugh either way.

We spend the next two hours working on the outline. Every five minutes there's a new heated debate between Emma and Oliver, and each time they look to me to give the answer. We micro-analyze from every possible angle. It's a rush—I feel strangely all-knowing and mighty, like these aren't just fictional ideas, people and words made of ink and paper. They are as real as the three of us.

It's so different from when I work with my dad, and it feels like exactly what I'm supposed to be doing, today, right now, in this messy basement with Oliver and Emma and stacks of dusty old books.

When Siobhan shouts down that it's dinnertime, all three of us startle, necks snapping up from our huddle around the papers on the coffee table.

"You should stay," Emma suggests, her eyes still glued to the notes. "We could work more after dinner."

"God. My brain actually hurts, I swear." Oliver stands to stretch, massaging his temples with his fists. "Is that a serious thing, Thistle? Do you get a brain ache on your writing days?"

I laugh, tossing a pillow at him. "You're such a lightweight." My brain doesn't hurt—it's the exact opposite. My brain feels like it's firing from all sides, every last synapse lighting up like a firework. I've never felt this completely and totally awake before. "We can hit Pause for tonight, though. I should get home, check in on my dad."

Emma shrugs and pushes my papers into a pile. "As long as you promise you'll come back tomorrow to finish the outline. I feel way too freaking invested to miss anything."

"Of course! I wouldn't leave you dangling now."

We head up the stairs and Emma hugs me bye and goes into the kitchen to see what *god-awful but acceptably healthy* foods she's going to be eating tonight. Oliver walks me out to their front stoop.

"I can't remember the last time I saw her this perky," he says, once the door is closed and it's just us. "Seriously, you make her forget how rough everything else is at the moment."

Oliver is standing so close to me, maybe too close considering Liam. *Liam.* His eyes are pinned to mine, his lips parted, like there's more he wants to say, but it's not coming out.

I remind myself that I've known Liam for thirteen years. That my allegiance lies elsewhere, not on this stoop with this boy I barely know. I take a step back, though it's a tiny one. My brain says to keep going, to keep backing away, but my body decides to stay still.

"It was amazing today," he says, like my movement has triggered his brain back into motion. "To see the look in your eyes when you were plotting everything out. I would've thought you were on some crazy drug if I didn't know better."

"It's not always like that," I say quietly. "It's much more fun with you two."

"If only we'd met you during the first book," he says, grinning. "Though I might have been demanding royalties after that much work."

He hugs me then, his arms reaching out and around me before I understand what's happening. His body is so warm and solid against mine, I let myself fall into it, my arms looping tight around his waist. I rest my head against his chest—soft, not as muscular as Liam's—for a moment before I make myself break away.

"I should get home," I say. "I'll see you tomorrow?"

Oliver nods. He doesn't say anything, but his eyes are studying me, a thoughtful frown creasing his forehead.

I turn and start down the sidewalk before he can tell me what he's thinking.

☙❦❧

I see Liam on my front steps from a block away, lit up by the streetlight.

I consider backing up, turning around—he hasn't seen me yet, I don't think—but whatever this is, it feels inevitable. I have to go home sometime.

It's bad enough that I'm about to be caught in a lie, but then I see what's on the step in front of him. A take-out box from Franny Rosa's, my favorite pizza place in the city. The arugula and pro- sciutto pizza, I'm sure, because Liam knows that's what I like best. Not the crimini and sausage, his first pick. It's a small thing, I know, but I hope I'm wrong. I hope he at least wasn't entirely selfless.

I'm three feet in front of him, and he still hasn't looked up.

"Hey," I say, my voice sounding just as shaky and pathetic as I feel. "It's so cold. I hope you haven't been out here long."

There's an excruciating pause before he looks up, and each sec- ond makes my stomach twist just a little bit tighter.

I want to throw myself at his feet, tell him that I'm sorry I lied, and I'll never do it again.

"Why?" he asks, his voice cracking. "You were never sick. Your dad's nurse looked confused when I said that. Said you've been up and about every day as far as she knew."

Thanks, Mia. "She's right. I was never sick." I sit down on the stoop next to him, leaving enough space between us that he doesn't have to touch me if he doesn't want to. "I don't know why I lied, really. I just . . . I needed time to be alone." Not alone. That's not true. There was Emma. Oliver. "I needed space away from every- thing." That's more accurate. Except I don't want to say the biggest truth. *I needed space away from you.*

"You could have just told me that. I would have understood."

"Would you have?" It comes out snippier than I intended. "I just mean . . . you would have been hurt. But you're hurt now, even more so because I lied. I'm sorry for that."

"You might have to lie to the rest of the world every day, but you're not supposed to lie to me, too." He can't look me in the eye when he says it. I can't look at him either.

"I know. And I'm really sorry. I just—I feel so lost right now."

"What have you been doing then? Where have you been?"

"I've been working on the book. Writing an outline for the last few chapters. I was thinking I'd show it to Dad, motivate him to try to finish with me, though he'll have to change some of his earlier stuff to sync up. He could talk it through, I could type it out—"

"So you were what, at a coffee shop or something these last few days?" He looks confused still, his eyebrows in a knot, but his frown has eased slightly. The edges are softer.

This is my moment: I tell the truth, the whole truth. Or I lie, and make this much easier.

And I know what I have to do, without having to think about it.

"I was working on it with Emma. The girl I visited, the superfan. And her brother, Oliver, he read the books, too. I wanted to brainstorm with them, get their thoughts on how it should wrap up." I sound calm when I say this, like it's the most reasonable explanation in the world. No room for any feelings of hurt or betrayal.

Liam is silent for a moment. He's staring down at his scuffed sneakers, not at me, and I have no clue what's going through his mind.

"You've been working with *them*?" he says finally. "I didn't even think you'd talked to them again after the hospital." He sounds more sad than accusing, which is infinitely worse.

"You never asked," I whisper. "And I didn't want to fight anymore."

He looks up at me now, and I wish he hadn't. There are tears welling up in his eyes. "I want whatever makes this easier on you. I hate seeing you so upset. You could have told me. You should have. Instead of just lying and hiding from me these past few days. I've read the books, too . . ."

I don't know what to say, so I wrap my arm around him instead. He stiffens, the hard muscles along his back going tight at my touch. He doesn't move away, though.

"Is this . . . over?" he asks, still refusing to break eye contact. "Are we done?"

"Of course we're not done," I say, the words tumbling from my mouth.

And it's true—I'd considered a break maybe, but I don't want this to be *done* for good. I definitely don't want that. This is just a rough patch. I've loved Liam for as long as I can remember, and I won't throw our relationship away now because of Marigold.

"I know I hurt you, and it was entirely selfish of me." I take a chance, lean in closer, my leg brushing against his. He still doesn't move away. "I should have been honest, but I was afraid of making things worse. Talking about my dad, about the books—it always leads to us fighting. But that wasn't fair to you. I should have told you how I felt and we could have worked through it."

"I get that," he says quietly. "I'm tired of fighting, too. I know you're not going to change how you feel about your dad. And I'm not sure I can either. But I can at least try to make life better for you."

"I need you, Li. Now more than ever."

He leans in, brushing my curls back from my face. We're kissing then, and it feels okay—better than okay.

We stay like that for a little while, pulling our jackets tighter and leaning in closer for warmth. My stomach grumbles and we break apart, laughing as we tear into the pizza box.

Arugula and prosciutto.

The cheese is hard and congealed by now, but we eat all of the pizza, dipping every last bite of crust into the chili oil Liam asked for on the side, my requirement, not his. We kiss good night when the cold is too unbearable, and then we go our separate ways.

And I wish I could feel happier than I do.

twelve

Marigold needed time and space between that awful gravestone and Colton's smiling, inexplicably alive-looking face. So she avoided the Afterworld and then Jonah, too, when he texted or called.

It was too confusing. Colton's kiss. His name and death date, so permanent there etched into granite for everyone to see. Jonah's hand in hers at the cemetery.

She wanted to talk to Abby and Sam. Needed to. Maybe it was time to tell them everything. Even if they might not believe her. Marigold had ignored their attempts to pull her back into their orbit, and she wanted to undo it all now, apologize for the months of neglect—she couldn't lose a decade of memories and secrets and sacred allegiances.

But how could she say: *I'm so sorry, I chose dead people over you.*

She didn't know what she *would* say, but she'd try. And so she called them both that night. Once. Twice. Three times. She left pitiful voice mails. Begging with no dignity. And then she fell asleep crying, but still hoping.

There were no messages waiting for her in the morning.

—EXCERPT FROM *LEMONADE SKIES*, **BOOK 2: BETWEEN TWO WORLDS**

I feel even guiltier the next afternoon as I walk the brisk thirty minutes it takes to get to the Flynns', despite the fact my secret isn't a secret anymore. And I feel the guiltiest yet when Oliver opens the door and tells me that Emma forgot she had a doctor's appointment today, and that he made a sacred oath that we wouldn't work without her—and I hear myself saying, "That's okay," and asking him if he wants to go grab a coffee or a cookie or something instead.

I don't think I could explain this decision to Liam quite as easily. I don't think I can explain it to myself either.

"If you could do anything right now, what would it be?" Oliver asks as we start off down the sidewalk. "I'm in the mood for adventure."

"Oh, I don't know, trek up Machu Picchu maybe."

"Yeah, that's on my bucket list, too. I guess I was thinking something a bit less adventurous for today, though. Maybe within city limits. And within the boundaries of the law. Though I'm flexible on that last bit." He flashes me a grin, and I smile back, and it's all so easy. "Seriously, though. Let's do something fun. You deserve it after the hard work yesterday. Your brain needs a day off."

"I spent the morning reading. So my brain's probably even more pissed at me now."

"Reading what? Some *Lemonade Skies*?"

I laugh. "I don't sit around reading my own books for fun, you know. I was reading an early copy of a book coming out this spring that the author wants me to write a blurb for."

"Are you friends with lots of other writers then?" he asks, watching me curiously.

"Nope. None. I know them, yeah. People ask for favors. But *friends*? Nah." He's quiet for a beat, so I turn the conversation to him. "How about you? Why are you hanging out with me every day? You must have lots of other friends who are wondering where you disappeared to."

"I told them I was way too busy hanging out with a gorgeous bestselling author to board or play *The Legend of Zelda*. They understood."

I feel my cheeks burn red-hot, but I don't acknowledge the word *gorgeous* otherwise.

I suggest that we go to the Mütter Museum—a vast collection of medical oddities—because it's the least romantic thing I can think of off the top of my head. I've never been, but I know the gist: jars of abnormal organs and deformed fetuses, brains and tumors and skulls. Nothing will say *This is platonic* quite like gazing upon a chunk of Einstein's brain.

"Awesome, yeah. I haven't been there since a field trip in middle school. In hindsight, it seems like a bizarre place to take kids. I had nightmares about the Soap Lady for weeks after. Have you seen her? Looks like a mummy, but it's because the corpse must have been in a super airless, alkaline environment. All the body fat turns into this gross waxy covering." He's shaking his head in disgust, though his eyes are lit up with excitement.

"Great. I've actually never been, so I'm psyched," I say, though the museum suddenly sounds like a completely terrible idea, nothing to actually be psyched about. I don't like thinking about death, ever, even if it's a total stranger who died hundreds of years ago. But it's too late to take it back, and I have no other suggestions, so we keep moving toward the museum. It might be inspiring, after all, for these last chapters. A different take on the afterlife, much darker and less fairy-tale than Marigold's version.

We make small talk for the rest of the way, though it's mostly Oliver doing the chatting. He's telling me about his classes that day, his best friends Pete and Jamie—how it's supremely dorky but they've had Friday-night sleepovers almost every week since they met in fifth grade. "I'm a sucker for tradition," he says. "Ritual. I can't think about breaking it off for college without getting the shakes."

"Where do you want to go?" I ask, realizing for the first time that this friendship already has an expiration date. He'll be—we'll *both* be—leaving next year for college. I'll be flying, up, up, away. Gone.

"I don't know. I have a list, but I haven't applied anywhere yet. I'm going to major in English—amateur, I know, since you wrote awesome books without it. If I had real talent, I'd know by now."

"Shut up," I say, bumping against his shoulder. There's no bitterness in his voice, though, not even a sliver of jealousy. He glances down at me and grins, and I fight the urge to push back the thin strand of coppery-red hair that's gotten caught in his eyelashes. I make myself turn away.

"It feels like I could go anywhere, really. I used to think about heading out west and going to school in Colorado, Oregon, Washington. Somewhere far away, more mellow. I don't know, though. I'm going to apply to local schools, too. Temple, Drexel, St. Joe's. I hate thinking about leaving Emma. I know it's silly, and not what she would tell me to do. She's going to be fine. And it's not like I can really help. But we've gotten so close these past two years. We have each other's backs. It seems much harder from across the country."

"Yeah, I get it." That's how I'd always felt about Liam, even if I didn't want to admit to myself that he was a factor in my college decisions. And maybe I would have felt that way about leaving Dad, too, if things hadn't gone so terribly downhill. "You have to do what feels right," I say, forcing my thoughts back to Oliver and his life, his choices, not mine.

We're at the museum then, thankfully, passing through the grand wrought-iron gate and pillared wooden doors. I push forward into the lobby, toward the visitors' stand, paying for two tickets before Oliver can stop me. "It's payback for your help with everything. I'd be hacking away at the writer's block forever without you and Emma."

"Well, you made it through two other books without us, so I'm not so sure we're that essential, but I'll still take that ticket, don't worry." He winks—a graceful, seamless wink—and starts off toward the exhibits, motioning for me to follow. "The museum closes at five, so we have a lot of awesomely creepy things to see in the next ninety minutes."

We start with microscope slides of Einstein's temporal lobe, and then we move on to the Hyrtl Skull collection, 139 human skulls. Oliver looks enthralled by it all, but I can't shake the feeling that 278 black eye sockets are staring out at me. I'm relieved when we move on, down a flight of steps, into a new room.

But I shouldn't be, because it only gets more unsettling. Jarred fetuses. Massive cysts. Shrunken heads. I keep moving and skim through most of the displays, focusing on the text, not the visuals, as Oliver pores over every last jar and mounted skeleton. He seems especially entranced by a large gangrenous foot.

What feels like hours later we're finally headed back up the stairs, the gift shop safely in sight, when—

"The Soap Lady," Oliver calls out from behind me. "Just like I remember her!"

I turn to see him standing over something that resembles a coffin. The Soap Lady is lying behind a red velvet curtain, her display set up like a viewing at a funeral home. The room seems quieter than the rest of the museum, too quiet. My skin prickles.

"Come see!" He waves me forward, and I pause for a beat before moving toward him. I don't want to see her, not really, but this is *science*. Real life.

I step up next to Oliver and look down, squeezing my hands into fists.

The woman—she does look like a mummy. Black and stony like charcoal, caught in a tortured pose: her face contorted, mouth gaping open, like she's forever stuck mid-scream. There are holes where her nose once was, her eyes. I could almost believe that she's just an old, dirty statue, some grotesque work of ancient art—not a real human being, never a real human being—except there are strands of hair matted along the side of her head. Brown maybe, or strawberry blond, it's hard to say. The last bit of life that still clings to her.

Is this what my mom looks like now?

As soon as I think the words, I feel vomit rise up my throat and start to back away. I think of the pictures of her I've seen, that curly dark hair just like mine, the warm, happy smile. I think about my beautiful mother morphed into this terrible monster of a corpse, any last remaining curls rotting off her head.

Oliver wraps an arm around me and I let myself fall against him, focusing my energy into not throwing up all over the pristine tiled museum floor. In a minute he's led us outside and is setting me down on a wooden bench.

"God, I'm so sorry, Thistle. I knew how bad my nightmares were, I should never have made you look. It's freaky to see death like this. To remember the Soap Lady was a real person once. It really gets in your head."

"I'm fine—" I try to say, but the words catch in my throat. When I close my eyes I can't stop seeing her face, my mom's face, a horrific, twisted amalgam of the two together.

I force my eyes open. We're in a sunny garden. Out of hell, into the light. It's cold out here, but I don't mind. The cold is good. I feel more alive.

"What is this place?" I ask.

"A medicinal plant garden. I remembered it from last time. Seemed like the best bet."

We're both quiet for a minute. I'm pretending to study the plac-ards noting the many different varieties of herbs all around us: thyme and sage and Lady's Mantle. The back brick walls are covered in columns of ivy, and trees and bushes block us from the street. A plane rumbles overhead, but otherwise I could believe we're in our own bubble away from everything and everyone. Like this garden was put here specifically to be our refuge.

"What happened in there, Thistle?" Oliver asks, the words soft, gentle.

"The Soa—" I stop myself. I can't bring myself to even say the name. "She made me think about my mom. In a coffin. It's stupid, I know. I don't remember her funeral, and the two have nothing to do with each other, but . . ." I shrug.

"That's not stupid." He reaches out and wraps his fingers around mine. His hand is solid and warm and everything that I need right now, even if I shouldn't.

"I think I have the opposite view of death," he says, keeping his eyes steady on mine, barely even blinking. I don't blink either. "I like to remind myself of it so that it seems less scary. Make it more just a part of everyday life, so it's less shocking when it actually happens, if that makes sense." He pauses, squeezes my hand tighter. I squeeze back. "I was with my grandma when she died. I was twelve. We were in the kitchen together, making her famous corned beef—she grew up in Ireland—and she said she felt faint, and then . . . I was glad I was there, but I hated it, too. I hated that I was stuck with that as my final memory of her forever."

"What's worse, no memory at all, or a shitty memory?" I ask, even though the answer is obvious.

"I want to remember everything," he says.

We're both quiet for a minute, but it's an okay quiet now. Peaceful.

"I really do love gardens," I say, smiling as I look out over the courtyard, even though most of the plants are long gone for the winter. I can picture what summer must look like from this bench. "I've thought about going to college for botany, maybe."

"I guess English would be a waste of time for you, huh?" He smiles at first, but then he cocks his head, his eyes squinting down at me. "I figured you were going to be an author forever. Would you be going just to get the college experience? Or to do botany as a hobby?"

"I'm not sure I want to settle on one definition of myself at this point. What if there's something more than writing? I hope there is." There has to be.

"And I hope I grow up to be even half as interesting as you are right now. You definitely don't need me to tell you this, because it's so obvious but—you're pretty special."

I want to soak in the words, loop them over and over and memorize the exact sound, the exact weight of them, so I can replay this moment always. But I don't deserve to feel proud. I don't deserve much of anything.

Oliver must sense that his words didn't have the desired effect, because he lets go of my hand and stands up from the bench. "So how about we go get some doughnuts and hot chocolate, blow out of this death hole? My blood is starting to freeze."

"Sounds perfect," I say, jumping up beside him.

Oliver starts asking me about what plants I grow, how long I've liked gardening, and suddenly we're out of the museum, away from the Soap Lady. We sit at a nearby café talking until Oliver's mom calls, telling him he needs to get home for dinner. I'm loopy from the six brown sugar–coated cider doughnuts we split and a huge mug of foamy hot chocolate. Loopy, I tell myself, from the sugar overload. Nothing more.

That night, when Liam comes over and kisses me and asks about my day, I don't tell him about the Soap Lady or the medicinal-plant garden or the best cider doughnuts I've ever had.

I lie. Again. Maybe it's an addiction now. Maybe this is who I am. Liam would be right to judge me. Because instead of the truth, I tell him that I got loads of work done.

That I'm even closer to being finished. *For good.*

❁❁❁

I knock on my dad's door after Liam leaves.

"Hey," I say quietly, anxiously, as I push open the door. No response. He's sitting up in his wheelchair, his back turned to me. Sleeping, I assume. I tiptoe over to check, afraid to jolt him awake, but when I step in front of him I see that his eyes are wide open, clearer and more alert than they've been for a while.

"How are you feeling?" I sit on the edge of his bed and lean in close, but not too close.

"Terrible." He sighs. "Physically terrible to start. The occupational therapist came by today and I felt useless. But emotionally, I'm—I'm not so great either. I keep thinking about how much I'm failing you, and I can't stand it."

"That's not true," I say, even if it is. I look at him, really look at him, for the first time in days. He's lost some weight—which would be a good thing ordinarily, if it was attributed to green smoothies or laps around the block, fewer parakeet-shaped cookies. But it's too much, too fast, and his face looks pale and thin and saggy.

"It seems like you've been pretty busy, though? You haven't been around much lately."

"Yeah, some new friends. A fan I met at my reading at the bookstore, actually."

"Oh," he says, his mouth twisting downward. "*Marigold*. Did you see the e-mail we got from Elliot this afternoon?"

I shake my head. I hadn't checked the e-mail on my laptop since before I'd met up with Oliver.

"Well, he loves the chapters he's read, but he said he *really* must have the rest of the pages next Friday. He suggested he come to Philly in the next few days to help you hash through anything that's left to do and start talking about edits. Susan was invited to join in, too."

"What?" The room spins in front of me. "No. No way. They can't come here."

"I know." He sighs again. "I called Elliot as soon as I read the e-mail. I said that you would be much better left to your own devices—can't mess with genius—but that it's imperative you're given more time. I told him I'd been distracting you. It was my fault."

"And . . . ?" I ask.

"He said he has to have the chapters next week. Martin Davis is breathing fire down his neck. He's insisting on the visit."

My breath hitches. "You were so sure you could get more time."

"I know, Thistle. I tried with Susan then, too, and I got the same story. I don't—I don't know what to do. I'm beating myself up about it, trust me."

"Well, luckily I'm working on a potential solution." My heart is pounding. It's my dad, I shouldn't be nervous, but—this is it, my chance.

"Oh?" He raises both eyebrows.

"I've been outlining the ending for you. It's not exactly how you envisioned it, but I think it'll work. I think it's how it should be. Maybe if I share that with Elliot first, we can—"

"Sweetie," Dad says, interrupting me, "I appreciate that you're trying to help. I do. And I don't mean this to be offensive, but . . . *I* have to be the one to write it. There's just too much riding on these last chapters. You're a great second in command. The best. But this is too important. And the ending needs to stay the way I've envisioned it. It's the only way."

I stand up. I need space. "But I don't get it. You're telling me there's no more time. And you're also telling me that you can't write it yet, but you're the only one who *can* write it, period. So where does that leave us? Where does it leave *me*? How can I have a meeting with Elliot and Susan if I don't have anything to show them?"

He scowls up at the ceiling, shaking his head. "Let me keep thinking about it. I'll figure something out."

"I don't think either of us believes that." I don't recognize my voice. It's cold. Empty.

He's silent for a moment, and I turn toward the door.

"Maybe," he starts, and then pauses, breathing heavily. "Maybe we shouldn't have done it."

These are words that, before, I would have felt so satisfied to hear. So vindicated. But it's too little too late. His regrets do no good now.

"Maybe we should tell them the truth, Thistle."

"And then what?"

"I don't know."

❀❀❀

I throw myself onto the bed, yank the blankets high up over my head. I want to sleep for the next few weeks, erase myself from everything that's happening.

My phone rings, vibrating next to me on the bed. I check it even though I don't want to. Liam. It stops for a beat. Rings again. I pick it up this time.

"Hey," I say, sniffling and gasping into the phone.

"Thistle? What's wrong?"

"Everything. Same as always. My dad. Susan. Elliot. This goddamned book. Susan and Elliot want to come to Philly to help me, and I don't know if I can do it. If I can keep pretending." I'm babbling, words flowing as quickly as the tears.

"What can I do?"

"Nothing, Li. It's all on me. It's my mess. I just need you to be here for me."

"I was calling to say good night, but I can sneak out if you want? Come back over?"

"It's okay." I take a shaky breath, trying to pull myself together. "Tomorrow?"

"Tomorrow." He sighs. "I have a water polo game, but I'll come over when I get back. I just wish . . ."

"Me too."

"Good night, Thistle."

"Good night, Li."

thirteen

If Colton was curious about why Marigold had stayed away from the Afterworld for a week, he didn't ask. He just looked relieved when she found him, swimming laps in the Purple Pool—and surprised when she leaned over the edge for a kiss. He grinned when she pulled away. "I guess you missed me, huh?"

They lounged, legs touching, on the fake blue grass surrounding the pool.

"Remember Finley?" Colton asked. "My bunk mate who told you about dying in a boating accident? His one-year anniversary was yesterday, and he just disappeared. It'll be my anniversary in a few months . . ."

Marigold turned to him, heart thudding. There was too much about the Afterworld that neither of them understood. There were whispers about what happened next, that kids "moved up" after their first year—though no one knew how it happened or what "up" would be like.

And Colton's anniversary meant it was also her mom's anniversary, and she'd probably move up from wherever she was.

"We've never been able to find a way to the upper floors," Marigold said. "Maybe this is as far as I can go. Maybe I won't see Mom again. Maybe I'll lose you forever, too."

—EXCERPT FROM *LEMONADE SKIES,* **BOOK 2: BETWEEN TWO WORLDS**

E mma isn't there at the Flynns' house the next day either.
But this time, she's not just at an appointment. She's back in the hospital. Oliver had waited for me to get to their house so we could go visit her together.

"What happened?" I ask from the passenger seat of his old black

Jetta, my palms hot and slick against my jeans. I don't want to go back to the hospital.

"It's another flare-up," he says, his jawline rigid as he stares out over the steering wheel. "Maybe it's fine, but I don't know. She might need surgery. Medication's more of a temporary fix at this point."

"What kind of surgery?" I should have wondered, worried about Emma more since my first visit, googled Crohn's so I could talk about it without sounding like a total neophyte. She'd pretended she was fine, so I'd pretended she was fine, too.

"I'm not sure, really. I know they've talked about an ileostomy as a kind of worst-case procedure—that's when they make an opening in the stomach and they bring the end of the small intestine to form a stoma . . ."

He continues talking, but I can barely keep up, the terms are all so foreign to me. Emma might have to use an exterior pouch to collect her digestive waste. I understand that much.

"I'm so sorry," I say when he finally goes quiet. I'm the one who reaches out to squeeze his hand this time.

"I'm glad you're here." He glances at me for a moment before turning back to the road. His hair is messier than usual today, scraggly strands pulled up into a loose bun. "My parents are difficult to communicate with during times like this. They shut off and go to this entirely different place, where nothing exists but Emma and what needs to be done next. Step one, two, three. Which is fine, they should be thinking just about Emma, but it's hard sometimes, being in total action mode and not being able to talk about how I'm feeling, too." He cringes, his lips wrinkling up in disgust. "Ugh. Gross. That must sound so incredibly selfish. I'm the worst."

"Please. You seem like one of the least selfish people I know. You vent if you need to—scream out some bad words, if that helps. I hear it works wonders in times like these."

Oliver snorts, almost smiling. "Do you know the old band Blink-182?" he asks, lowering his window. It's cold outside, and I hug myself tighter as the wind whips into the car.

"Vaguely," I say. My knowledge is limited to the name of the band and the fact they were popular a decade or two ago.

He clears his throat and starts screaming one shockingly long string of extreme profanities, loosely sung to some kind of tune. It's more profanities than I've used in the last year, combined, probably.

"That's an awful song! Stop!" I yell, trying not to give in to my smile. "Is it even a real song, or are you just making it up?"

"Of course it's real." He glances over and grins at me, left dimple flaring. " 'Family Reunion'! Google it! I mostly hate it, but I kind of love it, too."

I start to protest again, but he's laughing now between words, and I can't help but laugh with him.

He draws out the last note, voice cracking, red-faced from pushing out every last bit of air from his lungs. He turns to me again, still beaming, his eyes glistening.

"I feel *so* much better."

❀❀❀

We only have five minutes with Emma before she is going to be whisked away for a test. She's quiet. Way too quiet. It's unnerving to see her so still, even when Oliver baits her with bad jokes about Jon Snow's parentage again. She should have screeched in outrage, but instead she just gives him a sad smile and shakes her head.

A nurse comes in to wheel her away, and I wave as she and a very subdued Siobhan disappear down the hall.

"I should probably leave," I say a few minutes later. Oliver and I are lingering outside her room, not speaking, not making eye contact. "This feels like family time. We can pick up where we left off whenever Emma is up to it."

That's not true, not really. Because: deadline. There's a deadline. One week. But I'm not sure there's a reason to keep working anyway, if Dad continues to insist he's the only one who can write it. I can't even think about what would happen if we told the truth. It would be too awful.

I haven't e-mailed Elliot and Susan back about their visit, which I really should do. I'm sure there will be at least one new e-mail from them by the time I get home. I can only put them off for so long. But the idea of seeing them in just a few days, here, in Philly—it doesn't compute. The image doesn't fit into any part of my brain. I've never seen them without Dad. I've never led any of the conversations. If they've noticed, they haven't cared. As long as the books were getting written—and getting written well—they didn't seem to ask any questions.

"Yeah. Sure," Oliver says, interrupting my thoughts. "I'll give you a ride. It'll probably be a late night here, anyway. No Friday-night sleepover with the boys."

"Don't worry about me. I'll just hop in a cab."

"I dragged you here. It's fine. I want some fresh air."

Before I can insist again, he's already started off down the hallway, and I'm following.

We don't talk during the drive, short of me giving him directions.

"It's this one," I say, pointing to my house, and Oliver pulls to a stop.

"Okay then." He's smiling and there's a soft crinkling around his eyes that I haven't noticed before. But we're so close now, side by side under the bright streetlights, it'd be hard to miss. I'm seeing everything—the flecks of amber in his green eyes, the constellation of freckles scattered along the tip of his nose, the curve of his lips. I'm seeing too many things. More than I should.

He sees me looking, and now he's looking, too.

I need to leave, need cool air, but I'm waiting for something that I shouldn't be waiting for, that I'm not sure I want to be waiting for.

That last part's not true, is it?

I do want it.

I do, or I would be backing away right now, wouldn't I? Backing away as he leans in closer, closer, his eyes on my lips, his hand on my hand, our fingers flaming together like small torches. Instead, I lean in toward him.

"Can I kiss you?" he whispers.

"Yes." I gasp as I say it. But I don't take it back.

Our lips touch and somehow I'm still surprised, even after the yes, after all the clear-as-day signs that carried us to this point. Maybe I'm surprised because it's only the second pair of lips I've ever touched, and they feel so like Liam's and so different at the same time. Oliver's lips are fuller, rounder. They move more slowly over mine. The kiss is soft and hesitant and shy, and it's so much more beautiful than I deserve.

I let it happen for a little while. For too long. And all I can think about is that maybe this—*this* is my happy place. Not just the Flynns' house, like I'd thought before. But Oliver. Him. Us.

As soon as I think that, though, the hard truth slams into me.

Oliver likes me because of who he *thinks* I am.

He likes me because he thinks I'm a seventeen-year-old wonder-girl. Talented and confident. That's who Thistle Tate is to him.

But that isn't me. Oliver likes a person who doesn't actually exist.

I draw back as quickly as I can, my hands dropping from his neck and the tangled hairs I've unknowingly tugged out from his bun.

"I'm sorry," I mumble, grabbing my purse from the floor.

"Why?" He's trying to smile, but there's panic in his eyes. "There's nothing I can see to be sorry about . . . is there?"

Liam, I think shamefully. How could I do this to Liam?

And why was Liam not the reason I stopped?

It's wrong, all of it. Me and Oliver, we can't be anything. Because of Liam, yes—but even without him, I can't be with someone who doesn't know the truth. Liam knows, and he still wants to be with me. He may not like it, but he doesn't define me by one lie.

I can't tell Oliver, though. Could never tell him. It's the basis for our friendship. And Emma, too. He'd have to tell Emma. He couldn't hide something like this, not from her. I refuse to take away this good piece of her life, this one bright spot.

"I like you, Oliver. I do, and I'm so glad that we're friends," I say, talking without breathing, forcing it out before I lose my nerve. "Meeting you and Emma, it might sound pathetic, but—it was one of the best things to happen to me in a long time. Which is why we shouldn't complicate things. There's so much going on right now, and . . . honestly, I'm kind of a disaster. Maybe I'm good at hiding it, I don't know, but trust me. We're better off as friends."

I always thought that, underneath the lies about Marigold, I was a decent person. I was loyal. I had morals. I was a good daughter, a good friend. But now? Now I don't know anything anymore.

My brain is calling me a long list of nasty things: *Cheater. Liar. Traitor. Fake.*

Oliver opens his mouth, but nothing comes out. He's looking at the steering wheel, not at me, which makes this marginally easier. I grab the door handle and push, just as he turns and says: "We're all messy, Thistle. I know it's a stressful time for you. We can wait. Okay?"

I nod. A silent yes, but still. A yes. I'm a coward. The worst kind of coward.

I start for my house, head tucked low, a walk of complete shame. I avert my eyes from Liam's house, thanking the universe it's too early for him to be home from his game.

I should tell him, though. I need to. It *feels* wrong. Which means that it *is* wrong.

If a girl kisses a boy when no one else is around to see it, does that mean it didn't happen?

No.

It still happened. It definitely happened. And even if Liam and I hadn't put an official label on our dating, I know it was implied. We are together. And together means exclusive.

In a masochistic downward spiral, I force myself to picture the reverse scenario: Liam in the car with another girl, a kiss that lasts for far too long to be unreciprocated. The image scorches a hole in my mind, white-hot and irreversible.

I want my mom. I want a female best friend at least. An aunt. A cousin. I'm not picky—I'd take whatever I could get. But there's no one.

I take deep breaths, open the front door, and head to the kitchen for a glass of water. Mia is there, making dinner for my dad, a salad and some sort of greenish pasta. Lucy's at her feet, waiting with bated breath for a lettuce leaf to drop. I've been ignoring Lucy, too. Another betrayal to add to the list. I reach out to tickle her ears, but she doesn't react, not even a quick side-eye. She keeps her focus pinned on Mia. The dismissal stings. She may be a dog, but she's probably the most loyal living creature in my life. I take my hand away, rub it against my jeans. Pretend it didn't happen. It's the food! It's all about the food! Nothing to do with me. At all.

I look up at Mia instead.

"Hey." It's an effort to say even that much right now. I fake smile—the training coming in handy yet again—and turn toward the sink, hoping she's not in the mood for chitchat either.

"How was your day?" Mia asks.

"Good," I respond, with a false cheeriness. "You?"

"Okay."

Mia wants to talk more, I can tell, but I get my water and practically jog across the kitchen to the stairs, taking the steps two at a time, and hurl myself into my room. I try to read—a new book about a teen witch whose very mortal boyfriend gets captured by her aunts' rival coven—but even though I was loving it yesterday, the words are a tedious slog now. I'm stuck on the same two pages for twenty minutes before I throw it across the room. I move to the computer instead, scan through my e-mail. There are messages from bloggers, fans, etc. People who don't know me. I see the e-mail from Elliot about his proposed jaunt to Philly. *The powers that be are very anxious to see how the book ends. I have so much faith in you, Thistle. WE ALL DO.*

Tomorrow. I'll respond in the morning. Maybe. It feels inevitable anyway, if they're determined to come. They'll show up without permission. But I'll try to stall until the bitter end.

I close my e-mail and pick up the outline notes from my desk and begin to read. They're good. Really good. Between the three of us, we've come up with an equal amount of expected and unexpected moments, enough balance to keep fans satisfied and surprised at the same time. There's symmetry to it, an order that feels just right.

I don't care that Dad doesn't want me to do this. I want to. I *need* to have something to show Elliot and Susan. One of us has to do something, and that someone won't be him.

I begin to type my messy notes into neat lines, adding in new ideas as I go. My fingers are moving faster than my thoughts, like it's somebody else in control of my hands—not me, not my brain. This is how Dad feels, maybe. How real writers feel.

I write, I delete, I write more. I eat some chocolate and stare at the ceiling for what could be five minutes or thirty, mentally talking through what Colton might use to stake his argument for trying the portal to get back home, how he'd say it.

I write, and I forget. I forget about everything else going on—like dreaming while I'm wide awake—until suddenly it's after nine and my phone is ringing, Liam smiling up at me.

My stomach pinches, because even though I'm looking at Liam, all I can think about is Oliver, his lips, eyes, hair, the way he kissed me, the way I wanted him to. But I pick up anyway, because none of that is Liam's fault, and I can't just run away from my mistakes.

"Hey, Li," I say, trying to sound cool, the phone blazing hot in my hands.

"Hey. I tried pinging you earlier, but you didn't come to the window. Your light's on, though. I guess you're pretty busy?"

"You did? I'm sorry, I must have missed it." I don't think that's ever happened before. My ears are usually highly attuned to even the gentlest tap of a Ping-Pong ball on glass.

"I'm worried about you. Have been all day."

Liam was worrying about me, and I was kissing another boy. I can practically hear my heart snapping down the middle. Not a clean, easy break, but one with a thousand little splintered edges.

"I'm fine," I say. "I've been working on notes for Marigold." Start with one truth. Maybe the rest will come, too.

"Oh."

I keep going. "I visited Emma in the hospital again . . . she's not doing well."

"Seriously, Thistle?"

"What?"

"It's just . . . why do you really need to see them so much? I mean, ever since you started working with them, you've seemed, I don't know, different. Not yourself."

"Not myself?" I bristle, immediately defensive. "No. They're good for me. They believe in me, and . . . it helps with the writing. Honestly, I feel more myself than ever."

"Right. More yourself. I get it," he says, and then he's quiet.

I could do it now—I could tell him about what happened with Oliver today. But it doesn't seem like a conversation for the phone. Better to wait until tomorrow. Give myself more time to reflect, too, on what I even want to be saying. Why I did it. Why it will or won't happen again.

"I—I really was thinking about you all day," he says. "About us. I like you so damn much, Thistle. But I can't tell what you're thinking anymore. I know I was the one who said we shouldn't rush into labels, but I was just being dumb and scared. I'm all-in with you, you know that, right? I guess the real question is, do you still want this? Do you still want *me*?" He sounds small and desperate and wounded, and I want to curl into a ball and never hurt anyone else ever again.

"Of course I want you, Li," I hear myself say, the words stiff and robotic and entirely unlike me. Liam must hear it, too, because we're both silent for an uncomfortable amount of time.

"I didn't think you'd throw away a Machu Picchu trip that easily," he finally says, and I can't tell if he's smiling, but I'm not. "I guess I should let you go. You have work to do, right?"

"Yes. No. I don't know. I'm probably doing all this for nothing. I'm doomed. Dad won't like my ideas, and he'll ruin it somehow. Or I'll ruin it on my own."

"We'll figure something out."

I agree even though I know there's nothing he can do. I'll tell him tomorrow. I will. I should.

I'll try.

❀❀❀

I have another *new* nightmare.

I'd almost prefer my old nightmare now, the crash—that was the past, at least. Over and done. This is the present. The future.

I'm in a courtroom again, though this time Liam is the judge, and Oliver is on the stand. The case seems to be about Marigold at first—with Oliver passionately insisting that *of course* it was all me, I'm brilliant and talented and there's not a chance in hell the book came from anywhere but my brain. My one-of-a-kind, beautiful brain. Liam is snickering. My dad is next to me, and he starts laughing, too. The whole room is laughing then, Susan and Elliot and my publicist, bloggers and fans and booksellers. They're all cracking up, hysterical at the thought that anyone could still believe I'm brilliant or talented.

When my eyes finally snap open, I see my room, the white morning light streaming in through the windows. Everything is quiet. Peaceful. Normal.

I sigh in relief and reach for my phone on the nightstand.

There are fifteen missed calls from the last few hours.

There are two texts, too, from Susan. She's never texted me before. Not once.

With a prickling sense of unease, I tap to read them.

First, a link to a blog, *Elisabeth Early's Books*. One of my harshest critics.

And then Susan's second text: *I'm sure none of this is true, Thistle. Ugly, outrageous gossip. But everyone is talking and we need to make a statement ASAP. Theo is clearly not the real author! We know you're the star. We just have to make sure everyone else knows it, too. Call me!!! As soon as you wake up!!! XXX P.S. I tried to call your dad, too, but he's not picking up either.*

I click the link, my finger on autopilot. I see the headline, though the words are fuzzy, the dark teal words bleeding out over the screen.

LEMONADE SKIES FANS: MEET THEO TATE, THE REAL AUTHOR OF YOUR BELOVED SERIES.

I drop the phone.

fourteen

Christmas morning. The first one without her.

Marigold's dad was sitting by the tree when she came downstairs. He'd put it up at least, stringing lights around the plastic branches, going through the motions.

"Merry Christmas," he said, smiling—smiling too much, in an unexpected and forgotten way. "Open your gifts!"

And so she did. Bathing suits and a snorkel, an ocean-scented candle.

"I'm sensing a theme here," she joked. *Vacation*—she dared to let herself hope. "Are we . . . going on an exotic trip?"

Though it wasn't a good time to leave—Colton would be moved up next month. She wanted to be there, with him. She wanted to be there, just in case his move would mean finally finding new information about where her mom could be.

"Not quite, sweetie. We're doing what your mom and I always dreamed about," he said, his eyes misting over as he leaned in to grab her hand. "You and me—we're moving to Florida in two weeks. We'll leave all this behind. For good."

—EXCERPT FROM *LEMONADE SKIES*, **BOOK 2: BETWEEN TWO WORLDS**

I'm out of bed, my bare feet slapping against the cold floor.

I pinch myself once, twice, three times. I can't be awake right now. Dreaming, I'm dreaming, *this is a dream*. One more new nightmare to add to the list. That's all, nothing more.

I yank my nightstand drawer open and closed a few times, slamming it back in so hard that my lamp teeters and falls to the floor, the bulb breaking and splintering across the wooden floor. I bend down to scoop up the biggest pieces, and a shard slips and slices through my skin. A single drop of blood stains my comforter as I lean back against the bed for support.

I can feel the sting of pain. I can feel everything—the fresh cut on my finger, the cool air on my bare arms and legs, my throbbing, constricting chest.

This isn't sleep. I'm not just dreaming.

Which means that the blog post, the text from Susan: it's all real.

I blot my finger on a tissue and run to my desk, flip my laptop open. *Elisabeth Early*, I type, and her too-familiar homepage pops up on the screen. I try not to look at her blog, but I can never stop myself. She's one of the only bloggers who actively dislikes *Lemonade Skies*. That hadn't prevented her from coming to my first-ever reading in Philly—she lives in a suburb just outside the city—to smile at me and shake my hand, as if she hadn't already said that the first book was "trifling and sophomoric and tired." My dad was of course more offended than I was—rightfully so. In a strange way, I was thrilled that she'd called the writing *sophomoric*. It meant she believed the book was actually written by a teenager. Her review was nastier for the second book, though, her growing bewilderment about why in the world other readers cared so much. "There are a *million* other books more deserving of that bestseller status."

I'd hurt for my dad when I'd read that line. I'd hurt for Marigold, too. She was my literary sister, after all.

As bad as that post was, it has nothing on this latest one. I stare at the screen. Stare at those words again, those terrible, horrific, true words.

LEMONADE SKIES FANS: MEET THEO TATE, THE REAL AUTHOR OF YOUR BELOVED SERIES.

I can't breathe. Or blink. Or move my finger to scroll the mouse. So I keep staring, the swirly teal letters bold and underlined and looking so very certain and confident. Just below I can see the top half of a photo of Dad and me from this last tour, him smiling down at me as I sign a big stack of *Lemonade Skies* inventory. Seeing it now, with that glaring headline above it, his smile looks maybe too proud. Too territorial. I'm sure that's what our thousands of fans—*former* fans—are thinking right now, too, in exactly this moment, all across the globe.

My finger is pressing on the mouse, scrolling, against my will. I read it all, every last hideous word. I have to. I have to know.

Well, now, this is a twist none of us expected, right? (Not even me, one of the only *Lemonade Skies* detractors on the Internet!!!) I'd always chalked up the saccharine voice and paper-thin, almost nonexistent character development to the fact that the author was a teenager. Sure, considering her age, Thistle was above average. That didn't make her books any more entertaining or more readable, *but* it was a reasonable excuse. (I mean, heck, I could barely manage to scrape together ten pages for an essay when I was her age!) I figured she'd probably develop more polish and depth with age. That maybe I'd actually like later books down the road. But in light of what I know now— that *Thistle's 55-year-old father, THEO TATE, is actually **the author** of these books,* just color me downright confused. I guess the writing is just mediocre because it's mediocre, independent of age or actual life experience. Huh. Go figure.

Thank god I never liked these books to begin with, because *boy would I be pissed as hell right now.* Theo and Thistle, heads up: lying isn't cool. It isn't fair. And I think I speak for many of your fans when I say that I hope you have to return your ridiculously oversized advances and that the third book never sees the light of day. Even if I'd been planning on reading it (let's be honest, I wasn't, but still), you couldn't pay me to do it now. There are way too many infinitely more deserving books out there.

What do you all think about it? Very curious to hear your thoughts!

Perhaps a petition to Zenith is in order . . .

I apologize profusely if I'm wrong. I will write the longest apology ever to be seen. So believe what you want to believe. But me . . . I'm going to believe this until proven otherwise.

XX Elisabeth XX

I had wondered what it would be like—what *I* would be like, how I would feel—if the worst ever happened. But right now, I feel nothing. Not yet. I am still, quiet, numb. Empty. I want to feel something, anything, but there are too many things I could be feeling, and I can't seem to process which one to pick. I can categorize them all neatly, ticking off my options:

I could feel furious. Outraged that someone betrayed me. Who, though? An image of my dad pops into my mind first—our last real conversation. *Maybe we should tell them the truth, Thistle.* But I don't let myself think about it more, not yet.

I could feel ashamed. The world knows I'm a fraud. A talentless nobody.

I could feel scared. What will Zenith do to punish us?

I could also feel . . . relieved. The secret is out. I can stop pretending.

Instead of deciding, I take a long shower. I tilt my face into the too-hot stream of water, lather my body and hair in floral-scented bubbles. My skin is bright red when I finally step out and towel myself off. I pat my hair dry and comb through the tangles. I consider what to wear.

It's this moment, this one insignificant decision, that starts to break me. The first crack.

Because what do I wear on a day like today?

What clothes are appropriate for when your entire world is imploding?

Certainly nothing tainted by Marigold. I want to pull out every tour dress, skirt, blouse from my closet—douse them in gasoline in a trash bin out in the backyard, watch until the last marigold-colored frill burns up in smoke. For now, I content myself with tossing them one by one into a towering heap on the closet floor.

I put on my mom's gray wool sweater again. I can still remember exactly how I felt the last time I wore it, the morning after my first kiss with Liam.

Liam. He's one person I can talk to at least. One person whose entire opinion of me won't be blown apart by this public revelation. He probably hasn't even heard the news yet, since he has no interest in the YA world beyond me. To him, the YA canon consists solely of Harry Potter (loves), *Twilight* (hates), and *Lemonade Skies* (likes by default). But now doesn't feel like the right time to lean on him.

Oliver, though . . . Oliver and Emma. They would know. Emma would no doubt have seen it blasting through her social media feeds.

I shatter all the way through now, every last lucid piece of me sliding away. I'm sobbing so hard I can barely see through the tears as I storm downstairs to Dad's room.

"*Was it you?*" I scream, flinging open his door without knocking.

He's watching me with confused, sleepy eyes. This only makes me angrier. Much angrier. I slam the door shut behind me and he jolts forward, pushing the button that shifts his bed into an upright position. He shakes his head back and forth, like he's clearing out the fog from his brain.

"What the hell is going on, Thistle? I just woke up. What are you talking about?"

"Elisabeth Early. She posted this morning about how it's all a lie, that *you* are the author. Not me. Never me. You."

His mouth gapes open. "Everyone knows? And you think . . . it's because of *me*?"

"Probably. Maybe."

"Can you bring my laptop over to me? I need to see the post."

I walk over and pick the computer up from his desk, drop it unceremoniously onto his lap without his usual mouse. It's propped at a difficult angle for him to navigate with his arms still in slings, but I don't offer any additional help. He shifts against the bed until his fingers hit the keys, and I can tell when he finds Elisabeth Early's page because his whole face suddenly crumples in on itself.

I have to look away. "I mean, you're the most logical answer. Who else would it be?"

He stares at me like he's never seen me before. "Even if I had decided that you and I would be better off if we just ended this whole charade—I'd have had a quiet conversation with Elliot and Susan first. Maybe it wouldn't have stayed quiet, but I would have tried. And I certainly would have talked it through with you before I did anything."

"But who else is there?" I whine, desperate and needy. I sound like I'm five years old again, begging for another bowl of ice cream before bed. "I mean, has Mrs. Rizzo been spying? Or, no, wait—oh my god, oh my god, *Mia*. It's Mia! She's overheard us talking about it. She *lives* here. She knows what's going on. She obviously was the one who—"

"Why would Mia care about this?" Dad interrupts, squinting up at me.

"Mia!" I jerk the door open and lean my head out into the hall— "Mia!"—yelling much louder than necessary because she's standing in the kitchen just a few feet away.

"Yes?" I can't read her tone, if it's panicked or curious or confused.

"Was it you?" I step out into the hallway, directly facing her. "Did you blow the whistle? Tell the whole world that I'm not the real author?"

"Excuse me?" Her brow wrinkles and her usually friendly face is now anything but. "Whistle-blowing? What are you even talking about?"

"Don't lie to me."

"I am *not* lying to you. Is this about those books all over your dad's room? The writing he tried to do? I wondered what was going on, the way you stomp in and out of there and the way he carries on about disappointing you, but honey, that's none of my business. And truth be told, I don't really care who wrote the books."

I don't want to believe her, I don't, but there's not even the slightest trace of guilt on her face.

"Oh," I say, wishing I could slip between the wooden floor-boards. "I'm sorry." I slink back toward Dad's room. "I really am."

Mia nods, already turned away from me, busy or at least pretending to be busy with some papers stacked on the kitchen counter.

Dad's studying me as I fall against the end of his bed, eyes filled with what I suspect is pity. I can't look at him. "Thistle . . ." He stops. Then, "Thistle, did you tell Liam?"

My body stiffens and I push off the bed. "Yes."

"I thought it was supposed to be our secret, like we discussed. But I guess a part of me wondered. He never seems particularly happy when I'm around. He definitely gives me the stink-eye sometimes."

"I tell him everything." I *did* tell him everything.

"I know. Wishful thinking on my part. But I guess you had to vent to someone, right? It was a lot to carry around."

I don't bother responding to that.

"What's done is done. But I'm asking because, I don't know . . . do you think there's any chance he could have done this? Was he upset with you about anything?"

My throat constricts. *Liam*. No. He wouldn't. Ever.

Liam.

"It's the only option," he says quietly. Carefully. "Unless you've told someone else?"

"Liam is my best friend."

Dad sighs, his brows furrowing into deep wrinkles as he closes his eyes. "I know he cares about you," he says, his eyes still shut. The words come slowly, each like a little weight being pressed off his tongue. "He worries about you, I can tell. Maybe in some twisted way he thought he'd be helping you . . . ?"

"That makes no sense. He wouldn't. No way—"

I have to ask him. Now. Before I can do anything else, before I can breathe again.

I'm flying out of Dad's room, down the hall and through the front door. It's cold and rainy and gray outside, exactly the kind of ugly weather I'd expect from this day. I leap up the Carusos' stoop two stairs at a time and pound at the buzzer.

The door opens, and Liam's there, eyes wide. "Thistle," he says. He looks like he just rolled out of bed, ratty pajamas and messy hair, his normal Saturday-morning look. But it's not a normal Saturday morning. "Are you okay?"

"Why wouldn't I be?" I slip past him and into the house.

"I mean—you seem . . . upset?" He sounds conflicted, like he's not sure what to give away yet. Just in case I don't know.

"Was it you?" It comes out more as a gasp than actual words. I can feel myself crumbling, tears welling, but I will them back in. I take a deep breath, make myself stand up straighter.

He shuffles his bare feet on the thick Persian carpet, staring up at the ceiling.

"Was it?" I'm louder this time. Too loud to be ignored.

"Yes."

"How?"

"I met Elisabeth at your first event here, remember? Though she'd already been such a witch about the book that I hardly said two words to her. But she remembered me from that night. She trusted me, especially when—"

I cut him off. "I didn't mean *how* as in the logistics of it, Liam. I'm not an idiot. You met her, you remembered that she wasn't one of my biggest fans, so she'd be way more easily swayed to believe a story like this. Good work."

My voice sounds cold and cutting, cruel enough that Liam physically recoils, taking a few steps back to get farther away from me. I watch as he steadies himself again. He looks at me straight on.

"I saw you," he says.

"You saw me what?"

"I saw you kiss him. I saw you kiss Oliver yesterday."

"Oh." The words pound me in the stomach, sharp and jagged and deep. I lean against the wall because I'm not sure I can keep standing without it.

"I was hoping when I called last night you'd admit to it at least. I came home early to see you because you'd sounded so down the night before. Skipped a big game and pissed off my coach royally, but I didn't care. And then you weren't home when I stopped by, but I was looking out the window—"

"I'm sorry," I say. And I am.

"Are you?"

"I'm sorry that it happened that way. And I'm sorry that I wasn't honest about it. I was going to tell you, though. I didn't want to do it on the phone."

"Sure."

"I promise. I was going to tell you today."

He snorts. "You told me it was all about the book. Another lie. It's all lies with you now. Do you even know how to be honest about anything?" He rakes his hands through his hair, shaking his head. "It's scary. Like I don't even know you anymore. Those books, your whole charade, it was ruining our relationship. So I thought you needed something to make you stop lying. Something that would make you realize how messed up you'd become. How many people you were hurting."

"What I did with Oliver was wrong, and I apologize for how that went down. But it was no excuse for you to go running to the enemy."

"Are you mad because Emma will find out the truth? *Oliver?*" Liam's voice tightens around his name, as if it's foul-tasting bile that needs to be immediately spit out. "Now he'll know who you really are?"

I slide down the wall to the floor, hugging my knees tight in to my chest. "People will *hate* me, including Oliver and Emma. People will tear me apart online. Can you even imagine the things fans are saying right now? Can you imagine the hate messages I'm going to be getting for weeks? Months?" I shake my head. "You don't have a clue. You just stormed in like a vindictive monster crushing everything in its path. You were jealous, and you decided to ruin my entire life because of one stupid kiss. You had a right to be mad at me. But you didn't have the right to destroy everything."

He's on his hands and knees now on the floor next to me, head ducked down. "You're right. I was jealous. And pissed. But honestly? I thought it was only a matter of time before the truth was out anyway, since your dad wouldn't be able to finish it. I thought at least you could get the shitty part done with so you could move on with your life. So you could be free. It wasn't all about revenge."

"That's what you're telling yourself? And what am I going to do with all this freedom?"

"You—you be you. Be honest. You do whatever you want to do, not what someone else is pushing you into. All those crazy expectations—they're gone."

"Dad could go to jail, Liam. That's not freedom."

"They're not putting him in jail. Worst case I bet he has to give some money back."

"You don't know anything."

"I know that I love you. We both messed this up bad, really bad—but we can work this out. It's you and me. We can fix this."

Love. He's leaning in toward me, his arms reaching out to pull me closer. I jerk away, pushing back up to my feet. *Love.*

Had I loved him? Do I love him now? Or was this whole thing out of . . . *convenience*? Because we're neighbors. Because he was all I knew of the outside world. I don't know. I can't know. Especially now, because whatever it was—it's over.

"There's nothing left to fix. With us. Or with the book. I was handling that just fine, for the record. Our ideas were really good, just as good if not more so than anything my dad could've come up with." I feel a flash of pride as I say it, even though it doesn't matter. None of it matters now. "I might have messed up, but I didn't do it to hurt you. That's the difference between you and me. I never wanted to hurt anyone. And if this is what love is, I don't want love, ever. Not yours, at least."

I'm shaking, I realize, my legs wobbling. I might faint if I move, but even fainting would be better than staying here with Liam. I don't say a word as I start to leave. There's nothing else to be said. Liam must realize that much at least, because he doesn't try to stop me.

Back inside my house, Mia is standing by Dad's closed door, actively not looking at me as I walk in her direction toward the stairs.

"I'm so sorry," I say, not looking at her either. "I was terrible. You didn't deserve that."

Before Mia can respond—if she's even going to respond—the doorbell chimes.

"Shoot, that's Liam, I bet . . . I know you don't owe me any favors, but can you just tell him to leave?" I ask, eyes pleading with her.

She pauses for a moment, nods. "Sure. Whatever you want."

"Thank you," I say, already halfway up the stairs when the door opens. I dive for the landing, pulling my legs quickly out of view.

"Hello there, I—" Mia breaks off. Is it not Liam? Could it be Oliver? No doubt he'd want the truth straight from me. He'd hold out on believing any nasty gossip until he heard it from my lips.

But it's not Oliver's voice that carries up the stairs, paralyzing me against the railing. This voice is female. Cool and clipped.

"Hello. My name is Susan Van Buren. I'm here to see Thistle."

fifteen

The movers were coming tomorrow, and Marigold couldn't leave the portal. Not before she found her mom.

She called Jonah to say she was coming over, and he was waiting for her, bundled up on his front steps.

"Are you okay?" he asked, his breath a white cloud.

"I have to leave for a little while," she said.

"So the Afterworld, I'm guessing, not Florida. For how long?"

"I'm not sure. I'm going to leave a note for my dad tonight. Tell him that I'm staying with a friend he doesn't know, in Philly. That I won't move."

"Will you pack food and water?"

"I put some water bottles and protein bars in my bag, just in case. But I told you, I don't get hungry or thirsty when I'm there."

"I'll miss you. Tell Colt I love him and miss him."

"I will. But he knows."

And before she could stop Jonah—but no, she wouldn't stop him if she could, would she?—he was kissing her.

Marigold was kissing the person Colton loved most in any world—his brother.

—EXCERPT FROM *LEMONADE SKIES, BOOK 2: BETWEEN TWO WORLDS*

I t's not true, is it?"

Susan's eyebrows lift dramatically high as she asks the question, her sharp eyes squinting from behind round tortoiseshell frames.

We're sitting at the kitchen table, Susan and I, so close that I'm sure she can hear my heart slamming against my rib cage. After Susan introduced herself at the door, Mia came up and took my hand, eased me down the stairs. She led us both into the kitchen and poured glasses of water before heading upstairs, away from this. Susan and I gave each other cold, detached hugs and settled onto our chairs in silence. There was no pretense of chitchat, no asking about my dad or compliment on our house, which she'd never seen before today.

"Can I get my dad?" I ask, desperate for some sense of protection. I don't want to do this alone. "I feel like he should be here for this conversation, and—"

"*No*. Right now I'm interested in hearing what *you* have to say. I'll talk to your father later if need be. My pleasant Saturday morning was imploded by this story, and I dropped everything to be on the next train down here. So again . . . Thistle, tell me, please, that this isn't true. Tell me that I overreacted when you weren't picking up my calls."

It occurs to me now that I could lie. I could say that *of course* it's not true, that Elisabeth Early never liked me, that there was no evidence whatsoever to prove her claim. What was Liam's word against mine? My dad would back me up. Fans would want to trust us— would want to believe so they could preserve everything they loved about Marigold, about me.

I could say that Liam had lashed out after I'd broken his heart. I could undo everything he'd done. I could make this all go away.

I could. But I don't. I can't.

"It's true," I say instead. "All of it."

"How dare you?" She stands from her seat, towering over me. She's not yelling, but she doesn't have to—her lack of composure is scary enough. I've never seen this side of Susan, red-faced and eyes bulging, her mouth gaping open, fumbling for what words to say next. "How—how—how *dare* you and your father lie to me all this time? After everything I've done for you? You haven't just ruined your career, you know. You've ruined mine, too. *My* career. What will my other clients think of me? You've destroyed my name. My agency. And for *what*? Why lie? These books were good. No—they were fucking *exquisite*. No one had to lie."

"That's not true," I say quietly. I make myself look at her as I talk. I deserve to suffer. "Dad queried agents with other projects for years. *Years*. My whole life, really. And he never got a single bite. He was just one of thousands of wannabe writers, and it was eating away at him. Ruining him. It was bad. Really bad. He thought that maybe if agents believed a teen wrote *Girl in the Afterworld*, there'd be a hook. He was so happy when it worked, and I—I couldn't take that away from him. We needed the money. And I needed him to be happy."

Susan tilts her head, considers this for a moment. "But did he ever try to send *Girl in the Afterworld* to other agents first? Had people rejected it thinking it was Theo's?"

Had they? "No. At least I don't think so." It all feels so long ago now.

Susan sighs. Her face is slightly less red, her breathing slower. She looks more deflated than angry. I preferred the anger. Her rage made sense to me—it was her well-earned right.

"That's what I thought," she says. "No competent agent would have rejected it, whoever wrote it. You never had to lie, Thistle. That's the most frustrating part of this whole mess."

This—somehow this is worse than anything else Susan could say. The idea that my dad could have been a success in his own right, proudly taking credit for his own masterpiece—it razor blades right through my gut. I could have had a normal life, been a proud daughter watching her dad's career from the sidelines. Not *this*.

"I don't even know what else to say right now." Susan turns away from me, her gaze fixed toward the window in the back door, my dead garden. "I have to speak to Elliot. Tell him everything. Unless . . ." She pauses for a beat, shakes her head. Sighs again. "No. *No*, I will not in any way suggest maintaining this silly lie. I don't know what Martin Davis and Zenith will do next. I really don't. In my thirty-five years of experience, there's never been a case quite like this. Legally, I'm sure they'll go easy on *you*—you're the minor who was pushed into this unethical disaster. But your dad . . . I don't know. And the *fans*. God help you with the fans, Thistle, because I guarantee that it won't be pretty."

I can't see her face, but I wonder if there's a tiny smile on it now. Satisfaction at the fact that I have no plausible chance of escaping unscathed.

Susan turns around sharply, and if there was a smile, it's already long gone. "I'm leaving. I'll call Elliot from the train, ruin his weekend, too. I imagine he won't have any immediate answers. He'll have to go straight to Martin." She grabs her purse from the table, giving me one clipped nod before starting across the kitchen. "I'll be in touch."

"But—" I jump from my seat, following her into the hallway. It seems like there is so much more to say, to be decided and strategized. "Are you sure you don't want to talk to my dad? We can get him in the wheelchair and bring him out to—"

"I have nothing—*nothing*—to say to Theo. I can't see his face right now. I wouldn't trust myself if I did. Just assure him that he'll be hearing more once Zenith has decided how to handle things."

"Susan? Is that you?" my dad calls out from behind the closed office door, just a few steps from where Susan stands. "I'm sorry, I had headphones on. I didn't know you were here. Can we talk? I just need help getting into my wheelchair."

She stops for a beat. Takes a deep breath. And then she keeps moving forward. The door slams behind her, picture frames rattling against the walls.

"It's over," I say, not bothering to open Dad's door. "I told her everything. And you were right, by the way. It was Liam who did this. So, *congratulations.*" I turn away from his room and walk slowly up the stairs.

My phone's ringing as I walk into my bedroom. I let it ring through to the end without seeing who it is. It stops for a few seconds, rings again. And then again. I grab for it. *Oliver Flynn.* There's no point in putting off the inevitable.

"Hello?" I answer cautiously. I can hear my voice shaking.

"Thistle! I'm so glad you picked up, I've been trying you all morning."

"You have?" Of course he has. He's been just waiting to tear into me. "I'm sorry, things have been crazy here, as I'm sure you—"

"No worries, it's fine. I'm sorry for being so needy. It's just . . . Emma's not doing well. They decided on surgery for sure, and I'm a total wreck."

"Oh my god, Oliver. I'm so sorry."

He doesn't know.

There is more to this universe than the plight of Thistle Tate and Marigold Maybee.

There is chronic sickness and suffering, blood and needles and risks—cutting open a girl's body, sewing it up again in a way that hopefully, *fingers crossed*, makes her at least a little bit better.

"What can I do?" I ask, desperate to do something, anything, during this small grace period before everything is destroyed for good.

"Can I come over? I need to escape the hospital. Escape everything."

"Of course," I say, before I think about the many potential ugly complications of this decision: Dad, no doubt fretting downstairs in his lair; Mia, a relative stranger who now despises me and who also knows my deepest, darkest secret; and Liam, who could come over at any moment, begging for forgiveness or yelling at me more for cheating, for the lies. It's too late to take it back, though. I'll have to sweep Oliver up to my bedroom before anyone else has a chance to lunge.

"I can be there in ten minutes if that's okay."

"Sure . . . yeah, that'd be fine."

"Super, see you soon then," he says, and hangs up.

I glance around my room, taking in the chaos. It would be abundantly clear to any observer that this is the nest of a recluse who rarely has contact with the outside world. I start shoving dirty underwear and pajamas in the hamper and chocolate wrappers and tissues in the trash can. I pull my blankets up over my pillows in a weak attempt at bed making, push books into stacks off to the side of the room and old plates and cups under my bed. I turn to my laptop then, powering it off before snapping it shut and burying it under some piles of papers on my desk. I can't take any chance of him seeing the morning's big news.

The window—the clear view to Liam's room. I yank the curtains shut, blocking any unwanted surveillance. It's not his business who comes over, not anymore, but I don't need to add fuel to his fire. I'm lucky I have a second window along the back of the house for light, because I think this curtain will be closed for the foreseeable future.

I give the room a last once-over. It's messy still, a layer of dust glistening on my nightstand and bookshelves, and with decor that looks decidedly more thirteen than seventeen: framed Harry Potter posters—including two personally signed prints from J. K. Rowling, which I'll have on my wall until the day I die, when they'll be ceremoniously taken down to go in the coffin with me—a glow-in-the-dark galaxy on the ceiling, a unicorn lamp and bobbleheads of Archie and Betty and Veronica on the dresser, a framed picture of me and Liam in Mickey ears. Only Dad and Liam have ever seen my room. I've never had to look at it with fresh eyes.

It's fine, though, or as fine as it will be, so I run down the steps and wait by the door.

Oliver drives up a few seconds later, exactly ten minutes after our call.

"Thistle!" he says when I yank open the front door, and the look he gives me tells me everything—I'm the person he wants to be with when he's having a bad day.

But this will be the last time he looks at me this way. He's going to find out. And that'll be it. This will be done. Before we barely had a chance to start.

He steps inside and I fall into him, hugging him against me as tight as I can. "I'm so sorry," I say, and I mean it in so many ways.

"She's going to be okay." He hugs me back, just as tight. "It's scary right now, but I know it's going to work out. I just hate seeing her like this."

"I know." I'm fighting back tears that aren't fair to cry. He'll think I'm crying about Emma—and I am, partly. Though I'm crying for me, too. Crying because I'm so terrified for this hug to end. I don't want to let go. But I need to. I need to tell him.

We stand that way for a few minutes, Oliver rubbing circles on my back, a feeling that is so beautiful and so perfect that I want to sear it into my neurons and remember the sensation forever. This day has had so much ugliness: Elisabeth Early, Dad, Mia, Susan. *Liam*. But just a few minutes with Oliver makes the rest fade.

I hear a shuffling noise coming from the hallway behind us, and I jump back, pulling free of Oliver's arms as I spin around. It's only Lucy, though, giving me a long, slow look before she turns toward the kitchen.

"Let's go upstairs. My dad's sleeping down here until he's able to do steps again."

We walk up in silence. I close the bedroom door behind us—a gesture that I hope Oliver doesn't assume means more than it does—and finally bring myself to face him. My cheeks feel too flushed. Standing this close to him, five feet from my bed.

"When is the surgery?" I ask, desperate to think about other things. Emma is why he's here, why he's standing next to me in my bedroom, looking frazzled, his messy red hair shoved into the hood of his black sweatshirt. Emma is what matters.

"Monday morning." He moves toward my bed, perches on the edge. I sit next to him, close, but not so close that we make contact.

"Can I come see her?" *One last time*, I don't say.

"Of course, but probably not until after surgery. She's exhausted, and I know all she'd want to do if she saw you is to keep talking about the outline. I swear, even when she's asleep she's mumbling about Jonah and Colton and destiny. I just hope she's relatively healthy when the book comes out, because she's going to lose it when she sees any of the things we talked about in actual black-and-white in a published book."

He grins at me but I can only nod, pretending it doesn't feel like I'm falling apart on the inside.

"I'm loving these sick Harry Potter posters, by the way. Can't say I read the books—I'm more a *Lord of the Rings* guy—but the movies were pretty sweet. How come you don't have any *Lemonade Skies* posters? Are they framed in gold in an office somewhere?"

"Ha. I spend enough time with Marigold. I don't need her staring at me while I sleep."

I could tell him now. I could. While we're talking about Marigold. I open my lips, the words somewhere deep, deep down in my throat.

"I have to—" I start, but Oliver is talking, too, louder than me, my words disappearing under his. "Do you want to go for a ride?" I drop my sentence, relieved and disappointed in myself.

He should be at the hospital with his sister, and I should stay home . . . doing what? Waiting to hear more from Susan and Elliot. Scrolling through social media and the blogosphere to see just how badly my fans are taking the news. Read the scathing e-mails that are no doubt flooding my in-box. I have no actual work to do, not anymore. No schoolwork until my dad is up for it again—if that ever happens—and for the first time in years, no *Lemonade Skies* deadlines. Because there won't be a third book.

I laugh out loud. All that work, the planning, the fighting with Dad over how it would all end, the brainstorming session with Emma and Oliver, the outline that I had felt so very proud about. It was all for *nothing*.

"What's so funny?" Oliver asks, cocking his head, studying me with those catlike eyes.

"Oh, nothing. Everything. A ride sounds great. I need a break."

He stands up, bowing like a perfect gentleman before offering me his hand. His hair has fallen out of his hood, red waves across his forehead. I want to brush it back, run my hands through it, tug it out from his bun, and lose myself in it.

I resist, though. I reach out and just take his hand instead.

He smiles and I nod, and off we go, escaping this day for as long as life will let us.

sixteen

Marigold couldn't look Colton in the eyes when she got there.

"I'm so tired," she lied. "And I feel guilty about leaving Dad."

"It's the best thing for both of you," Colton said, hugging her with arms that felt exactly like Jonah's arms, arms that would always remind her of betrayal. "He would want you to find your mom, if he knew. And besides, being here means you and I have more time together."

Marigold dreamed about the accident that night, her first full night in the Afterworld. But the dream was different: it was before the crash, and her mom was yelling from the driver's seat, telling Marigold how selfish she was, how needy and spoiled.

She had said all those things exactly, hadn't she?

Somehow in the aftermath, Marigold had forgotten those details. She'd forgotten a lot of things: how many other times they'd had similar screaming matches—how many times she'd seemed to be a disappointment to her mother. She woke up, crying and breathless, with the most terrifying question playing over and over through her mind: What if her mom didn't want to see her again?

—EXCERPT FROM *LEMONADE SKIES*, **BOOK 2: BETWEEN TWO WORLDS**

So do you have an actual destination in mind? Just curious."

We've been driving for maybe an hour, out of the city and onto the highway, though we've just pulled off onto a winding country road that I've never seen before. The drizzle has stopped and it's a bright white November day. Only a few last hazy wisps of fog hover above the trees and fields, blue sky peeking out from behind the clouds.

"Not really," Oliver says. "I just knew that I wanted fresh air. I love the city, but it's definitely not a forever home for me, you know?"

I hadn't thought much beyond college. I'd just assumed that I'd go far away for school, probably with or at least somewhere near Liam, get some distance from my dad, from Marigold—but that we would both come home again eventually. Liam had always said he was a Philly boy for life. I guess I'd expected to be a Philly girl right alongside him. But now?

"I'm not sure what I think about Philly," I say, eyes focused on the blur of nature beyond the window. "I just know I want to go somewhere else right now. See something new. Meet different kinds of people. Meet any people at all, really, since I've spent the last twelve years of school at home with my dad."

"For sure." Oliver nods. "I can understand that. You need to get away for a while."

A new and extremely unpleasant thought occurs to me, clawing at my stomach. My SAT scores were decent, but I'd been assuming my applications would hinge on *Lemonade Skies*, of course—the fact that I was a *prodigy*. At least by their definition, because I would have two books under my belt before graduation and a third on its way. Three books from a prestigious publishing house. Books that had sold in thirty-five countries and had sales of over ten million copies worldwide. I hadn't bothered with any early admissions applications because, with credentials like those, all the top colleges would be fighting over me. *Would have been fighting over me*, I correct myself. Because there would certainly be no fighting now. No trying to lure me away from competitors. I'd be untouchable to every college I'd ever really wanted.

My future feels as empty as the rolling fields around us, harvested for the season, corn and wheat and whatever else was growing there long gone now. The earth is brown and barren, ready for a deep slumber until the spring.

I don't need college to be a gardener, I remind myself. This helps. Slightly.

"I wish we could pick apples," I say, "but it's too late . . ."

Oliver glances over at me, smiling. "Look at you, you're secretly a country girl, too."

"I'm just amazed by anything that I can eat straight from nature. Pick it off a vine, a tree, from the ground, whatever, and just pop it right in my mouth. It's a mini-miracle to me."

"How about a Christmas-tree farm? I'm sure we could find one of those."

"I love Christmas and decorating our fake tree, don't get me wrong, but I never loved the idea of murdering a gorgeous pine and watching it slowly die for the next month. Needles turning brown, dropping one by one, the last bits of lifeblood draining out. I'm a hypocrite because I'd never say no to a gorgeous bouquet of flowers, but they're so temporary anyway, even in the ground. They live, they die, they come back again, at least in some cases. But that tree—who knows how long a life it could have had otherwise, you know?" I shudder dramatically to make my point, though it's really how I feel. "It's just kind of gross to me. The annual slaughter of so many tree souls. But no offense if it's what your family does," I tack on politely at the end, just in case.

"We do engage in the mass slaughter, I'm sorry to say, but maybe we'll have to reconsider this year. You've made me realize the error of our ways." He's trying hard to look somber, but he's biting his lip to keep back a smile. "I'll just be sure not to buy you any flowers unless they're in a pot. I wouldn't want you to be a hypocrite on my account."

"Fake flowers are fine, too, as long as they're made with fine silks," I say, reaching over to grab his hand. It feels bold, touching him now, me initiating. I squeeze, and he squeezes back.

But he will never give you flowers, not now, will he?

"I keep seeing signs for something called Green Hill Reservoir Park," Oliver says, and I force myself back to this: this moment. "Should we try it out?"

"Green Hill sounds pretty idyllic. How can we pass up a name like that?"

We're driving deeper into the woods now, bare tree limbs raised like twisting old arches along the road ahead of us. There's a sign directing us down a long, gravel-covered entrance, and finally a parking lot that is empty except for one lone Jeep. The park ranger's, probably.

I zipper up my puffy black coat and put on my green wool hat and matching scarf before I open the door. I'm glad I wore my mom's sweater today—it's the warmest piece of clothing I own and adds a solid extra layer. I step out of the car, the cold biting into me, but in a divine, exhilarating way. Oliver was right about leaving the city. If I were a religious person, today would have been a good day to go to church. Confess to a priest or pastor that I've sinned—a big sin at that—and be told I'll be forgiven, that I can atone, purify, start again. That I am not above redemption.

But I haven't been inside a church since my mom's funeral, and I don't remember that day.

This park, though, is how I imagine a church would feel. I'm in awe of the trees circling us, their trunks too wide to hug, branches stretching high into the sky, three times as tall as my house in Philly.

I catch glimpses of glistening water in the distance, off behind the trees. I close my eyes and breathe in as much pine-scented air as my lungs will allow. I hold it, let it flow through me, slowly breathe out.

"This is perfect," I say quietly, turning to Oliver. He looks peaceful, more relaxed than I've ever seen him.

We hold hands again, so effortlessly this time I'm not even sure who moved first, whose fingers led the way. We walk toward the reservoir leisurely, in no rush to pass through any part of this day. The air feels colder as we get closer to the water, crisper and more brittle. It pricks the back of my throat when I inhale too deeply.

"I feel like we own this place," Oliver says, leaning into me. Our shoulders touch, our hips, and I feel suddenly much warmer.

"Well, it is pretty darn cold out here. I guess most people are done with nature until spring comes around."

"The people who live around here are too used to this kind of beauty. They can probably just step out into their yard and get the same effect. We had to work harder to find it."

"It's like your car knew where we were going even before you did."

"It's true." He drops my hand, spreading his arms out wide, taking in the whole reservoir. I would have thought it was just a regular lake—it looks too entirely sure of its existence to have been created by humans. "Green Hill, Pennsylvania, we were meant to find you today. We needed you." He turns to me, his whole face glowing like the now brilliant blue sky above us. "Thank you," he says, to me, to the water, to this whole day.

I reach up and cup his cheeks, pull him in closer.

"What about last night?" he asks quietly, his lips grazing my forehead. "Wanting to stay friends to keep things uncomplicated?"

"I—I meant it, Oliver. Because it's true. But that doesn't mean it's what I really want. I like you, and that's why I'm trying to protect you. From me."

"I don't care, Thistle, I don't. I meant what I said. I'll take messy if it means being with you."

I could tell him now, but instead we lean in at the same time—my mouth finding his, our lips moving, fast and frantic, creating our own heat out here on this lonely beach. I feel more lit up than the winter sun, electric golden energy flowing through my veins.

We break away eventually, staring at each other. And then we walk farther along the path, until we're deeper into the woods, climbing to the top of a huge rock formation conveniently situated to overlook the reservoir. The water stretches out in front of us, a sheet of smooth gray metal glinting under the sun.

We're kissing again then, and even though I know this is wrong, that Oliver deserves the truth, I can't make myself stop. Because the only thing I know for sure is: if this is our last day together, I want to condense the future moments we won't have into *this*, beautiful glorious *this*. I'm not thinking, I'm doing. And he must be, too, because suddenly our jackets are off, other layers disappearing, too, scattered on the rock around us. I should be cold, my bare skin exposed, but all I can feel is Oliver surrounding me.

There are boundaries we don't cross. Won't cross. We both know there's a line without needing to say it out loud. But still, I want to enjoy as much of him as I can.

Only for a second, I think—that Jeep, that ranger, what if someone . . . ?

But then Oliver kisses me harder, and I am floating above the treetops, watching us from the clouds, hoping and wishing and praying that *this* . . .

This moment will never have to end.

❀❀❀

The ride home is silent. A good silent, though, at least for Oliver. He's cupping my hand like I am newly fragile and delicate. I am gripping back for dear life.

We stop at a Wawa for food on our way, and I pretend that my turkey-and-cheese hoagie requires all my attention, as if it is the most fascinating sandwich I've ever eaten.

I should tell him my story, my truth. I've made the treachery infinitely worse by letting him in closer. The guilt is settling in fast now, choking the words from my throat. I have never been more of a coward.

It's dark by the time we get back to Philly, the lights of our city twinkling at us, welcoming us home. But we're not the same two people who left earlier today. I'm not, at least. I already know this day will mark me for the rest of my life. *Oliver.* I keep sneaking glances at him as he drives. His eyes look serious, focused on the traffic, but there's a tiny smile playing at his lips. I try to make my lips move the same way, but it doesn't work.

He pulls up to my house and we sit there for a few minutes, neither of us saying the words or making the moves that will put an end to this day. His phone rings, somewhere in his pocket. He doesn't pull it out, but sighs. "It's probably my parents wondering where I've been. I should head to the hospital, check in with everyone. It's going to be a long few days coming up."

I nod, suddenly feeling queasy with dread, the knowledge that *this*—this will be our last moment together. No more Oliver. No more Emma either.

Just me. Thistle Tate, the great pretender.

"What are you thinking?" Oliver asks gently. I want to fling my arms around him and reassure him with a thousand kisses. But I don't. "I mean, today was pretty unexpected, especially after last night's talk. But it . . . also felt so natural. Unless you . . . ?" He breaks off, waiting for me to finish.

"This afternoon was—it was perfect," I say, turning to him, leaning in so that our faces are just inches apart.

Oliver's lips curl up into a too-happy grin. "It was pretty perfect. But I have a feeling it's only going to get better." He kisses me, saving me from having to fake a smile.

It's soft and lingering this time, and I try to feel, taste, savor every last second.

"Good-bye, Thistle," Oliver says, slowly pulling away. He looks reluctant, but I can tell that his mind is switching back to that call, whatever news is waiting at the hospital.

"Good-bye," I whisper, just barely. The word scratches at my lips.

I hear the car waiting as I walk, but I don't look back as I open the front door and step inside the house.

❀❀❀

Dad calls for me later that night, as I'm passing from the kitchen to the stairs.

I consider pretending that I didn't hear, but he tries again, and there's a brittle sadness to his voice that tugs at me, even after everything.

"Yeah?" I lean against the door frame, committed to not stepping in any farther. He's sitting in his wheelchair, looking out the dark window.

"How are you?" He turns to face me. The lighting in his room is dim, but I notice again how much skinnier he looks, how gaunt his face has become. For all the wrongs he's done, I've had my share of wrongs, too. That doesn't make it better, excusable, even if it makes us equals.

"I'm pretty shitty, actually."

"I am so sorry, Thistle." He lets out a sad sigh, and the sound, the feeling, snakes around me and pulls me down with him. "So ashamed of myself. And I'm angry that I let this much fall onto you, that I let career success come first. I really would undo it all if I could. I'd rather be a disaster who can't keep a rotten part-time job for more than two months than this person I've become." He shakes his head.

But I don't say anything back. I don't have to. I agree, and we both know it.

"I'll call Susan Monday morning—give her the rest of the weekend to cool down. I don't think it'll make any difference, but I want to reaffirm that this was my doing. That you were an innocent bystander."

"She knows, Dad. You're the one who signed the contract with Zenith. I agreed to it, maybe, but I was only fifteen. I was a minor. I was doing what my dad asked me to do. My sole guardian."

It's these words that make Dad break. *Sole guardian.* I'd said it purposefully; I'd wanted to hurt him, to drive the knife in deeper.

"I almost hope there is no afterworld. That this is it, this is all we have. Because the idea that your mom could be watching—" He sobs, the tears a steady stream. His wrinkles fan out in deep lines across his cheeks, his forehead. "She would never forgive me," he cries, so inconsolably now that I can just barely make sense of his words. "And you shouldn't either."

I have no reason to still be in here. I go up to my room, and my phone is buzzing nonstop—Oliver—but I don't pick up, I don't click through to his texts or voice mails.

I am nothing. I am no one.

Nothing.

No one.

seventeen

Marigold and Colton were standing in their spot in the atrium. "It's time for me to move up," he said, arms wrapped around her. "Wait here and I'll be back as soon as I can."

"What if you can't?" Marigold said.

"Don't worry, I'll find a way. Or . . ." His eyes lit up with hope. "I could try coming through the portal with you right now."

"But what if your coming closes the portal and then there's no hope of finding Mom?"

Colton sighed. "Fine. We stick to this plan. For now."

Marigold didn't say anything for a few minutes, then whispered, "I can't wait here forever. I've already been in the Afterworld for almost a week. I should go home." To Dad. And to Jonah. Because she thought about him every day. When she kissed Colton, when she twisted her fingers into his hair.

"If I'm not back in a day, go home. Beg your dad not to move. I promise I'll look for your mom wherever I am. Come to this spot in a month, and if I'm not here, the month after. And the month after that, until we find each other and . . ."

Marigold kissed him. She kissed him until he disappeared, leaving her with nothing but silence and her own breaking heart.

—EXCERPT FROM *LEMONADE SKIES*, **BOOK 2: BETWEEN TWO WORLDS**

I'm not surprised to find Oliver on my doorstep in the morning, knocking frantically.

I steel myself as I pull open the door. I'm too tired from crying all night, too empty of anything to feel emotional. This was inevitable. I'm prepared for this, I tell myself.

But I am not, in fact, prepared for how utterly destroyed Oliver looks. His skin is practically transparent in the early-morning sun, his freckles darker than ever in contrast. They usually look so per-fect on his face, just right—like there's a purpose for each and every one of them—but right now they look wrong. Everything looks wrong. His hair is matted back into a messy bun, strands falling out, brushing into red-rimmed eyes. Red hair, red eyes, red lips, red red red on an otherwise completely blank white canvas.

"You know." I can barely hear myself say the words.

"I know."

He doesn't sound sad, or angry, or hurt. He sounds like a flat line, a bare room, a hollow shell.

"I'm sorry."

"You're sorry," he deadpans. "You're *sorry.*"

I step back into the hallway, motioning for him to come inside where it's warm. He doesn't move, though. I stay put. "I should have told you yesterday. Or no, I should have told you before yesterday. But I couldn't tell anyone. And I—I had my reasons. Good ones, I thought. For my dad's sake. He was depressed, Oliver, so depressed. He never got over my mom dying. And we were running out of money. He'd had a string of failed jobs, failed manuscripts—this was the first thing that worked out. He lied to agents before I gave permission, but then it was—it was the first time I'd seen him happy in so long. Excited about life." I pause, shake away the sad memories. Shake away the excuses. "None of that matters though, not now. I lied to you, I lied to everyone, and I don't expect anyone to forgive me."

"You're right. I can't forgive you. I can't stop thinking about yes-terday, about how fucking great I thought you were. All lies. And Emma . . . the look in her eyes when she told me last night. Jesus Christ, it was bad." His voice is filling in now, the fear, the rage, the disappointment. I'm glad, because he deserves that—deserves to let it out. And I deserve to feel like the lowliest, dirtiest scum.

He looks like he's about to turn away, to leave for good. But he stops himself.

"Did anyone know? Besides your dad?"

I consider for a second. But there's no point in lying. "Liam. My neighbor."

"Right. So you could trust him. Just not me."

"That's not fair. I've known Liam since I was four. He knew everything about me."

"And you loved him, right? Still do, maybe."

"It's different. Besides, he's the one who outed me, so—"

"Never mind. None of it matters. I don't give a shit who you love, and who you tell your deepest, darkest secrets to. I don't want any of it."

I reach out to him, but he steps back, just out of reach. "I really care about you, Oliver. Everything we felt yesterday was still real."

He shakes his head, backing away even farther. "I don't think you even know what *real* is. Everything about you is a lie."

He's down the sidewalk then, opening up his car door. "Tell Emma," I start to yell, but then I realize there's nothing she'd want to hear. The best thing for her is to forget about me. But it's not just me she's losing. She's losing Marigold, too. She'll never be able to read another word of her favorite books, the world and the people she loved so much. I've ruined that for her, too. Her refuge.

I hope her parents let her use every dirty word under the sun today.

❀❀❀

I log on to Twitter. I type five words: *It's all true. I'm sorry.*

If yesterday was about self-indulgence and denial, today is about punishment.

It's time for me to face it head-on, to see everything that fans are saying about me online. To read all the e-mails—though, this, I realize, might have to be a more extended punishment, because there are already over two thousand new messages in my in-box. Enraged fans, of course, and what looks like a slew of media requests, too. Everyone wants an exclusive interview. Including, I see, from a quick scan of subject lines, the *New York Times*.

The *New York Times* knows. Everyone knows.

I close my e-mail and search for my name online, click the "news" option to bypass my website and best-seller listings and all the good and happy things that people have said about me over the years. The news updates—they are not so good and happy.

Thistle Tate, International Bestselling Author, Accused of Fraud.
Theo and Thistle Tate: Their Lemonade Skies Conspiracy
In Depth: The Undoing of Thistle Tate.

I sit at my desk for over six hours. I can't make myself stop. It's like rubbernecking at my own accident scene—I'm bloody and broken and somehow watching from outside my body. And I can't look away, no matter how gruesome the sight.

My name is mud. My dad's name is mud. The Tates will never again have a home in publishing. I'm not sure we'll have a home anywhere.

The direct tweets and personal messages are the worst—there's no limit to what someone feels comfortable expressing online. I've been called: *a conniving bitch, a fame whore, a talentless piece of shit.* They seem rather unanimous in thinking that my dad and I should be shipped off to jail. After we return all our money, of course. There are calls, too, for an international *Lemonade Skies* Book Burning Day. There's even a new Twitter account dedicated to rallying my enemies: Ban Marigold Maybee!

When I finally seem to have covered most of the posts from the last twenty-four hours, I close down my computer. Maybe I'll read more tonight. Tomorrow. The day after that. The day after that, too. Because there's nothing else to do. No homework, no book, no friends or boyfriends. Just a dad who I can't bear to even look at right now. There's Mia, too, but I'm sure she wants nothing to do with either Tate anymore. I can't believe she's even still here.

I rack my brain trying to think of one other person, someone else who might actually care about how awful my life is right now.

Mrs. Rizzo.

I laugh. *Care* feels like a strong word. But she did say I should knock if I needed anything, and I need to talk to someone. Plus I've eaten nothing all day, and one of her parakeet cookies sounds perfect right now.

I'm on her porch knocking before I can change my mind. There's a pause, and just as I'm about to try one more time, the curtain gets yanked aside. Mrs. Rizzo is staring at me, her snowy brows raised. She looks surprised at first, but then alarmed.

"Is everything okay?" she asks, nearly knocking me over as she throws the door open. "Is your father in trouble? Do I need to call 9-1-1?" Of course she would assume that my face on her doorstep must mean something terrible has happened. I've never once initiated contact, not in seventeen years of living right next door.

"No, he's fine. I'm fine. Well, not *fine*, but not in dire medical need. Can I—would you want to have tea or anything?"

She lifts both eyebrows, lips pursed. Like she's waiting for the joke to land. She pulls her housecoat tightly around her chest, blue-and-white parakeets flapping in the cool breeze. "Okay," she says, her sharp eyes observing me warily. "Come inside from the cold. You're still in your pajamas, you know."

I look down. She's right. Pink-and-yellow-plaid top and bottoms. Slippers on the cold concrete stoop. "I apologize for my indecency. I can change if you want and come back?"

Her gaze softens, just a bit. "Don't be silly. Get inside. You're letting the cold in!" She mutters about outrageous oil prices as she heads down the hallway, leading me to where I know her kitchen will be, seeing as it's an exact mirror image of our house. Structurally, that is. Nothing else is the same. I could have guessed from the housecoat and the cookies, but any color that Mrs. Rizzo lacks in her dour demeanor, she more than makes up for in her home decor. It's like sparkly rainbow vomit everywhere: the floors, the walls, the countertops. There's hardly a square of white to be seen anywhere. The hallway is lined with canary-yellow and Barbie-pink and sky-blue frames displaying pictures of kitties and puppies and lambs and—of course—parakeets. There are no baby pictures, no family photos. There is just one portrait of an actual human: a man in an army uniform. The photo has that old-timey brownish golden tint, but I can still tell that he is quite handsome. *Was* quite handsome. I assume this must be her late husband, but I don't ask.

The kitchen counter is a mess—canisters and whisks and wooden spoons, dapples of flour and sugar all over the faded silver-speckled Formica. I remember that countertop from when I was younger— replacing it was the one home improvement Dad made with our first *Lemonade Skies* advance. Mrs. Rizzo points at a kitchen chair, giving a grunt that I take to mean: *Sit down*. I obey. She's busying herself with a kettle, filling it and putting it on the stove, rustling around in her cabinets for boxes of tea and mugs and what I suspect is a tin of cookies.

She comes over to me, tin in hands, and takes the lid off. It's her typical parakeets, but this time—this time there are mini–chocolate chips on top, no sprinkles. "I tried something new today," she says. "I usually like to keep my chocolate separate, but I figured, why not? Who knows how many days I have left? Might as well try everything once."

I take one cookie, but Mrs. Rizzo keeps holding the tin in front of me. "It's not rude to have more if you're hungry, you know."

I take three more, and she seems content, closing the tin and putting it down on the table. We smile at each other politely, silent for a moment, before the kettle lets out a low, squeaky whistle. She walks to the counter and collects a tray with two steaming mugs of hot water and every kind of tea bag under the sun.

"I suspect the black cherry would taste especially nice with this particular cookie," she says, settling the tray at the table and easing into the chair next to me. "And I'm personally very keen on adding a generous drip of cream to my tea. Makes it taste like a real treat." I take a black cherry tea bag and steep it, adding two cubes of sugar and cream, just as Mrs. Rizzo does. She seems pleased by this, nodding at my cup approvingly as we both dip our cookies.

"These are fantastic," I say, only after I've chewed and swallowed the entire first cookie. "Seriously, the chips were a phenomenal decision. Game changing."

"I thought so, too. This new recipe might be the death of me. Or my waistline at least."

I wouldn't say that Mrs. Rizzo is slim necessarily, but she's certainly not morbidly obese. I'd be thrilled to make it to her age—and if I could pick a way to go, death by shortbread chocolate chip cookie seems pretty great, all things considered.

"So you're in my kitchen to talk about something, I imagine? Given you've lived here for, oh, your entire life, and you've never set foot on my doorstep. This feels like quite the occasion."

It's not accusatory, the way she says it. More an observation. It's not like she was seeking me out either. She was too busy peeking over the backyard wall and lecturing me on the sidewalk—but now doesn't seem like the time to point those things out.

Except . . . she did knock on our door sometimes, didn't she? With cookies for Dad. Maybe for me, too, even if she didn't expressly say that. And I was always too snotty to eat one, let alone thank her.

"I'm sorry about that. I've been . . . a pretty shitty neighbor, I guess. I'm a shitty friend and girlfriend, too, so it's nothing to take personally. Really, you've been better off. A shitty neighbor from afar is better than a shitty neighbor who's too in your business."

"That was quite a lot of 'shitty,' dear." She's smiling, though. A small smile, but still easily the biggest one I've ever seen on her face. It's like seeing a beak on a kitten, whiskers on a bird. "But there is something you're good at, no?" she says. "I've followed along for all of Marigold's adventures, you know. You're a rather talented writer."

"You've read them?" This stuns me. More than the chocolate chips on her parakeet cookies, more than the fact that I was allowed to say *shitty* four times without being scolded.

"Your father always gives me a copy hot off the press. Repayment for the cookies."

"But you never told me. You never once brought it up when you saw me on the street."

"True. I could have acknowledged it. But you never seemed interested in talking to me, so I suppose I was a bit reluctant to praise you. I can be quite the crotchety old hag, you know."

She winks at me. Mrs. Rizzo *winks* at me. I laugh so hard the milky tea spews out of my mouth, and instead of looking at me in disgust, she's laughing, too. The moment feels so bizarre, so completely surreal and at odds with everything Mrs. Rizzo and I had established in our nonrelationship as neighbors, that suddenly I want her to know.

"Mrs. Rizzo, about that writing thing—"

"Call me Dottie," she says, cutting me off.

"Dottie," I say, tentatively. It feels odd on my lips, but no more odd than anything else that's happening, so I might as well embrace it. "Dottie it is."

"Thank you."

"So Dottie, the thing is . . ."

And just like that, I'm telling her everything. My dad's unhappiness, his money woes and failed attempts at getting published, his one shot at success. The lie that felt like our only choice. Though maybe Susan had been right—maybe we'd never needed to resort to deceit. But now we'd never know. I tell her about the years of faking my role, faking it so well that no one, not my agent, my editor, my fans ever suspected. I tell her about the deadline, my dad's mental state, my fights with Liam. Working with Oliver and Emma. The big exposé.

"I've lost everything," I say at the end, miraculously still free of tears. I guess I'm all dried up, nothing left to shed. "No friends, no career. Probably no college prospects, either, since I've just been caught in one of the biggest literary scandals in history. Mrs.— Dottie . . . what do I do now? What's next?"

"More cookies," she says, yanking open the lid of the tin and shoving them into my hands. "Eat more cookies."

"That's your solution?" I laugh. And then take a few cookies, of course.

"The best I have at the moment. I'm still processing your rather extraordinary tale." She takes some cookies, too, her already very wrinkled face creasing even more deeply as she chews, considering. "From what I'm hearing, this situation has been awfully toxic. Probably hurt your relationship with your father more than helped it, despite your good intentions. And you were planning on cutting all writing ties after this last book, correct?"

"Yep. This book was it, for me at least. I was scared I was going to be pressured again, by Dad, by the publisher. But I wanted no part of 'writing' another book."

"Do you think," she starts, then takes another large bite of cookie, and continues: "Do you think that—despite the immediate consequences, yes, and the ugliness of what everyone is saying about you on that darn Internet—maybe it's for the best? 'The truth will set you free.' That's John, chapter eight—"

"I'm not very familiar with the Bible, but I know that line." I don't need biblical fire and brimstone—I'm miserable enough without the idea of hell lurking around the corner. I've had enough afterworld with Marigold to need any more of my own.

She sighs, reaching out to pat my hand. Her palm is warmer and softer than I expect—she's always looked so stiff, I imagined her skin would be brittle and leathery. Dottie is nothing but surprises today.

"I know I'm just a crazy old lady to you. And it's mostly true. My parakeet obsession! And I'm a lot old, too. Eighty-seven, to be precise." She looks smug as she says it, proud of every single one of those years. "I've told some lies in almost nine decades. None of them as much of a whopper as yours, but they add up. I don't think lying makes you evil. And considering the reasons for this lie in particular . . . no, I don't think you're an awful person. It was a mistake. And you're paying for it. But you're only seventeen. It may be hard to see now, but this lie won't define you forever. You can't let it. You have to go on and do so many other good things that this just seems like one blip in a long life of happy truths. You know what I regret about life? That since my husband, Sammy, died thirty-six years ago, I have barely left this house or talked to anyone but these walls. I've learned too much about life from the television screen, not from being out there in the wild. So whatever you do, don't do that. Don't you dare keep hiding yourself." She gives my hand one last squeeze and stands up, unceremoniously clearing away our teacups and cookie crumbs.

I'm too dazed to offer to help, which I realize only after the table looks perfectly clean and orderly again. She's already moved on to the countertops, sweeping up the flour patches and dumping the baking utensils into the sink.

"Can I help you with anything else?" she asks then, wiping her hands on a dish towel. "Do you want more cookies to take home to your father? Or for your dinner?"

I nod, even if my stomach hurts from too much sugar and it feels greedy to ask for more. But I don't have a mom or a grandmother to make me comfort food. Dottie Rizzo is as good as it'll get for me, and maybe it's not such a bad alternative.

"I'm glad you came," she says, handing me a plastic bag of cookies. "You know, if you want to pop over tomorrow, or any day really, you're more than welcome. It seems like both of these houses can be a bit solitary sometimes. We're a sad little row, aren't we?"

Liam, me and Dad, Dottie. A sad little row indeed.

"Of course I'll be back," I say as I move toward the door. And I mean it.

She nods, a bit tight lipped as she pretends to shoo me away. But her eyes are smiling and shiny. I'm about to walk down her front steps when she says, "You look so much like your mother, you know that?"

It occurs to me, for the first time ever, that Dottie would have known Mom. She grew up here, right next door. All along I've had another source to be drilling for information, and I was too indifferent toward her to realize.

"Do you think sometime . . . we could talk about my mom?"

She frowns at me, her eyes even shinier. "Sure. I don't know much about her life after high school, mind you, but I remember her as a young girl. Sweet thing. Sassy, though, like you. Had some fire to her. By the time she passed, I'd shut myself off in here. She tried to reach out a few times after she moved back with your father, but I pushed her away. I'll always regret that. I will."

She closes the door then, and I'm glad, because she can't see that I'm crying as I trudge back to my own house.

Mom. I'll finally know more about Mom.

I read for a bit that night. I don't check my phone or turn my computer back on. I replay my conversation with Mrs. Rizzo—Dottie, which I'll probably never get used to—and start to think that she's right. I hate the way it happened, that Liam betrayed me, that

I betrayed him, too. But maybe it was all for the best. This is *worst*. There can only be better. For the first time, I let myself feel it:

Relief.

I fall asleep thinking about my mom, wondering what she would say to me if she could somehow send me a message down here on earth. I may hate the Afterworld when it comes to Marigold, but that doesn't apply to Mom. I want her to still be existing somehow, her soul some beautiful, untouchable orb of light.

My dreams that night are Marigold's. I'm climbing again, higher and higher through that great big building in the sky. But it's my mom at the top. My mom. Rose Lockwood Tate. *Mommy*. We lock eyes and I reach out. She reaches back. We hug so tight I can feel her heartbeat, her *heartbeat*. I'm in her arms, all night long.

I'm in her arms until the sun comes up.

eighteen

The third month.

The third time she'd go back to the Afterworld, looking for Colton, hoping things would be different—that he would be there waiting, armed with news about her mom. Marigold kissed her dad good night, went up to bed, and then slipped out just after midnight.

She called Jonah on her walk to the old house.

"I'm on my way now. I wanted to say good night."

"You'll come back by tomorrow morning either way?" he asked.

"I'll try my hardest. I don't want to scare Dad, not after I've convinced him to stay here. And I can't be grounded again. I don't want to sneak around to be with you."

"Will you tell Colt? About . . . us?"

"I probably won't even see him," she said, her voice dropping to a whisper as she passed her neighbor's house. "It's been three months. I might never—"

"You didn't answer."

"Yes. I will. I'll tell him."

—EXCERPT FROM *LEMONADE SKIES, BOOK 2: BETWEEN TWO WORLDS*

I wake up weary and ragged, my bones aching deep down. It's like I never even slept, like I really was up hugging my mom the whole night.

I want to know more about Mom. But I don't want to hear it from Mrs. Rizzo. *Dottie.* I want to hear it from Dad—I deserve that much. He can't give me anything else right now, but this? It should be easy.

If he says no—well, then I'll go next door. And I'll steal that old box from Mia's room, too. I'll put it together for myself, every scrap of my mother that still exists on this earth. I can't have my mom actually here with me now—patting my back, pushing my hair behind my ears, letting me drip tears and runny snot on her shoulder without flinching. But filling in the blanks would still help—a connect-the-dots to find even a hazy shape of the woman who once was my mother. A human-shaped constellation.

"Dad," I say, barging through his door without knocking. I've waited fourteen years for answers, and suddenly I can't wait a second longer. As soon as my foot is in the room, I unload: "Everything really sucks right now. But you know what sucks more than anything else? More than lawsuits or losing my best friend? Not having Mom. Not having Mom to hug me and tell me that things are going to end up okay. And not only is she not here, but I can't even picture her in my mind. I can't ask myself: *What would Mom say? What would Mom do?* Because I don't know. I don't have a clue how Mom would react in this situation, because you refuse to talk about her. That's not fair, Dad. You've taken everything else away from me, but please—please don't take this."

Dad sits in his wheelchair looking at me, stunned. He doesn't respond, so I keep talking.

"I want to see that box, too. That red box with Mom's old things, her letters and pictures. I may not have known her—not like you did—but I'm pretty sure she'd want me to see what she left behind. She'd want her own daughter to remember her."

When he still doesn't say anything, I keep going. "I want to know about the day she died, too. I want to hear exactly how it happened. I don't care if it's hard. She was my *mom*. I want to know, the good and the bad." I pull the desk chair over and sit next to him and we stare at each other for what is surely seconds but feels more like hours.

"Okay." He sounds broken and defeated, but despite this, my hope soars. *Finally.* "I loved your mom. So much." He closes his eyes, but I keep my gaze pinned on him. I want to see his expression, feel every part of this. "And she loved me. She loved you. Your mom loved you more than anything in this world. Don't forget that, with everything else I'm about to say."

Don't forget that. My mind races to think of what he could say that might potentially undo my knowledge of this seemingly obvious fact.

"I'll remember," I say—anything to keep him going.

"Your mom...had always struggled with depression. That was no secret when we first started dating. She had it mostly under control at that point, but there were ups and downs throughout the years. For a while she didn't feel ready for a baby, and then when she finally did, getting pregnant was much harder than expected. We weren't sure it would ever happen, to be honest. And then you showed up, our miracle baby. But after she had you . . . well, she was blindsided. She'd been on a high during the pregnancy, confident that she'd beaten down her demons. Things were good. Really good. She was determined to be the best mom. Took a year off from her job at the ad agency so she could stay at home with you full-time. But after you were born, the depression hit again. Hard. Harder than ever, she said, though she didn't admit that for a long time."

He opens his eyes, and I wish he hadn't. I can see just how sorry he is to be telling me this—he kept her secrets to protect *me* all these years, not himself.

"She tried to pretend it got better. And I believed her at first. There were good days. But there were more bad days. She never ended up going back to work. She insisted it was more important to be with you, and that she could freelance if we needed the money at some point. But she probably should have gone back for herself. She was so smart, so energetic. She needed a reason to get out of the house, to get dressed every morning. Three years out, she was still struggling, but just as hell-bent on the idea that she would handle things on her own . . ."

There's a slow *click click* sound growing louder. Lucy. She's poking her head in, looking up at me with those permanently mournful hound eyes. I reach out and she comes over, nuzzles her ears against my legs. My sadness must have been radiating from me in such powerful waves that she was helpless against its pull.

"She . . ." He hesitates, glancing down at Lucy. Whatever he's about to say, I'm pretty sure it will tear me apart. But we're too far gone now to turn around.

"Dad . . ."

He nods, grim-faced. "She admitted to me . . . near the end . . . that she could barely remember her first year with you. Could barely remember first steps, first words. But she told me she'd been getting better. She *promised*. Looking back, I can tell how much she must have hidden, the severity of everything she was feeling. She was ashamed to talk, even to *me*—it wasn't until I read the letters that I really saw—" He breaks and I break—we're breaking together.

"Dad," I manage to choke out, reaching to squeeze his hand. "You don't have to—"

"I need to finish. I started. And I need"—he pauses, taking a breath—"to finish."

I nod, rolling my chair over so that I'm even closer to him, as close as I can be without crawling onto his lap like a helpless little girl. I'm so mad at him still, but I also need him so much it aches.

"The day it happened, the day we lost her, you and I were at home. Your mom had told me she needed a shopping day, and she drove to some outlet stores outside the city. She said she wouldn't be gone long. But then it started pouring rain. Sheets, I remember. I could barely see out the windows. You'd just fallen over a toy in the living room and were hysterically crying when the police called. I couldn't hear the officer at first—I had to ask him to repeat himself. He said she'd veered off the road into a tree. She was gone when they arrived."

I feel dizzy. Nauseated. "Why am I always in the car with her in my nightmare? And why did you write that Marigold was in the car with her mom?"

"I don't know, sweetheart. But soon after it happened, you talked about the accident like you had been there with her. And in my mind, you *were* with her, in her heart. In her mind. We both were. I think that's why you have the nightmare—it connected you to her, and it still does."

"But it was an accident?" I ask, even though I'm not sure I'm ready to hear the answer.

"Oh, sweetheart." My dad's face is twisted into a grotesque caricature of himself, familiar but still so strange and unknowable. "I don't know. No one knows. I'll be asking myself that question every day for the rest of my life. She easily could have just lost her grip in that rainstorm—it was so nasty out there. Or—or it could have been a bad day for her. A really bad day. I wish more than anything in this world that I'd understood the full extent of her illness from the beginning. That I'd pushed harder for the treatment she needed. She'd been seeing a counselor in those last few weeks—I'd begged enough, and she'd finally relented. But it was too little too late. I'd wanted to believe her when she said she could work through it. She was so independent, so strong willed. Just like you, Thistle."

His fingertips coil around mine, and for now at least—for this one fleeting, slippery moment—I don't care about everything Dad's done wrong. I'm just glad that he's still here, that his fall from the ladder didn't take him away from me, too. We have time. We have a future.

"I'm sorry I've held this all back from you. I'm sorry that I kept your mother a stranger for so long, but having you was the best thing that ever happened to her. I want you to read her letters—her diary, really. I always knew I'd tell you, but the longer I waited, the harder it got to say anything. I wanted you to have the mom you dreamed she was—because she *was* that mom. There was so much good to tell you, but it was hard to tell you about her at all without telling you everything. All the strings still come together in the end."

He stares at me, waiting for my reaction. I don't have words, though. I feel everything. I feel too much. Guilt and shock and sadness and anger. And above all else: disappointment.

The myth of Rose Lockwood Tate is gone.

It's what I'd always wanted. But I'd never pictured it like this.

"The box is under my bed. I had Mia bring it down for me. I read the letters sometimes, as you discovered. More than I should probably."

I don't speak. I don't make a move toward the box.

"Say something, Thistle. Please. Tell me what you're thinking. I know how hard this must be to hear, but your mom loved you so much. You'll see that for yourself in the letters."

"Okay." It's the best I can do. I unwind my fingers from Dad's and somehow manage to stand without collapsing on top of Lucy.

The box is right there, just a few inches from my feet. I pick it up, holding it out in front of me as far as I can, my arms stretched like it's a box filled with spiders.

"Thanks," I say, not able to meet my dad's eyes as I turn toward the door.

"I love you," he says.

"I love you, too."

I'm on the stairs then, in my room. I stare at the box on my lap. There will be no going back: once I see, once I read, I won't be able to erase my memory. I take a deep breath, pop the clasp, and open the lid.

Mom. The scent is so strong, springtime and sunny flowers.

If I close my eyes, I can almost remember the way her voice sounds.

Almost.

☙❦❧

I pull out the notes first, saving the pictures and knickknacks for later.

Each page is dated at the top. The first date I see is from just a few weeks after I was born. I flip through the pile, all in chronological order, my eyes jumping around her loopy, tangled words. There are notes, lists, letters that Mom seemed to have written to herself. I only have to skim to see that the handwriting gets more gnarled as time goes by, almost indecipherable in the later notes. I straighten the pile, tucking pages into neat and orderly lines.

I start reading.

The letters are sparse in the first year. There's a lot of talk about how cute I am, how I ate my first Cheerios, took my first step, saw my first snowflake. Happy stuff. Each note at least starts that way, fluff and sunshine. But then she'll start to talk about how tired she is—how she can never seem to sleep anymore because her mind is *flooded with questions and fears and terrible, terrible dark and hellish and haunting images* that she can't understand.

She writes six months after my birth:

> *Sometimes I doubt that Thistle will ever love me.*
>
> *How could she love me, when I have no idea how to really be a mom? I cry most days after Theo leaves; I cry most nights after he falls asleep. I cry rocking her, feeding her, changing her. I worry that Theo won't love me as much now that he has Thistle, that he won't need me anymore. I worry that he'll see I'm a bad mom and take her away from me. I worry that I'd be glad if he did. Relieved. Because surely I'll mess up fiercely as a mom and she'll end up hurting. Emotionally, that is. Never physically.*
>
> *I'm a good person. I love my daughter. I vow to be a better mother tomorrow. I vow to be the mother that this beautiful baby deserves.*

Every word sears my mind, but I keep flipping through. Hoping for brighter, lighter notes. I find a pretty piece of floral stationery dated around my second birthday. Orange and yellow flowers. The first line seems promising: *Things that should have made me happy today.* But then I realize that *should have* negates any chance of an uplifting letter.

> *Things that should have made me happy today:*
>
> *1. Waking up to Theo kissing my eyelids, two butterfly flutters against my skin.*

2. *Listening then as he crept into Thistle's nursery, singing—on loop—his totally off-key but adorable rendition of "Hakuna Matata" (her favorite song, this week at least).*

3. *Thistle climbing into my bed when he left, her soft little baby arms wrapping around my neck and holding on tight, so tight.*

4. *Making chocolate chip pancakes with Thistle, smearing chocolate on my lips as she screamed and clapped her hands. I let her smear chocolate on her lips, too, and of course it ended up all over her clothes, the table, the chair. Conveniently it was raining, and we danced outside to clean ourselves off.*

5. *Napping together after our rain dance, listening to the pitter-patter against the windows, knowing we were safe and dry and warm.*

6. *Theo coming home with beautiful marigolds for my garden. Clipping two—one for my hair, one for Thistle's.*

7. *Putting Thistle to bed and splitting a bottle of wine with Theo, watching a few of my favorite episodes of Seinfeld. Theo kissing me and telling me that I've never looked more beautiful.*

Things that actually made me happy today:

(Must try harder tomorrow.)

I consider stopping. What good will this really do? Will I be better off for having read all of it? For having had this peek into my mother's troubled mind? I'm not sure if the answer is no or yes, but it doesn't matter. I have to get to the end. I need to see every good word there is—every single time she says she loves me, that I'm precious, that I'm beautiful or bright or kind. Even if there are ten bad words for every good, I'll take those odds. This is all I'll ever have. It's like a cup of salt water in the desert, and I don't have the willpower to not drink it in when there's not a drop of anything else in sight.

So I keep reading. I dig in, deeper and darker. The next few notes seem to be letters to me, personally. *Dear Thistle.* Almost as if—almost as if she *knew.* Knew that there was even a tiny shred of a chance that she wouldn't be around to tell me these things herself. I could be wrong. I hope with every piece of my soul that I am. That the car accident was exactly and only that: an *accident.*

I start reading one of these letters, her scrawl much messier now, harder to unravel.

> *Dear Thistle,*
> *Have I ever told you about the day your father and I found out I was having you?*

Of course she hadn't. These aren't conversations a mother has with a toddler. She must have intended for me to read it when I was older. But why not wait to tell me for herself?

> *I had been suspecting it for a week or two, though I can't say exactly how I knew, just that my body suddenly felt different to me. Like it wasn't only mine anymore. I didn't feel alone, ever. Not like I usually did.*
> *I took the test in the bathroom at work one morning and—I was right. You were there. It wasn't just me*

now—it was me and you. I told myself I'd wait until that night to tell your dad, think of some cute way to do the reveal over dinner. We had waited so long for you, I wanted it to all be perfect. But an hour later, I left the office and drove over to his school. I parked by the faculty door and waited two hours for the last class to end. He saw me before I saw him, tapping on the window and making me scream. I looked up at him and started crying. Happy tears, of course. And he didn't even have to ask. He just knew. He yanked open the door and pulled me up into his arms, swung me in circles around the parking lot.

It was the best day ever, Thistle. You'd already made me the happiest I'd ever been, just by existing. If only I could have stayed that happy.

If only I could be different.

The letters start to blur, and I slide from one to the next, caught up in a fast-moving current of misery. It's like I'm riding high on a rushing river leading to a waterfall, watching helplessly as the edge gets closer, closer. The tears are coming quickly now, and I don't notice I'm at the end of the stack until I have just one flimsy piece of that god-awful flowery paper left in my hand. It's dated a few weeks before she died.

> *Dear Thistle,*
>
> *We were at the park this morning, the two of us. I was pushing you on the swings, and things were good. You were laughing, and I felt okay. But then I had that terrible feeling that washes over me like a tidal wave—that feeling*

of total hopelessness, like I will never be able to do any-
thing right, that I will never be able to protect you, that I
am an unfit mother . . .

The next thing I remember clearly is me on a bench,
a woman shaking me—Is that your little girl? She was
angry. Yelling. I looked up and saw you then, and it pulled
me out of my fog. You had slipped from the swing, your
elbows bruised, bleeding. You were crying hysterically,
and I started crying hysterically, too. The other mothers
were watching us. The judgment on their faces, confirm-
ing my worst fear—that I cannot take care of you.

I thought I was getting better. I'd promised myself
I was. I'd promised your dad, too. I'm still crying now,
making a total mess of this letter. What am I going to do?

Forgive me, Thistle. Please. Because I'm not sure I can
ever forgive myself.

That's the end.

Those are the last words from my mom that I will ever have: *I'm not sure I can ever forgive myself.* We have one thing in common at least. I'm not sure I'll ever be able to forgive her either.

nineteen

Colton was there, waiting for her. She opened her mouth, Jonah's name—the truth—on her lips, but before she could speak, Colton said: "We're all together after the first year, but cliques tend to form around ages and death dates, so I think—based on that and the photo you showed me—I've found her." And then he led Marigold to a luminescent tunnel she'd never seen before, up glimmering spiraling stairs. Into a high-vaulted room filled with music and flowers and people. A party.

And across the crowd, Marigold saw her—Violet. *Mom.*

"Mom!" Marigold shouted, but the chatter stole her words away. Colton hoisted her onto his back and started plowing through the crowd.

"See, football wasn't a waste. Couldn't have done this with Debate Club!"

"Shut up and move faster!" Marigold waved her hands above her head as they ran, closer and closer until—

"Shoot," Colton said, "she's headed toward that door."

"Violet Maybee!" Marigold yelled as loud as she could, her throat burning.

Her mom stopped and turned. Their eyes met, locked in place.

And Marigold felt like she was finally home.

—EXCERPT FROM *LEMONADE SKIES,* **BOOK 2: BETWEEN TWO WORLDS**

I open my eyes to bright white light pouring in through my window. The sunshine feels good, merry and pleasant and the opposite of everything else in my life.

For a few seconds I wonder if I'd maybe dreamed it all. But then I glance down at the floor, see the sheets of paper scattered around like remarkably uncelebratory confetti. I'd dumped the letters there last night after I finished reading through them for the fifth time. I'd contemplated tearing them to shreds and flushing them down the toilet—I came close, ripping the last letter nearly in half, before some shrill voice in my head screamed: *No! Thistle, stop! This is all you and Dad have now.*

I hadn't left my room since yesterday's conversation with Dad. I should be starving now, but my stomach feels like it's shriveled into a particle of dust.

Before bed last night I sorted through the rest of the contents of the box: photos of Dad and Mom at their wedding, photos of Mom pregnant, of Mom and newborn me, Mom and toddler me. There was some jewelry, too: a slightly green-tinged golden locket with my dad's much-younger face on one half of the heart, mine on the other, grinning big through my chubby baby cheeks; a charm bracelet with one lone pendant, the outline of a pigtailed girl; and a plain gold wedding band and a sparkly yellow sapphire engagement ring. At least I assume it's her engagement ring, because it's the only other ring there. Jammed at the very bottom of the box I found some ticket stubs to concerts and movies I've never heard of, a few seashells, a pinkish heart-shaped pebble, a package of Junior Mints that no doubt expired sometime during the past fourteen years.

And that's it—the full list.

That's what I have left of my mom to tide me over for the rest of my life.

I wish now that I'd read the letters gradually instead of devouring them whole. I could have read one a week, picked each apart carefully to be sure I wasn't missing anything important. Absorbed the bad news more slowly, savored each gem of good that I could find.

Or maybe it's for the best that it's over. That my illusions were stripped away all at once. Because that's the worst part of this: the reality that my vision for all these years was so wrong, that the towering pedestal I'd placed my mom on had been part of some silly childish fantasy. It was make-believe, coloring in my world in the way that made me feel happiest.

I'd missed her, always, but I'd missed my perfectly conceived version of her—the golden mom who would have baked elaborate birthday cupcakes even before Pinterest was a thing. The mom who would have encouraged me to play the violin, or the flute, or the drums, whatever I wanted to play; to take ballet, sign up for soccer, join the swim team. She would have believed I was capable of anything, and she would have shown up at every recital or game, even if it meant skipping a meeting at whatever high-powered job she would have been juggling on the side. I would have been her number one, always. I would have filled her heart with a joy so sparkly and bright that she couldn't even remember how existence was possible before I landed in her arms.

I don't know where Mom belongs now. I know—deep down I know, I do—that it's not really her fault. She didn't ask for her depression. I'm sure it wasn't the life she would have chosen for herself, if biology had given her a say. But staying angry feels like my best shot at survival right now. I'm mad at my mom for not magically fixing herself, for being too proud to ask for help sooner. Mad at my dad, too, for keeping these secrets for so long—and mad that he hadn't found a way to rescue her somehow before she got as low as she did.

What do I do today? Where do I go? Who do I talk to?

Nothing, nowhere, no one.

Emma's surgery should have happened yesterday. I've been too busy pitying myself to worry about her. Because I am a terribly self-centered human being. Maybe after she's had time to process and recover I'll write her a short e-mail, thank her for everything and remind her that she's better off without me and Marigold.

I wonder how Oliver is holding up. I wonder if he's thought about me at all.

I wonder how long it'll take to stop wondering these things.

As much as I want to avoid the Internet, it's all I have right now. I check my in-box because I'm masochistic and can't stop myself. There's another few hundred e-mails since yesterday. The subject lines are filled with angry words. I don't click on any of them because I already know what they'll say, and it's nothing worse than what I'm already thinking about myself. I do a search to make sure there's nothing new from Oliver or Emma. Nope. Of course there's not. Nothing from Liam either. I don't know if I'm more relieved or disappointed that he hasn't tried to reach out, not that it would change anything.

And then, because I'm already on a vicious downward trajectory, I google *Oliver Flynn*. There must be some photos, some tweets, some snippet of him that I can hoard for myself. The first thing that pops up, though, is an article in his high school newspaper about a writing scholarship he won last month. Five hundred dollars, and his short story will be reprinted in a collection with those of other talented high school students from across the country. He never mentioned it, probably because he thought it was nothing compared to the millions of copies of *Lemonade Skies* books out in the world. This was small change, comparatively.

Except his was *real*. His was earned.

I wallow, clicking through all the pictures of him I can find on social media. He has a lot more friends than I would have expected, given how available he was to spend time with me. They look friendly. Normal. Like people I would have wanted to meet, if I'd had more time. There's one picture in particular that I can't stop looking at: Oliver and two guys, two girls, baking for some kind of fund-raiser. They're in the Flynns' kitchen, and there's flour in their hair, flour on their faces, but they look so happy in the mess, arms around one another, mid-laugh when the flash went off. One of the girls, a pretty blonde with very pink lips, is leaning against Oliver's shoulder, grinning up at him instead of at the camera.

I will never know what these high school moments are like—big laughing friend groups, people who have known you since kindergarten, who have witnessed the most embarrassing bits of your history and still love you anyway. Even if I come around eventually, an awkward late bloomer, I'll have missed these years. I'll never get them back.

After I've scraped up every last picture of Oliver on the Internet, it's time to admit defeat. My stomach is howling at me and for the first time in my life the idea of more chocolate makes me feel ill.

It's quiet downstairs—safe. Even Lucy must be sleeping. I step into the kitchen, mind completely focused on the egg-and-cheese sandwich I'm going to make, the one thing that might help me feel better right now.

"Thistle."

I spin around, my hands clutching at my chest. "Dad, Jesus Christ! You scared me." My dad, out of his bedroom. It's so unexpected that all I can do is stand and stare, openmouthed.

"I'm sorry," he says, fighting back a smile. "I've been waiting down here all morning. I knew you'd give up the hunger strike at some point and sneak into the kitchen."

"It's—it's good to see you moving around."

"Mia's been pushing me to be less of a disgusting sloth for days. And Melissa, my occupational therapist, was here this morning, too, and she gave me some exercises to do. I can't be up on crutches until these slings are off in a few weeks, but I want to be around more. I need to do better. For you."

"It's a little late now, isn't it?"

He sighs, deflating into the wheelchair. "I am so sorry, and I'd redo everything if I could. The books, the fame, all of it. I'd have sent you off to school to make friends. I'd have pushed you to join the band or the choir or sports teams or the theater—I'd have chaperoned on field trips, hosted big sleepovers here with your friends, even if I would have been the bumbling, clueless single dad. I'd have given you all the normal things you deserve. Maybe I would have written a book with my name on it that would have sold. Or maybe you would have grown up to be a writer yourself, been a big success in your own right. Maybe some of those things can still happen, I don't know. You still have a wide-open future in front of you. But I am sorry."

"I would never have grown up to be a writer," I say, ignoring the rest, the apologies I can't stand to hear. "I mean, I have no shot now that my name will be blacklisted from the world of publishing for good, but—I am not a writer."

Dad looks at me, eyebrows drawing into one long fuzzy line. "Why do you say that?"

"Why would I *not* say that? I didn't write a word of *Lemonade Skies*, in case you forgot. I suggested a few things that made it into the story, but even most of my ideas were vetoed."

"You had hugely constructive input. And you nitpicked at every single sentence I wrote. You made me streamline and stay true to the voice. You're seventeen years old, Thistle. And you've had a hand in two bestselling books. Don't downplay your role. It wasn't nothing."

"Yeah. Whatever you say." I turn away toward the fridge, back to my initial project, eggs and cheese.

"I don't expect you to take my word for it, not right now. All I'm saying is: Don't rule it out. Don't let me ruin the whole writing thing for you."

"Well, given that no decent college will probably take me at this point, I don't see an English major or any majors in my near future."

He's quiet for a minute, and I revel in the small joy of shocking him into silence.

"You haven't applied yet," he says finally. "There's still time to strategize. The story will fade, schools won't recognize your name—"

"I'm the most recognizable cheater in the country right now, Dad. I couldn't even run away to Australia or England, they'll know me, too."

"We'll figure something out. It'll be fine."

Fine. It's meaningless—everything he says. I'm done listening to it. I'm done letting him feel better about himself.

"No, Dad, *I'll* figure something out. You just figure yourself out, okay? You've already ruined my life. Don't you get that? You can't fix anything for me. You're a total disaster."

My dad jerks back in his chair. I'd sounded colder than I intended—it's maybe the meanest thing I've ever said to him. But I don't regret it. He doesn't get to pick and choose when to be Supportive Dad. Life doesn't work that way.

"I'm going to Dottie's," I announce, because I can't bear to be in this house with him.

"Thistle, please—" he calls out, but I'm already halfway down the hall.

I don't turn back before slamming the door behind me.

⊛⊛⊛

Dottie—I'm getting better at calling her that—seems only moderately surprised to see me again so soon.

She insists I eat a sandwich first, tuna with cheese and pickles, when I admit I haven't eaten real food in what feels like days and I'm starting to feel dizzy. It tastes like the best tuna sandwich I'd ever had in my life. I finish every crumb and then shovel a few cookies into my mouth—chocolate and bright pink sprinkles today, another interesting variation. And then I tell her about Mom, the letters, my fight with Dad. She's silent the whole time I ramble on, nodding and nibbling at cookies.

"I feel so guilty," she says after I finish, frowning as she puts down her cup of black cherry tea. "I should have been a better neighbor. I should have talked to her when she came around, I should have helped her more with you."

There are so many more questions I want to ask, more about Mom as a kid, but my head is already too heavy with new knowledge. I linger longer than socially appropriate for an unannounced teatime, probably, but I can't stand the idea of going home. I consider asking her if I can stay here tonight, but even with our new buddy bond it feels too weird. And I'm not sure I could ever sleep with all those puppies and kitties staring down at me from the walls.

My dad is in the hallway when I come back in, like he's been waiting for me all this time.

(217)

"I'm glad you and Dottie are hitting it off," he says casually, as if we didn't have a massive blowup a few hours before. "Your mom always did worry about her."

"Well, I have no one else these days, so I figured why not? Lose one neighbor, gain another." I start toward the stairs.

"I talked to Susan while you were gone."

I turn back to him. "And?"

"She said Elliot and Zenith are still figuring out how to *handle* things. I think as much as they hate our guts, they're wondering if there's a way they can spin it that would get even more sales for this last book. Or if it's better to quit now, save face, make the whole story blow over sooner. She said it's maybe a good fifty-fifty chance right now."

"They . . . would maybe want to publish the book still?" This possibility had never once occurred to me in the last few days. We were done. *Lemonade Skies* was over. For good.

"Maybe." He shakes his head. "We'll see."

"Right."

"I'm going to try, Thistle. To be better. For you. For me. For both of us."

"Okay."

"Because you're right, I've been a giant mess, and I've had my pity party long enough."

I feel too numb to respond. My feelings are too complicated. I'm relieved he's holding himself up mentally and emotionally, but I'm tired of having to worry about that in the first place. I don't run right back up to my room though. I settle on the couch, and Dad rolls in behind me, and without discussion we're back to *Sherlock*. We order

Thai food a few hours later, and Mia pulls up a TV tray and eats next to me. Maybe she doesn't hate both of us.

It doesn't feel normal, but it feels better than the last few days. I'm too weak to fight it. Hiding out in my bedroom, rotting away in loneliness—like Dottie said, it's not a sustainable plan. But just because I watch some TV and eat food in the same room doesn't mean Dad's forgiven or that we're okay again. It means that I need *someone* to keep me from imploding with misery, and—for better or for worse—Dad is the only real someone I have. He's my only family.

We've both hurt people. We've both made mistakes.

Like father like daughter.

❀❀❀

I've been in bed for hours, but I can't sleep.

I keep hearing Dad's words from this afternoon, as much as I want to write them off as meaningless obligatory groveling: *Don't downplay your role. It wasn't nothing.*

Is that at all true? Do I have at least some basic writing skills? Maybe that rush I felt working on the outline was something real—something rare and golden. Or maybe it was just a garbage fantasy fueled by my need to feel productive. Either way, there's only that fifty percent chance there will even be a third book. There's no point in working on it more until we know.

But still . . .

I hop out of bed and open my laptop, find the document that's now buried in layers of folders to prevent myself from doing the exact thing I'm doing right now. If I'd been serious about never seeing it again, I would have deleted it. But I hadn't.

The document flashes open, and my eyes scan hungrily,

possessively over the words and ideas I wrote just last week, though last week feels like months ago now.

Suddenly, I know exactly what Colton should say in his final scene. I jot it down before I forget, and just like that, I can *see*, *feel*, *hear* how Marigold will approach her mom, how their last conversation will go. It's like I'm standing there watching and listening, and my hands are flying over the keyboard so that I don't miss a thing.

From that scene on, the rest fits in easily, until there's just one thing left to be done:

Send Marigold home from the Afterworld.

twenty

It takes me a week.

A week to bring my outline to life, to create the world, the people, the conversations I'm seeing play out as clear as a movie in my head. I feel like I'm not myself as it's happening, or like I'm above, around, outside myself somehow. Words come to me, to my fingers, but I don't think them first. They just happen. I can't explain it, and even though I see the words coming from my hands on a keyboard, I almost don't believe it—I feel guilty, sneaky, like I'm stealing from someone or somewhere because it doesn't feel like this, *all of this*, could possibly be coming from *me*.

I don't stop to question it, though.

I'm running on a manic new energy. I don't do anything but write, except for the basic necessities. I eat only when I can't go another word without a bite of something, usually granola bars or a quick sandwich or one of Dottie's cookies—from a plate that magically appeared on my desk one morning while I showered. Showers are rare, too, so Mia—acting as Dad's legs, or on her own—must have jumped on a small window of opportunity to make the delivery. There was a bowl of vegetables and hummus and some apples put on my desk, too, probably because a nurse couldn't in good conscience feed me cookies alone.

If Dad suspects what I'm up to, he hasn't said anything. He's kept his distance, even though I hear him whirring and puttering downstairs. He's still up and about. Trying.

I haven't had a single interaction with anyone from the outside world. My phone's been on airplane mode to avoid any calls or texts, and I disconnected my laptop from the Internet. If there are any practical matters to be taken care of, hopefully Dad's on top of it. I'm trusting in him, but only because I honestly don't care what's happening on the business end. It feels separate from me, from *this*. Even if I'm the only person who ever reads these pages, I won't regret the time I've put into them. There's nothing else in the world I'd rather be doing right now.

I've rewritten parts of Dad's old chapters, and the new chapters are mostly done, too. Marigold tells Colton the truth about Jonah sooner now; he's angry and hurt, of course, and even more determined at first to come through the portal, to confront his twin face-to-face. But he has more space to come to his senses, and by the time he finds out about the house being demolished and the portal likely closing for good, he agrees that messing with destiny is wrong. And if someone else has to love Marigold, he's glad it's Jonah.

There's one scene that I can't stop tinkering with, though, coming back to it again and again in the last seven days: Marigold and her mom, their last moment. It's down in rough, choppy words, but it still doesn't feel true enough. There's something missing, some inner light—or inner darkness, or maybe both.

I stayed up until three last night piecing together an inspiration board on the corkboard above my desk. It's the worst and best parts of my mom's letters typed out in quotes, her photos, her charm bracelet and rings. The locket is around my neck as I type—heavier than I expected, a weight that doesn't allow me to forget I'm wearing it. I contemplate putting on her sweater again for good measure, but I can't do it. All I see when I look at it now is my perfect day in the woods with Oliver, and the morning after my first kiss with Liam.

My phone is propped up on my dresser next to my desk, the camera turned on, just waiting for me to press Record. I've been filming myself in clips throughout the process, addressing fans—or former readers, more accurately, since *fans* feels like a long shot now—explaining the process, the whys and hows of my deciding on a particular scene or conversation. Just in case these chapters ever do see the light of day, or even if they don't, I want the world to know: I'm not totally useless.

It's been two days since I showered and my hair is a gnarly, greasy knot and I'm wearing a faded *Calvin and Hobbes* T-shirt that's exclusively for sleeping—but I tap the red Record button without inspecting myself in the mirror first and flip the camera around. If I can't make this video completely genuine, then there's no point in making it at all. My eyes focus on the camera lens on the back of my phone. I clear my throat. I feel my cheeks flushing before I say a single word, but I start anyway.

"I never knew my mom, not really. I was three when she died, too young for memories, and my dad rarely talked about her—the details came like bread crumbs. It was too hard on him, and I didn't want to make him sadder than he already was. So I had to fill in the blank spaces on my own. I built my mom the way I wanted, the dream mom who always did and said everything right, who never would have yelled at me, who would have let me eat two desserts if I asked nicely enough, and would have let me stay home from school some days just for fun. She was so beautiful, this dream mom. She was all I had, and I loved her more than anything."

I can feel my eyes watering, but I keep going. I don't shut down the camera. I pretend it's Oliver on the other end, not just the other side of my empty room. I've used that method all week—talk to these nonexistent-but-maybe-someday listeners like they're Oliver. Like they have every reason to judge me, but I still hope they'll understand at least some piece of what I'm saying. And maybe they'll still hate me after they hear my story, but a little bit less.

"Last week, Dream Mom died. I lost a mother all over again. My dad told me that my mom suffered from depression her whole life . . . He wanted to help; she insisted she could handle it on her own. My mom was a strong woman, but it takes more than that to live with depression. Especially when you have a small child sapping all your energy, needing you, clinging, demanding, crying."

I stop for a minute to catch my breath. I feel as though I've been running up and down the stairs, not just sitting at a desk talking to an invisible audience.

"I lost my mom in a car accident. That's what I was raised to believe. And maybe it was just that—an accident. But maybe it was my mom at the end of a very thin rope. Maybe it was a dark moment. The darkest moment. My dad and I—we'll never know. I haven't found Marigold's magical portal, and I don't think I ever will. I can't ask Mom any last questions, tell her the things I never got to say. All I have is what Dad can tell me, and a pile of letters I read for the first time last week. Notes that my mom wrote for herself in the years before she died. Letters about me. About how much she loved me. Even if motherhood made her unhappy sometimes, if it scared her more than anything in the world. If I could say one thing to my mom, I'd tell her that I loved her for trying—that I still love her now and I always will."

I look away from the camera to Mom's notes, needing reminders, black-and-white evidence:

I love my daughter. I vow to be the mother that this beautiful baby deserves.

Making chocolate chip pancakes with Thistle, smear-ing chocolate on my lips as she screamed and clapped her hands. I let her smear chocolate on her lips, too, and of course it ended up all over her clothes, the table, the chair.

It was the best day ever, Thistle. You'd already made me the happiest I'd ever been, just by existing.

Forgive me, Thistle. Please. Because I'm not sure I can ever forgive myself.

The words feel new every time I read them—just as surreal and beautiful, just as cruel and unfair. I'm gripping the locket so tightly it's warm in my fingers. My eyes are stuck on Mom's eyes in my favorite photo of the two of us, making chocolate chip pancakes just as she described. There's chocolate on our chins, our hands, *every-where*, but clearly neither of us cares, because we're smiling so big our whole faces are being swallowed up. My dad must have been there to catch the moment, and I know now why he's made me choc-olate chip pancakes for all these years—but it must have squeezed his heart again every time, that sugary smell wafting through the kitchen and jolting him straight back to *this*.

I can smell it now, that sweet batter hot on the stove, just a splash of vanilla and a pinch of sea salt to set off the chocolate chips. I can't tell if I'm delirious from lack of sleep—from looking at the picture, reading Mom's words, her heart, literally, in my hands—or if Mia is cooking.

It doesn't matter, though, because the effect is the same, utterly gut-wrenching, and my hands are on the keyboard, deleting old words and filling them in with new.

"So you see how it is," Marigold said, her eyes on her hands, not able to meet her mom's gaze. "It's now or never. You try to come back with me, or—"

"This is good-bye," Violet filled in for her, voice quiet but still steady and calm.

Marigold nodded. The clear yellow sky beyond the window seemed brighter than ever, offensively bright when the world should be darker out of respect for such an awful conversation.

"What should we do?" Marigold asked in a whisper. She was edging closer to Violet, needing to feel that her mom was still as inexplicably solid as ever, still giving off heat, still taking up space. She was here, even if the fact of it would never make scientific sense. She was real, and maybe she could continue to be real, if only . . .

"I think we both know the answer."

It was like a fist punching Marigold's gut, even though these were the words she had expected, this was what she herself—if she had been forced to decide—would have said, even if it was not what she really wanted. What she wanted and what felt *right* were worlds apart.

"I want you to come, I do," Marigold said, her voice breaking as she fell into her mother's arms. "But it feels wrong, doesn't it? Like it's going against nature. We already cheated the system somehow, me being here. What would happen if you came with me? Would you be alive again, or would—?"

"Would I be some sad shadow haunting you for the rest of your life? Beyond that maybe, trapped in some strange in-between world forever."

"Yes. That." Marigold nodded, tears dripping across her mom's bright orange sweater.

"There is nothing I want more than to be the mother you deserve, for the rest of your life. To make you chocolate chip pancakes every morning, to be there with you every night, helping you figure out awful calc problems while your dad whistles happily in the background, cooking up his special barbecued chicken. I want it all. I want you. I want your dad. I want our whole life back."

"But," Marigold said.

"But," Violet repeated. "I can't undo the accident. I can't undo all the thousand little things we could have done differently. I shouldn't have lost my temper. I was blinded. Not thinking clearly."

"It wasn't just your fault," I said quietly. "Or my fault, for making you upset."

"Don't blame yourself. Ever. I can't explain why it had to happen that way, but it did, and my sweet darling, that's life. Life will be a whole lot of stuff that you can't change or undo or magically transform into something better or happier. We try the best we can, and we accept what we can't control. It's the most valuable thing I can teach you. So if I tried to rewrite this . . . I'd be undoing the most important lesson of your life."

"It's a terrible lesson, though. I don't want to learn it. I just want you."

"And you have me. Now, and after you walk back through the portal. You'll always have me. You have me in your mind, your heart. You have me in your blood. I'm in your eyes, the way you see the world. I'm in your lips, the way you speak to everyone around you. I'm in your ears, too, that funny little point we both have at the tip, Elvish ears, your dad always said." Violet pulled away to look Marigold in the eyes, their faces side by side, like a just slightly distorted mirror image.

"You have everything you remember about me. All the things your dad remembers, too. It's more than some people will ever have."

"I want so many more memories, though."

"Me too. But just remember the most important part: I wasn't always a perfect mother, but I always loved you, and I always will. I believe with my whole heart this isn't it for us. There will be more. Someday. When it's time. There will be more for your dad and me, too. But please hug him every day for me. Tell him you love him. Will you do that?"

"Yes." Marigold hugged her even tighter, trying to remember everything about the sensation of that moment—how their arms and hips lined up seamlessly, the way her chin fit just right into the crook of her mom's neck. "I'll remember that you love us," Marigold said, "if you promise to always remember that I forgive you. That even if you weren't perfect, you were the perfect mom for me."

"I'll remember that," Violet said, crying now, too. "I will always, always remember that."

I don't notice until I type the last word that I'm full-on sobbing, messy tears dripping down my face and onto the keyboard. Marigold said bye to her mom, and this is the closest thing I'll get to good-bye, too, and the enormity of that feels too big to comprehend. I leap from the chair, throw open my back window. Cold air whips into the room and I inhale deeply, closing my eyes, the chill feeling so good and necessary. It's much cooler than the last time I was outside—like I blinked and winter swooped in. But then, it would be December now, wouldn't it? Which means Dad and I forgot about Thanksgiving. Or I forgot at least, and Dad and Mia didn't want to disturb me. We usually celebrated with Liam's family, anyway. Maybe Dad decided it would be too depressing to start a new tradition this year. He was right.

I wrap a scarf around my neck and leave the window open. I sit back at my desk, save the document, close it for now because I'm not sure what else I can do. The camera is still running. It saw everything, the breathless typing and the tears. Thistle a few months ago—a few weeks ago even—would have been incredibly embarrassed about this. She would have flicked it off, deleted the entire thing, started from scratch with much more composure.

But I'm not that Thistle now. And I'm not finished either.

"My dad was depressed for a lot of my childhood. I assumed that was all grief, that it was normal and to be expected. Of course he should be sad. He had lost the love of his life and was left to raise a little girl alone. I thought I could make it better, though. I thought if I let this book be published for the world to see, gave him the success he deserved, the money we needed—that I would make him happy forever. I would make our problems go away. What I did was wrong. It was unethical. And it was also not a solution. I'm not a therapist. There's no magic fix for these things."

I take a deep breath. I have so much to learn. Dad, too. The moral of these stories: You can't always keep fighting through alone. Sometimes the battle is too hard.

"I'm sorry. I hate that I deceived anyone. But I did what I thought I needed to do to make my dad less sad. I don't expect you to forgive me, but I just want you to think about this: What would you be willing to do for the people you love? The answer might scare you."

That's it. It's all I have in me. I grab my phone and turn the camera off.

I don't know what's next, what should happen now. My goal was to finish, and now I have. So I do the only thing that makes sense: I leap into bed and pull the blankets up to block out the rest of the world. And then I sleep.

twenty-one

I spend the next two days making up for last week's lost hours: I take long baths and afternoon naps and order takeout with Dad, though our meals together with Mia—poor Mia—are mostly silent. I'm too bitter still to say much, but I'm too lonely to ignore him altogether. And for all his mistakes, he did have some valid reasons. He wanted to protect me. Protect Mom.

I sort through my e-mail, too. Angry letters from readers go to a folder that I may or may not ever read. Everything that came in from Susan or Elliot or my publicist before the newsbreak gets filed away, too, because they're meaningless now. Old news from a different lifetime. There's nothing left then, no friends or concerned blogger, author, bookstore checking in. Not that I'd expected anything from anyone, but still. It stings.

Tonight Dad and Mia and I eat sushi and watch *Seinfeld*—my suggestion, because after reading Mom's note about *Seinfeld*, I wanted to see it for myself. It was an insignificant anecdote, maybe, but I wanted to see anything that was important to her. Dad seemed happy about it.

I wait until we're between episodes and Mia is on a call in her room when I say it: "I finished the book."

"Well, I hoped that's what you were so busy doing up there." He's playing it cool, eyes still on the TV screen, but I can see the cautious smile on his face. "I didn't want to bother you and ruin the process."

"You knew?"

"I didn't *know*. But I suspected."

We sit quietly for a moment.

"Well?" Dad asks, turning to me.

"Well?"

"Can I read the ending?"

"I thought you'd be mad at me. For writing it on my own. For doing it before we heard anything from Susan or Elliot."

"I'm not mad at all. To be honest, I think you might be the best person for the job."

I don't know how to respond to this, so instead I go upstairs and get my computer.

"I made lots of changes to earlier stuff, too, but just read the last few chapters for now. I want you to be brutally honest," I say, setting my laptop on Dad's wheelchair tray, moving the mouse toward his fingers to make navigating easier. "I wrote it mostly for myself anyway, so if it's bad, it doesn't even really matter."

But I don't really think it's bad, not at all. Maybe I'm delusional. It's personal, so it says something to me, of course. That doesn't mean it's universally good. But in my bones, I feel it: This is right. The way it should be.

While my dad reads, I pull on my jacket and step out to the garden. It's cold and dark, though there's enough light from surrounding homes that I don't have to flick on the patio lamp. Liam's house is glowing, every room lit up, and it hits me with a pang for the first time: *I miss him*. I miss what we had, what we could have been, if he'd handled things differently, if I'd handled things differently, too. But what he did—there's no going back.

I turn toward Dottie's house instead. I've neglected her this last week, too caught up in writing and reordering my life. Maybe Dad and I can have her over for dinner sometime. I'll cook for Mia, too. Four lonely people at one table won't seem as lonely anymore.

I pull my jacket around me tighter and lie down on the picnic table, staring up at the hazy city stars. My mind goes back to that park with Oliver—as it does way too often—and I wonder how much brighter the stars would look there. That tower of rocks would make for a spectacular observatory.

A *tap* startles me. At first I think it's a Ping-Pong ball and nearly roll off the table in a panic. I'm still not ready to talk to Liam, not now, maybe not ever.

But then another *tap*, and I see that it's Dad—at the back door. I hop up and move toward the stairs, Dad wheeling backward as I step inside.

"It's a brilliant ending—the only ending—and I couldn't have written a better one."

"I don't know if that's true," I say lamely, eyes on the ground, but inside I am a whirling, twirling skyrocket of joy.

"Of course it is."

The words are settling in, filling me to the brim. I look up, and Dad is crying.

"You're Marigold," he says, and now I'm crying, too. "Always have been. So it makes sense that only you could know what she would really do in the end. I was an old fool to ever think otherwise."

I've spent so much time resenting Marigold. But here it is, the truth I've always known:

Marigold is me, and I am her, and maybe we both need each other to survive.

"What's the title?" he asks.

"*World After World*," I say.

"Perfect."

"I want to deliver it to Elliot tomorrow."

❂❂❂

Dad asks if I want to wait until he can travel with me, but I tell him no. I want to do this without him, and besides, seeing him will just make Elliot angry. Seeing me might make him angry, too, but I'm hoping there's at least a little pity I can work with. Elliot feels like the best place to start—if I can get him on my side, maybe he can convince Susan. The publisher calls the shots. I debate e-mailing him to set up a meeting, but he has every reason to say no and I don't want to take that chance. I'll be harder to ignore in person—I hope—and the new chapters will be, too. He still might refuse to see me when I get there, but I have to try. I do know that Elliot is a complete workaholic—he rarely misses a day, and he hates to even leave the office for lunch. Odds are good he'll be in. I'll wait in the lobby all day if I need to.

But I don't want to take the train to New York alone. Not when I'm this anxious.

When I press his name to call, I don't expect him to pick up. I figure I'll leave a voice mail, and maybe I'll hear back a resounding *NO*, or maybe he'll just say nothing.

"Hello?" Oliver says, his voice sending shock waves straight through my heart.

"You picked up." It's all I can manage.

"I don't know why I did, to be honest." This burns, but it's truth, and it's what I should be hearing. I need a moment to gather my courage.

"So," Oliver says.

"Listen, I know I'm ridiculous for calling. But I revised the manuscript and wrote the last chapters—how we talked about mostly, just with new bits at the very end—and I need to deliver them to my editor. Face-to-face. I need to go to New York, and I don't want to go alone. It's childish and pathetic, but—I was wondering if you'd maybe, I don't know . . . drive me?" The request sounds so absurd out loud—Me! Asking a favor like this! After lying to Oliver, to *everyone*—that I want to laugh before Oliver beats me to it. "I realize I don't deserve any favors from you, now or ever, and that you'd have to skip school to take me on a weekday, so maybe I should just stop talking and hang up, because that's probably what you want?"

Lord. I should have rehearsed this. Not called on a whim at ten o'clock at night because I was on some high from Dad's thoroughly unanticipated seal of approval.

"You want *me* to skip school . . . to drive *you* . . . to *New York* . . . to deliver your *manuscript*?" The way his voice drawls out each highly unreasonable aspect of the sentence cuts like a knife, his smooth snarl at odds with his normally lovely voice.

"Yes. Sorry. It was stupid of me to call. I'll let you go, and I hope Emma is okay—"

"You must really be alone," he interjects, "if you're resorting to asking *me*."

That's true—of course I'm alone—but it's not the only reason. I'd trek to New York on foot in brand-new heels before I'd stoop to calling Liam for help. Oliver's the only person I'd *want*.

When I don't say anything he sighs and says: "Jesus, I'm insane to do this. *Insane*. But the idea of you going alone—" He stops, and I can just picture him tearing at his hair as he deliberates, a messy red cloud.

"You really don't have to," I say weakly, already pulling the phone away from my ear, finger hovering above the End Call button.

"Tomorrow morning. I'll be at your house at eight." He hangs up.

Oliver is coming. Tomorrow morning. And we're going to Zenith. It feels like a scene from an impossibly over-the-top New York City rom-com. It feels like nothing that could ever happen in my real life. But he is coming, we are going, and even though Oliver still hates me and Elliot might just turn me away—

There's possibility.

⊛⊛⊛

I'm up at five o'clock without an alarm.

I shower and put on makeup and blow-dry my hair to make the curls fuller and glossier. After days of holing up at home, I'm terrified to be back in the real world. The real world that now knows exactly who I am. And who I'm *not*. I don't want to look overdone, like I'm desperately trying, but I want Elliot to see me as the Thistle I am today, not the fifteen-year-old girl he first signed up. I'll be eighteen this spring. An adult. I tell myself that it's not about what Oliver thinks, too, but I know it's not true. I care. I care much more than I should.

There are only a few outfits still hanging neatly in my closet, and I go for a dress I'd worn for a Christmas charity event last year— dark green lace with an intricately buttoned neckline and a loose, flowing skirt. For one subtle pop of Marigold, I wear my mom's yellow sapphire ring.

When Oliver pulls up two minutes early, I'm already standing at the bottom of the stairs, waiting.

"I read the whole thing last night, and . . . it's exactly as it should be," Dad says, smiling as I lean in to peck his cheek. "Truly. So don't worry. Just avoid my name. Or throw me under the bus if it helps. But know that the work—the work stands on its own. Your mom would be so proud." He's staring at the ring on my finger, his already somber brow tightening even more. But before I can apologize or offer to take it off, he says: "I was thinking I'd save that for later—if you wanted it as your engagement ring someday. But keep it on. I think this moment is even bigger. This one's all about you."

"I love you," I say, because it's the only response that feels right. Life is short and fragile and unpredictable, and I choose to work this out with him, no matter how hard it'll be or how long it'll take me to completely forgive him.

"I love you, too." He waves me off then, as Mia leans in from behind him and says—"Good luck, Thistle."

"Thanks, Mia," I say, starting toward the door. But then I turn back. I walk over to Mia and I wrap my arms around her. She's rigid at first, but then she softens into the hug. "I'm sorry I've been so cold and unfriendly. It's been a rough patch, but that's no excuse. Thanks for putting up with us. Maybe I could make us all dinner some night?"

"That'd be nice," Mia says, patting my back.

I pull away and wave one last time, and then I'm out the door, running to the car before Oliver has to step out.

"Hey," I say, throwing myself into the passenger seat, eyes straight ahead.

"Hey."

"Thank you for doing this. You really didn't have to."

"I know."

He pulls away, and neither of us says anything as he navigates out of the city. I glance over a few times, and his eyes are focused intently on the road. His hair is smoother than I've ever seen it, brushed into a neat swoop that falls lightly to his shoulders. I can't see what he's wearing under his jacket, but he has on nice black suede boots with his usual black jeans.

I wait for him to ask me questions, but nothing comes.

"How's Emma doing?" I finally ask. "I've been thinking about her."

Oliver waits for a beat, then barely moves his lips as he says: "Okay."

I don't try again. The rest of the ride is uncomfortable silence, the kind of quiet that hums in your ears louder than any words. There's so much more I want to say, but it all sounds like excuses, and Oliver seems beyond that. He's doing me one last favor, that's it.

We park a few blocks down from Zenith. Every other time I've come to the office, it's felt like a festive celebration—sparkling apple juice and flower cupcakes and fancy cheese plates—my entrance into the building a kickoff to some grand parade. Today, it's more like a funeral march. No one knows I'm coming, and if they did, they'd probably bar the doors.

Oliver is lagging behind me when I stop in front of the terrifying revolving door.

"You don't have to come in with me. Honestly, they might kick me right out, in which case I'll be back in two minutes."

He shoves his hands into his jacket pockets and blows out a puff of white breath. It's frosty today, colder in New York than it was in Philly. There are light-up snowflakes and snowmen hanging from the streetlamps around us, but I don't think I've ever felt less Christmassy in my life. Dad and I might as well skip past this holiday, too.

"Well, I've come this far, what's another few feet?" He says it dryly, like it's a joke, but there's no laughter.

I'm relieved. I should be adult enough to face Elliot alone. But I'm not.

The stoic security guard at the front desk doesn't bat an eye when I present him with my state ID. News of the scandal must not have reached the lobby—a small comfort.

Oliver slips his license onto the desk, too, and then takes a few steps away from me.

"I'm visiting Elliot Archer at Zenith Children's," I say, voice shaking.

"Is he expecting you?"

"No. But I think he'll want to see me."

The guard looks entirely uninterested as he picks up the phone and dials Elliot. "I have Thistle Tate and Oliver Flynn here." A pause, and it takes all my willpower to not hop the counter and lean in close enough to hear the voice on the other end. Instead I study the shiny metallic Zenith Publishing logo above us: a triangle with an eye at the top, beams of light radiating out in a circle around it. The eyeball is staring right at me. Judging.

I am so far from any personal zenith right now.

After way too many seconds, the guard puts the phone down. "You're in. Tenth floor."

Elliot knows I'm here. And he's not sending me away.

Oliver and I take the elevator, still not talking through the ten flights. I peek over, though, to find him staring at me. He turns away and so do I, and it's almost like it never happened. But for that brief second, I swear it looked like he's as nervous as I am.

The receptionist glances up when our elevator door dings, indifferently at first, but then her eyes widen under her thick cat-eye glasses. She gasps.

"Thistle Tate," she announces for me, bright red lips in an O.

"Um . . . yes. That's me. Is Elliot coming to—?" I start to ask, but I don't have to finish because he's already swinging in through the glass doors from the hallway, looking immaculate in a light blue pinstriped suit.

"Thistle," he says.

"Elliot."

He glances briefly at Oliver, back to me. His face is tensed, jaw flexing. I can't tell if he's furious, or just ruffled because the black sheep has landed here with no warning.

"Can we talk for a few minutes?" I ask, sounding much meeker than I'd like.

Elliot considers briefly, and I prepare myself to turn right back around and go home.

"Sure. Okay. A few minutes."

We follow him, my head ducked down to avoid any glares. I can feel the whispers, even if I can't actually hear them.

"So how can I help you?" he says, closing his door behind us. He motions us toward two chairs, and then sits at his desk—stands up, sits again. "You know our legal team hasn't made a decision yet. This is a brand-new situation for us, quite a bit of logistics to think through. So if you're here to ask that we don't take back all advances, then—"

"No," I cut in, "I'm not. Quite frankly, you should do what you think is fair. We deserve whatever punishment you determine. What we did—what we did was atrocious and unethical, and I'm sorry. I am ashamed beyond words. But that's not why I'm here today. I'm here because . . . I did it. I reworked a lot of the chapters you already saw, and then I wrote the last two on my own. I finished the book."

"*You? You* finished the book?" Elliot's lips twist up into a very unattractive smirk.

"I did."

"How is anyone supposed to believe that?"

"Well, you're the editor, so I would think you'd pick up differences in my style. You can call my dad's caretaker, too—she knows he did nothing all last week and I was locked away in my room the whole time. Oliver here"—I point to him, and he gives a weak wave—"he and his sister helped me outline everything. And then I finished it myself. I recorded it—on camera—and talked through some of my process." It sounds silly out loud, because of course Dad and I could have easily orchestrated this. Who knows what I was *really* typing on camera? But I guess I have the stupid hope that people can see it in my eyes, hear it in my voice. Something intangible but still real and genuine. "I know it's asking a lot for you to believe me. And I know that there likely won't even be a third book. But I guess . . . I had to finish for myself. To know what happened to Marigold. I couldn't just leave her suspended between worlds forever."

If anything can convince him, it's this—Elliot wants to know, too. He's invested years of his life in Marigold. She's more real to him than I am at this point.

Elliot sighs. "Has Susan read it yet?"

"No. I figured there was no point in bothering her about it until I knew what you thought. Plus she's a lot scarier than you."

"That part is probably true. Do you have it with you? The pages?" Elliot's shaking his head like he can't believe he's even asking.

I nod. "I have two copies. It's the last two chapters, but there's also a list of changes I made leading up to that point." I reach for my *Lemonade Skies* tote and pull out two stacks of papers. I hand one to him. And then I turn to Oliver. "You can read, too, if you want."

He looks down at the papers, at my hands, considering. "Okay," he says finally.

The next thirty minutes are the most excruciating of my life. Is this what Dad feels like every time he has me send a new draft? The sudden overwhelming conviction that *of course* I'm totally unworthy, my writing is a joke, I'm a joke! I'm such a dope to think otherwise! I want to crawl under my chair and curl into a fetal position until the final reckoning comes.

"Well," Elliot says at last, and my whole body seems to explode with that one word—nauseated, sweaty, tingly with nerves. "Honestly, Thistle . . . if you wrote this, you did a fantastic job. This is *exactly* what I wanted to see happen. And I know for a fact it's exactly opposite of what your dad told me you were writing . . ." He squints at me, resting his chin on his fists. He's looking for something, for answers—as if the truth, or lack of it, is somehow written on my face. "Oh, hell. I don't know! I don't know what to do, and to be honest, this makes it even more confusing. Send me the full manuscript with your changes. It won't be up to me, but I'll read it and then talk to Martin and the rest of the team. Leave it in their hands. Because whoever wrote this ending—I'm impressed. Much more impressed than I like to admit, given the circumstances."

I nod, my body slowing down to a more normal pace of functioning, even if there are no real answers, because—*Elliot loves the ending.* He might hate my dad and me, but he *loves my chapters.*

Oliver shifts next to me, and I realize he still hasn't weighed in. He's done reading, though, or at least he's staring off out the window behind Elliot's head now.

"Thank you," I say, and I have never meant those two words more. I pull a small black flash drive from my bag and hand it to Elliot. "This has some of the videos I made, too. If you're interested. I'll send the manuscript when I get home and then . . . I guess we'll just wait to hear?" I stand up, and Oliver stands up next to me. "No pressure, though. I didn't come in here with this to force your hand. I just wanted you to have options. Don't worry about me. Do what's best for Zenith."

I start toward the door, but then I pause.

"And Marigold. Do what's best for Marigold, too."

❀❀❀

"I knew you could do it."

We're over halfway through the ride home, and it's the first thing Oliver's said to me.

"What?" I think I heard him, but I need to hear it again.

"I knew it. I knew that you weren't a fraud—at least not a total one. That you're a writer, whether you believe it or not. I could see it in the way you talked about Marigold."

"Then you definitely saw it before I did. I wrote it, and I'm still not sure I believe it."

"You helped your dad with everything, right?"

"Yeah. I mean, he wrote the actual sentences. But I was always there. I gave him ideas. I told him what worked and what didn't work. Sometimes he even listened."

He's quiet for a while, and I assume that's it, we've reached our quota for the ride. But then:

"You know what sucks, Thistle? I get it. I do. I get why you lied in the first place. Your dad was in a bad place. You were young, and you wanted to help. It's just the two of you. I mean, the fact you asked me to come today—*me*. The guy you knew for a few weeks, the guy you were kissing while you were lying to his face . . ." I cringe, wishing I could disappear into my seat, even if I deserve this, all of it. "I didn't come today out of pity. But I came because I realized how alone you really are. How alone you've probably always been."

I want to sob and howl from the truth of it, but—miraculously, somehow, I hold it together. If I have nothing else, I want to leave this car with my dignity intact.

"My whole life has been two people. My dad, who, despite being a good dad some of the time, created this whole disaster. And my neighbor Liam, who was my best friend—more than that when I met you," I add, because if I'm not fully honest now, what's the point of anything, "but he's the one who betrayed me. Partly out of jealousy—because of you—and partly out of some warped need to save me from my lies. So other than those two . . I've started having tea with my eighty-seven-year-old neighbor. There's that."

Oliver laughs, and then I'm laughing, too. I laugh until I can't breathe, and I'm suddenly way too hot to still have my jacket zipped all the way up. I lower the window a few inches, let the cool air ruffle through my curls.

"I'm sorry I lied to you, though," I say, my eyes pinned to the window, the Philly skyline peeking out along the horizon. "I was in too deep. Plus, I liked you, and I was pretty sure you only liked me because I was some supposedly amazingly talented writer."

"That's not true. I liked you because you were smart and interesting and unique, and you *are* those things. That's not a lie."

"Maybe, but still. I didn't want to let you and Emma down.

Maybe if I'd had longer—if the Internet hadn't done it for me—I would have told you, eventually. Or maybe I would have kept lying and put it behind me when the last book was out. I'll never know."

"I'd lie for Emma, too," Oliver says finally. I turn to him, our eyes meeting for a moment before he needs to look back at the road. "If it would make her life better or easier or happier . . . I'd lie for her. I'd lie to anyone."

I nod. He understands. It's even better than forgiveness. "Now that we're actually talking again—how is Emma really doing?"

"Not great yet, but better every day. Getting used to having a bag attached to her body—it's an adjustment. But she's owning it, just like she always does. And she misses you. She was mad as hell at first. It was good, actually, distracted her from the pain. But then she came around. She said I was being a jackass for not at least trying to hear your side of it." He snorts. "I told her she was a traitor."

"Maybe I can visit her sometime?" I try not to sound too optimistic, but it doesn't work.

He pauses, and I feel myself deflating, hope leaking out in a steady fizzle.

"Yeah. I think she'd like that."

I don't say anything else until we're pulling up to my house. Because I know what I need to say—and do—and I want to have an immediate exit strategy if it goes poorly.

I take a deep breath, balling my hands against the seat to steel myself. "I still like you, Oliver, I really do. And I love Emma, your whole family. You all made me feel more normal than I ever have in my life." I turn to him. He's watching me, his twinkly green eyes waiting to see if there's more to this grand speech. "You made me feel like I was better than even I knew I could be, and no one else has ever made me feel that way. I know there wasn't a lot of competition, but . . ."

Oliver laughs again. I can tell I must be flaming red now, the tips of my ears burning hot.

Before I can stop myself, analyze, second-guess, I lean in and kiss him.

And thankfully—thank the afterworld and all the sweet souls up there, Mom maybe, helping her little girl out—

He kisses me back.

twenty-two

Almost Nine Months Later

I had dreamed about California, New York, England, Australia. Moving to a college far away from this home I've lived in and loved and hated for these past eighteen years.

I leave tomorrow morning. But I won't need a plane to get there—it's about a fifty-minute walk, give or take, to get to Temple University. Yep. That's where I'm going, a nice *Philly* school—the last city I would have picked for myself at the start of all this. But the funny part is that it feels like exactly where I should be. I was rejected by some of the snootier schools on my list, as expected. Though they were polite about it, no reference to specifics, no *Lemonade Skies*, just brief and efficient form-letter rejections. But Temple must have liked my personal essay—about what led me to making the decisions I did, the gray between all the black and white. I was honest, and they took me in. Gave me a home.

If Dad or I or both of us get lonely, I'll only be a quick cab ride away. I can visit him—and Lucy—whenever I'm feeling homesick. But for now, we need some distance. I'll be in my dorm room, a space of my own, and I have a feeling that from there this city will be like a whole new world. I've lived here for eighteen years, but there's plenty I haven't seen.

My things are mostly all packed, piled up in the hallway outside my bedroom, ready for Dad to load into our rental van. I have too much stuff to fit into a cab for this trip. But hauling bags and boxes down the steps is no big deal for Dad these days. Ever since he made it out of the wheelchair and through rehab, he's been at the gym almost every morning. "Our bodies really are sacred," he's said too many times to count, usually while shoving a bright green smoothie into my hand. His new psychologist is thrilled with this outlook—the exercise is "fabulous for those feel-good brain chemicals."

Dad calls up from downstairs: "Thistle! Dinner! Mia's here and Dottie's on her way!"

We've had weekly dinners with Dottie, and Mia has been making increasingly frequent appearances, too—*just a friend*, Dad assures me, and I'm glad because he needs one. But tonight is extra-special. My big *farewell dinner*, though *farewell* seems a bit much when I'm only moving across town. I'm letting Dad have all his emotions, though—it's part of our healing process. It's okay that he's sad about me leaving, and it's okay that I'm happy to be doing something new, taking time for myself.

When I get to the kitchen, though, I'm immediately teary eyed from the loveliness of the scene—twinkly white lights strung along the walls, colored jars filled with candles on the table, glowing reds and greens and blues. There's a huge clay pot of flowers at the center—marigolds.

"It's beautiful," I say, swiping at the tears I was so sure I wouldn't cry. Silly me.

My dad is hovering over a steaming pot, but he spins around to grin at me. "Your mom used to hang tiny white lights up for all sorts of special occasions. She said it instantly added a touch of fairy tale. I need to bring the tradition back. She would like that."

He talks about her like this all the time now—the good memories, the less good, everything in between. I know my mom better every day.

"And," Dad continues, "since you don't want to do a big blowout bash here at home for the *World After World* pub day next weekend, I figured I had to make tonight even more of an event."

"I'm going to be too nervous on pub day to do anything but sit at my computer and refresh every ten seconds."

Next weekend the last Marigold installment will be out in the world. The books are on total lockdown now—not a single blogger or bookseller has had a sneak peek. A handful of select trade reviewers were sent highly confidential early copies, but only after agreeing in writing not to run any reviews prepublication. Zenith knew what they were doing, apparently, because buzz has reached frightening Harry Potter–like proportions. People still have mixed reactions about my dad and me. Zenith released some of my videos, and readers watched. Some of them get it. Some of them don't. But I have a feeling that even a few of our harshest critics will be too curious not to read. This isn't about just me, after all—it's about Marigold.

I hug Mia, and then I wander to the table, pluck off a marigold to tuck into my curls. I can still hear Elliot now, the day he conference-called Susan and me—*me*, not my dad—in January: "We might be making the biggest mistake of my career, but—but we're doing it. We're back on for this last book. It's just—it's too good not to put it out. But please do not let me down, Thistle. Please. Don't make me regret this."

I've been his and Susan's star author ever since. I sweated for weeks on revisions, putting more of my touches everywhere, starting from the beginning. I also poured myself into every blog post, every personal essay, blasted my soul out on display for the world to judge. I missed the deadline to have it published before school started. But we agreed that my first official launch event here in

Philly would be later next month, and I'll do a few long-weekend mini tours after that. I wanted time to settle into school, to adjust to this new life. And I wanted time to prepare myself if responses were less than positive. Otherwise I was too grateful to question anything about the process. I barely deserved to have this book out at all, so the least I could do was obey Zenith's every whim.

Dad has officially backed away from all things *Lemonade Skies*. He's started his own writing again—a second take at a memoir. I have a feeling he'll have much more to say this time.

Dottie steps up to the table, startling me from my trance. I hadn't even heard her open the front door. "I'd wager it's about a week's worth of cookies," she says, skipping the hellos as she hands me a big kitten-covered tin. Lucy pops up at her side, sniffing the air for treats, and Dottie pats her head lovingly. "If you want more, you have to come back and spend some time with an old crotchety hag."

I lean in and kiss her cheek. She grimaces, but I know better than to believe her displeasure. "I'll need the exercise after I eat these cookies, so a walk home would be perfect."

I had smelled the batter cooking from upstairs, but I still act surprised when Dad unveils the first course—chocolate chip pancakes covered in homemade whipped cream. There's more after, barbecued chicken and mashed sweet potatoes and roasted brussels sprouts, and to cap it off, a little champagne, because Dad says I should ease into the college way of life. He pops the bottle, only minimally spraying onto the sleeve of Dottie's bright blue dress—she leaves her parakeet housecoat at home for our weekly dinners.

"A toast," he says, clinking my glass, "to endings and beginnings."

It wasn't premeditated.

But as I'm packing up my last bag of toiletries after dinner, I see Liam's bedroom lamp go on. I'd opened the curtains again months ago, at the beginning of spring—I'd missed having all that natural light. Before I can follow my own train of thought there are three Ping-Pong balls in my hand, and suddenly I'm downstairs, sweeping through the kitchen door. I'd almost thrown out the Ping-Pong balls so many times—almost. But I couldn't. They were the start of too many good memories.

We still haven't talked. We passed on the sidewalk once early on and nodded at each other, but no words. Maybe if he'd tried reaching out, I would have responded. But he didn't. So I didn't either. I'd at the very least expected to cross paths outside this summer, me gardening, him grilling. But he must have avoided it, knowing the garden was my special place. That was nice of him, I suppose. Or cowardly. Maybe both.

I toss a Ping-Pong ball, and it feels so normal, so routine, that I can't believe it's been nine months. I give it a minute, throw a second ball.

Liam's window opens and he pops his head out, squinting down through the dim light. "I heard the first one but figured I must have been imagining it."

"Nope." I toss my last ball up in the air, trying to coolly catch it, like I am utterly unaffected by this moment. The ball misses my hand entirely, bouncing off the ground.

"Should I come down, then?" he asks, the words slow, uncertain.

"I'm leaving tomorrow." To go a few miles, but still. "I wanted to say good-bye."

He nods and disappears, and a minute later he's crawling over the brick wall, and for just a second I have to fight the urge to run and hug him and slip back through the last nine months to a time when we were still okay.

"Hey," he says, standing just a few inches away from me now—wearing that stupid *Reading Rainbow* shirt again, which, damn it, only makes me want to hug him more. I loved him for almost my whole life, and now he's gone, like he died and left me, too.

"I'm going to Temple," I tell him, cutting straight to the facts.

His eyes go wide. "But you were so ready to leave Philly."

"Yeah, I was. But when most of my dream schools rejected me because of . . ." I don't have to say it. "I had to reconsider my priorities. And the funny thing is, even though I've spent my whole life in Philly, I'm not sure I've ever really felt like I *lived* here."

Liam nods, his expression very serious as he seems to consider this. "I get that. I'm headed to Syracuse, probably for engineering. So not too far, but—"

"That's great! Congratulations."

"Yeah, you too."

We're standing there looking at each other, then at the stars, the moon, the grass below our bare feet. Maybe we'll run into each other over the holidays. Maybe not. I guess that's it, then?

It's not, though. There's more I should say. Want to say.

"Liam, I understand why you did what you did. It sucked, though—it was absolutely the wrong thing to do, don't get me wrong. But I kissed someone else and you wanted to hurt me. I know you wanted to help me, too, and you were right, there *were* way too many lies. To the readers, to you, to Oliver and Emma, to myself. It wasn't your job to fix me. I wish I could have made the decision on my own terms, but I'm glad the truth is out. I was so tired of lying. And of worrying and wondering about what would happen if we got caught. I finished the book, though. On my own. They're publishing it. Next week."

"I know. Of course. I still follow all your updates. And I'm so proud of you."

"Thanks." I take a small step back, closer to the house. "I guess I should—"

"Wait," Liam says, reaching out. His warm fingers graze my wrist for a second before I pull away. "Do you ever think about us? Because I do. I was an ass, and I am so ashamed of what I did. If I could take it back . . . I would. I'd do everything differently."

"Maybe that still wouldn't have been enough."

"What do you mean?" he asks, his voice catching.

"We were best friends, Li, and we loved each other. We had so much history. But maybe we should have left it at that. If it wasn't my dad and Marigold, maybe it would have just been other things. Eventually."

"You don't know that."

"You're right. I don't. But thinking about it that way, as some predetermined reality, makes it easier. Because we can't go back now."

Liam looks away. "I'll always miss you," he says finally. "I'll probably always love you, too."

My breath pinches in my lungs, a quick stab of heat—but I breathe through it. I'm okay.

I'm better than okay.

"I'll miss how things used to be." That's the truth. But not all of it. I say the rest before I can overanalyze: "Maybe someday we can be friends again. Who knows? Life is long."

"I would like that."

I step forward and hug him, because it feels like the right way to end this for now. And then I turn around and walk toward the porch.

I don't look back.

❁❁❁

Oliver shows up a half hour early the next morning to help us load the last odds and ends from my room into the van. He delivers a tray of Wawa coffee and doughnuts, too, as if he needs to work at this point to make my dad love him. If anything, it should be the other way around—but Oliver doesn't seem to hold a grudge against Dad. Thank goodness, because I couldn't do that again.

"Let's cut straight through the shit to the important stuff: Are you taking the signed Harry Potter posters, or can I snag them?" Emma pops up behind Oliver, grinning at me.

Oliver doesn't even bother to call her on her language. It's a lost cause.

She looks amazing today, bright eyed and glowing, already jumping past me to check out my bedroom. Her checkered summer dress flows loosely around her waist, her colostomy bag invisible to anyone who doesn't know to look for it.

"Well, I was going to take them with me, but then I got nervous that my roommate would steal them while I was at class and try to sell them for millions online, so yeah. Maybe they're safer at your house. Temporarily."

Oliver leans in and kisses me on the cheek. "Ugh. You're too good to her. Seriously. She's going to be such a brat. Have one grave medical condition and some seriously major surgery, and it's like no one can ever say no to you again, ever. It's disturbing."

"Shut the hell up!" Emma yells over her shoulder, already standing on my bed to pull her prizes down from the wall. "I'm not a brat!"

"Are you sure you have time to be helping me?" I ask, swinging my laptop bag over my shoulder. I saved the most important piece of luggage for last. "You still have to move into your dorm room, too, you know."

"Yep," he says. "I have half the stuff you do, it'll take no time. And I want to be there when you awkwardly attempt to befriend the new roomie. You need me there. I got the whole friend-making thing down. You on the other hand . . ." He beams at me, grabs the last box of books and my bag from my shoulder, and leaps down the stairs two at a time.

Emma follows Oliver, both signed posters clutched tight in her arms. I give the room one last glance—the half-empty shelves and blank walls, the cleared desk and nightstand, the cup of Ping-Pong balls on the windowsill—and then flick off the light and close my door.

When Oliver first told me he was choosing Temple, too, I panicked, worrying that it was solely for my benefit. But then I remembered what he'd said to me all those months ago—that maybe he should stay close to Emma. Phone calls just wouldn't be enough. I knew without asking *Why Temple?* And I was relieved.

The biggest surprise was that we'd both be English majors. The biggest surprise for me, at least. I'd grandly announced it at dinner one night, Dottie and Emma and Oliver packed around our table, and they'd barely looked up from their plates. I'm still not totally convinced about it—it could be a disaster. It's hard to say whether my work on *World After World* was a one-off. But if it's *real*, if it's in my blood—if I can feel that glittery magic rush from writing again and again and again . . .

Then I need to try.

⊛⊛⊛

Saturday, September 5.

Today.

Lemonade Skies: World After World is finally out.

By *Thistle Tate*, according to the cover, as per usual—only this time it's true. I wrote an author's note explaining that I did a lot of rewriting to make the book my own, but that I didn't change every single word of Dad's. It felt too dishonest not to give him some credit. But I'd earned my name on that cover.

Books are usually released on Tuesdays, but Zenith made an exception, picking a Saturday to make it feel more celebratory. Special preordered copies started arriving in the mail yesterday. Some bookstores held "Marigold at Midnight" parties last night. I didn't make any appearances, though. Not yet.

Trade reviews should already be in print and online this morning, and other reader responses could start coming in at any time now. I want to see it all, the good and the bad. My roommate—Jenny, from Maryland, a biology major who seems to have zero interest in *Lemonade Skies* or any other work of fiction, thank goodness—is away for the weekend visiting her girlfriend, so I have the dorm room to myself.

Dad's already texted three times, asking how I'm doing and if I've read any of the reviews yet. He wanted me to come home for the day so that he and I could "celebrate" together. But I'm not sure if it'll be a triumph or a failure yet, and I'd rather have a pity party alone. Especially because I don't think I slept at all last night, not a single damn wink. Every time I closed my eyes I saw Marigold and my mom, together, staring at me from below a lemonade-yellow sky, blue and red and purple stars sparkling bright.

I text Dad that I don't want any spoilers, at least not until I've chugged some mediocre coffee from the cafeteria. Or maybe I'll take my laptop and head off campus, treat myself to a more decadent cup with some froth in it while I start to read the reviews. It's a big day, after all. The biggest. I throw on some clothes—a dark orange romper, because I can't help but be superstitious—and am scraping my curls into a bun when there's a chipper knock at the door.

I swing it open to find Oliver—Oliver dressed in a neon orange sweat suit, to be precise. Brighter than a highlighter. Brighter than a safety cone. Brighter than a hazmat suit. It's the most un-black outfit he could ever possibly wear.

"It's pretty gloriously heinous, isn't it?" He does a little shimmy shake and then hugs me with one arm, whipping the other out from behind his back to hand me the most gigantic heart-shaped box of chocolates I have ever seen in my life. "Sustenance for your momentous day, since you insist on being a recluse. I have a thermos of hazelnut coffee and double chocolate chip cookies from my mom in my backpack, too. She insisted I come pick them up fresh this morning for you."

"I told you *explicitly* to avoid me this weekend because I might be a miserable wench," I say, pretending to frown, though I'm already jumping on him, both arms wrapping tight around his neck. I breathe him in—he smells like the Flynns' kitchen, toast and fried eggs and bacon, with a tinge of that chemically new clothes scent. My nose wrinkles. "I can't believe you actually bought this thing."

"Of course I did! It's a good luck charm for my lady!"

I pin myself to him even more snugly and we kiss for a few minutes, and I wonder for the thousandth time why I'm lucky enough to still have him in my life.

We settle in quietly, me at the desk, on my computer; him on my bed, with his iPad. Searching my name and *World After World*, clicking on the top news stories.

The reviews blur together. The *New York Times*, the *Philadelphia Inquirer*, *USA Today*. I read them all ravenously, repeatedly. It's hard to wrap my head around the words:

> *Fresh and exciting, a total emotional roller coaster.*
>
> *Thistle is young and her writing could use polish, but the spark—the spark is there.*
>
> *Hands down the best and only way Marigold's story could have ended.*
>
> *I still hate that the Tates lied, but—wow, she can actually write! Runs in the blood!*
>
> *Satisfying, smart conclusion to a series that no one will soon forget.*

I may be here, physically, reading words on the screen—but I am also not. I am somehow outside it all, hovering above, shining and twirling and combusting.

We celebrate by ordering falafel sandwiches and chicken kebabs for lunch, though Oliver eats most of mine. I barely even touch the chocolate. Coffee is enough.

At two o'clock, I see the first blogger post about Marigold. On Elisabeth Early's site, of course. I should let the trade reviews be enough. Elisabeth's words shouldn't have the power to make or break me. But I can't not look. I can't not care.

I tried to fight my urge to read this final book in the installment—the first that showcases actual pieces of Thistle Tate's own writing. I told you guys before that you couldn't *pay me* to read it. But . . . damn it, I couldn't resist!!! Partly because I wanted to see if Zenith was right in their decision to go ahead with what they called: "One of the most stunning series enders we've ever had the privilege of publishing." Partly because I had to know what Marigold would do in the end. (I love to hate that girl.) And maybe even just a tiny, tiny bit because I'd seen Thistle's videos (as we all have) and, well, I don't know . . . I won't say I forgive them for lying—it's still a hot mess of crap in my opinion—but I kind of sort of understand. Just a little. Why a girl would lie to make a parent happier. That's all I'll say. I do *not* regret that I outed her. I will never regret that because I think you guys deserved to know the truth.

Anyway, moving on: before I get too into the SPOILERS (!!!), I just want to say: all things considered, it was a surprisingly decent story. You know I've never loved the writing, and This-tle's writing doesn't have the confidence of her dad's work. But . . . to be honest? I like that. It worked for me. I felt like I was much more inside Marigold's head—feeling what she felt, rather than being told about it secondhand. There was a new raw style there. It was earnest and convincing. Probably because—duh!—the author really was seventeen this time.

WILD, RIGHT? And it shows. It really does. In a good way. If
only she could go back and rewrite the other two books . . . ?
Maybe I would have been a fan from day one. Ha!

She goes on to describe the plot twists in great detail, and I just skim
through for now. My eyes keep jumping back to the earlier lines: *Surprisingly decent. Raw. Earnest. Convincing.* I jump up from my chair
and shove the computer into Oliver's hands. He'd been lounging on
my bed, but he sits up arrow straight now, frowning deeply as he registers who wrote the post. But as his eyes flitter back and forth reading,
his lips slowly lift. "Wow. For her, this seems like an A-plus right?"

"An A-*super*-plus." I'm grinning and punching my fists through
the air, dancing in my seat. "This is as good as the *New York Times*
saying the spark is there. She's my toughest critic by far."

There's a steady stream of posts on Twitter and Goodreads and
other blogs as the day goes on. People who got the book yesterday or
first thing this morning and did nothing but read all day. And the
consensus? They like the ending. They *love* the ending.

There are negative posts, too, and people protesting the book's
existence, but that's fine—there have always been detractors. I know
the story's not *perfect*—no story is. I wouldn't trust a book if every
single review was glowing. That's not real life.

My dad calls crying, and I cry, too. I'm tempted to go home after
all, to jump in a cab and pop open more champagne, but—selfishly?
I want to celebrate this victory on my own, with Oliver. I'll see Dad
for the official launch. Home is so close, and I love that it's there—
when I need it. But I need to anchor myself in this brand-new Philadelphia. Dad and I both need to move on. We need to learn how to
exist apart. To be something to each other, but not everything.

We hang up and soon after Emma calls—reporting on her friends' enthusiastic reads, since she'd had VIP early access—and then I dive back into the *Lemonade Skies* wormhole. I'm so lost in it all that I don't notice when the sky goes dark and Oliver has to flick on the lights.

"Are we ordering dinner in, or could we maybe take a breather and go out?" Oliver asks politely, but I see him gazing longingly at this afternoon's empty take-out bag. His mom's cookies have been reduced to crumbs.

"Give me a sec," I say, tossing him a chocolate. "I just have one more thing to do."

I scan through the photos on my laptop and find it—a shot of the framed picture from Dad's office, Mom and me dressed in almost identical yellow sundresses, beaming at the camera. I upload it on Twitter, and write the only caption that makes sense:

Good-bye, Mom. Good-bye, Marigold. I'll miss you both—always.

Maybe I will see Mom again. Someday. Maybe Dad and I were onto something. I hope we were. Until then, I'll live. Here and now. But I'll never stop dreaming of lemonade skies.

I snap my laptop shut—like slamming a door, no peeking back to whatever came before. I get up and kiss my beautiful bright orange boyfriend.

"We can go now," I whisper. "I've said my good-byes." I close my eyes, waiting for more tears. But they don't come.

I'm okay.

Marigold's story may be over. But mine is just beginning.

Acknowledgments

Who knew a third book could be the hardest yet? Oh, Thistle, you were truly a labor of love. Emphasis on *labor*. There were days (weeks, months) I feared you would never see the light of day. But I couldn't let you go, and I'm so very glad I didn't.

A whole bright bouquet of gratitude for my dear agent, boss, and friend, Jill Grinberg, who kept on fighting for this story, and who believed in me and in Thistle all along, even when all I had was a few pages and a wild idea. Thank you to the whole beloved JGLM team, my darling work family: Cheryl Pientka, for live texting through your read, for planting the seed for this story so many years ago, for always being an unwavering advocate; Denise Page, for your sharp and valuable insights and boundless pop culture know-how, and for endlessly providing a listening ear during my various rants and raves; Sophia Seidner, for your fierce negotiations and candor. I feel immensely lucky to share my weekdays with such smart, kind, funny, passionate women.

Thank you, thank you to my marvel of an editor, Margaret Ferguson—you made Thistle who she is today, taking a decent but messy story and turning it into something special. Thank you for your tireless reads and brilliant notes, and for asking the hard questions I was either willfully avoiding or completely oblivious of before you. I've lost track of how many rounds we did (!), but I am so wildly appreciative for each and every one of them. I feel blessed every day that you came into my (and Thistle's) life.

To the rest of Holiday House—I'm honored to be a part of your special list, and so very grateful for all you've done in preparing

Thistle and Marigold to greet their readers. So many thanks to Terry Borzumato-Greenberg, Faye Bi, Michelle Montague, Emily Mannon, Emily Campasino, Kevin Jones, Kerry Martin, and Miriam Miller. You are truly a dream team. Thank you, too, to my thoughtful and meticulous copy editor, Chandra Wohleber, for giving that final shine, and to the incredibly talented Connie Gabbert for designing such a gorgeous (marigold!) cover.

My medical experts and sister-friends, Dr. Melissa DelVecchio and Dr. Christine Pulice Roy, thank you for keeping my health-and-body facts in check. Your razor-sharp scientific minds never cease to amaze me; your patients are lucky to have you. I'm pretty lucky, too. My beloved Philly girl, Sarah Yaskowski, thank you for ensuring I didn't embarrass my PA roots with any misinformation, and thank you for being a home away from home in my second-favorite city. And to Rob Spalding, thank you for reading in the final hour when all my perspective was lost, for giving me faith in this story and in my art—I'm so very glad our lives always connect when we both need it most.

To all my infinitely precious, treasured friends and family, new and old, the Detweilers and the Tamberellis, my valley and city loves—thank you always and forever for supporting, encouraging, believing in me. You ground me, but you give me wings. I would fly to any of you in a heartbeat.

Mom and Dad, I will never be able to say thank you enough for all you've given and continue to give, so unconditionally and gracefully, but I'll keep saying it anyway: *thank you*. You are my heart and soul, my beacons of bright light. Everything I do, past, present, future, is to make you proud. (And don't you worry! Even as a married lady, I'll always be your little girl. Promise.)

Danny, my cutie—sorry, couldn't hold that back!—my partner in all things for the rest of life, thank you for celebrating and cheersing with me on the good days, for holding me while I cry on the bad ones, for loving me, laughing with me, and nourishing my body and soul with delicious smoothies and dinners every day in between. You are my never-ending well of inspiration and joy, my edgy ginger dream love forever.

And lastly, my readers, thank you from the bottom of my heart for taking this journey into the world(s) of Thistle Tate and Marigold Maybee. I am eternally grateful.